MURDER AMONG THE ROSES

An utterly gripping cozy murder mystery full of twists

LIZ FIELDING

A Maybridge Murder Mystery Book 1

Joffe Books, London
www.joffebooks.com

First published in Great Britain in 2023

Cover art by Dee Dee Book Covers

ISBN: 978-1-80405-832-9

CHAPTER ONE

Red-faced and sweating with the effort, Abby Finch stabbed at the deep tap root, imagining that it was her soon-to-be ex-husband on the receiving end of her spade.

'Damn! Damn! Damn!'

The word echoed the jabbing until, beneath her raised spade, the white glimmer of bone brought her to a juddering halt. It wasn't the first time she'd disturbed the bones of a long-deceased pet, but the shock never lessened. She stuck her spade into the pile of earth she'd already removed and walked away, stretching her back, ripping off her gloves to scoop up some hair that had escaped the scrunchy and was sticking to her face.

Restoring this forgotten corner of the garden — where he'd made love to her, proposed to her — for the new woman in his life was Howard's punishment for defying him not once, but twice.

He might be done with her as a wife, but she was still useful in the garden, and with three children whose needs would always make her hostage to his demands, she'd had no choice but to concede.

For the moment, he had her over a barrel, but she took some comfort from the fact that she'd have an unlikely ally in Izzy Hamilton.

Once the divorce was sorted and Izzy was the new Mrs Finch, she wouldn't want her predecessor hanging around in the garden.

With that thought to console her, Abby took a steadying breath and, gloves back on and down on her knees, she reached into the cool, damp earth and took out a rib bone. It was a fragile thing, tiny against the clumsy thickness of her gardening gloves. She placed it carefully on the path beside her and then, using her hand fork, began to carefully scrape away the soil.

The animal had lain undisturbed until the roots of the rose had breached the box in which it had been buried, forcing it apart and curling through the ribs, scattering the neat curve of tiny vertebrae.

It had been wrapped in a knitted blanket, rotting now, with soil clinging to the strands of wool. There were damp-pitted brass hinges and, from a piece of the lid that had survived, she could see that it had once been inlaid with the same coloured wood and mother of pearl that she was turning up with her fork.

She put everything she found on the path beside the fragments of blanket and the bones, so that she could reinter it all together.

Then she found the skull.

Abby stared at it for a moment, struggling to equate what she'd expected to find with the reality of what lay before her.

Not the narrow, sharp-toothed skull of a small animal: it was round, with the unmistakable open fontanelle of a new-born baby. She felt her throat constrict, for a moment too shocked to breathe.

A baby?

Her hands were shaking so badly that it took her a minute to remove her gloves before lifting it out of the cold earth, cradling it gently in the palm of her hand as she had once cradled the heads of each of her children in the heart-stopping moment of pure love when first Lucy, then Tom and finally Sophie had opened their eyes and looked at her.

Had this infant breathed, been given a name? And who was the wretched mother? What had she been thinking as she'd buried her dead child in this secret grave?

Because it had to have been a secret.

She shivered despite the sun beating down on her neck, and, unable to bring herself to put the skull down on the stone path, she reached for her jacket and laid it on that.

A professional gardener, she knew that the discovery of human remains, no matter how old, had to be reported to the police, and fumbling for her phone, she made the call.

An officer took all the details, assuring her that someone would be along very shortly and warning her not to touch anything.

A bit late for that.

'Will they be long?' she asked, her voice seeming to come from a distance.

'Are you okay, ma'am?'

Okay? She had just found the remains of a baby, how the hell did he think she was feeling?

'Sit down, head between your legs,' he advised when she didn't answer. 'Someone will be with you very soon.'

Abby stumbled across to a bench in front of the summerhouse, but as she put her head down on her knees, she heard the clock on St Michael's church tower strike two.

She had been working through her lunch break, and now it was over. There were clients who would be expecting her and she began to make the necessary calls, apologising, promising that, somehow, she would find time to fit them in later. Or tomorrow.

Having done that, she called Aunt Molly.

Not a real aunt, but a friend of her late grandmother. She was widowed and living alone, so Abby visited regularly to cut her grass and to check that she was managing.

'I'm sorry, Molly, but I've been held up. I won't be able to make it this afternoon.'

'Don't worry, dear. I've made you a cake, but if you're going to be late, Lucy can pick it up on her way home.'

Not late . . . Not coming.

'I'm not sure whether she's got—'

'Tell her that Mabel's had kittens.'

Kittens?

'You didn't mention that she was having kittens.'

'No, well, I didn't want people pestering me for them. There's the prettiest calico. She's the spit of your Smudge. She's yours if you want her, and maybe one of her sisters. They can get lonely if you're out all day.'

'Actually, Molly,' she began, determined to put this one off until the weekend, 'I really don't think I can make it today. I'll be playing catch up—'

'I need to ask you a favour, Abby.'

'Are you okay? Is the house okay?'

'Yes, yes,' she said, impatiently. 'But it is important.'

'Right . . .' She'd been planning to fit in her paying clients this evening. Clearly that wasn't going to happen. 'It'll have to be after supper.'

Meanwhile, this was Howard's house. Much as she dreaded the conversation, she had to warn him about what she'd found and she called his office.

'Natalie Grant.'

His PA. 'I need a word with Howard, Natalie.'

'Howard is attending a business conference and left strict instructions that he is not to be disturbed except in the direst emergency.'

Direst? Abby mentally rolled her eyes. 'When will he be back?'

'Monday,' she replied, curt to the point of rudeness.

'Monday? But he promised . . .'

'I don't think his promises to you count for much these days. To any of us,' she added, not bothering to hide her bitterness.

Natalie had been infatuated with Howard for years and he'd used her to cover for him through who knew how many of his "indiscretions".

That he'd decided to make his latest extramarital adventure permanent must have come as a shock to the woman who'd never stopped hoping that one day she'd be upgraded from his "office wife" to the real thing.

'He promised his daughter,' Abby replied.

'Well, he's got a new family now. She's going to have to get used to taking second place.'

Abby took a breath, counted to three . . .

'Please remind him, when he returns, that he's supposed to give me a contact number when he's away. In case there's an emergency with the children.'

'You can always reach him through me.' There was a smug satisfaction in her voice.

'Apparently not,' she replied.

'Is it an emergency?'

If she and Howard had still been living together, Abby would have suspected yet another "indiscretion". But although sorely tempted to suggest Natalie save her cover technique for the inevitable moment when he started cheating on the new woman in his life, she let it go.

Hard as it was to swallow, she would have to deal with the woman as a go-between for the foreseeable future.

'Nothing I could classify as dire.' She didn't wait for a reply, cutting the connection as she heard someone calling her name.

'Down here,' she called. 'Follow the path through the shrubbery.'

A young woman wearing a police uniform appeared through the gap she'd created between the shrubs to reveal a long-overgrown path.

'PC Newcombe,' she said, offering her hand. 'Dee. And this is Shiv Kumar, from our forensics team.' She waved at the man who was following her, encased in a white body suit and carrying a large bag. 'He'll take care of the bones.'

He nodded in her direction.

'Abby Finch. Thank you both for being so quick. I haven't touched anything since I called the station, but I stayed close. The rooks will take anything . . .'

‘What have you touched?’ Shiv asked, glancing at the bones lying on the footpath, then peering into the hole.

‘I was wearing gloves until I found the skull. I took them off because it looked so fragile. I realise that I should have left it where it was, but I didn’t think . . .’

‘Not to worry, but I’ll have to take everything they might have been in contact with,’ he said, waving at her tools and gloves. ‘And I’ll need you to come down to the station for a DNA sample. For elimination purposes.’

‘Today?’

‘Someone will call to make an appointment,’ he said. ‘This isn’t going to be a rush job.’

‘You look a bit shaky, Mrs Finch,’ Dee Newcombe said. ‘Are you okay to answer a few questions?’ She took out her notebook as she headed towards the bench. ‘If I can start with your full name and address?’

‘Abigail May Finch,’ she began. ‘Oldfield Cottage, Mill Lane.’ She added her phone number.

‘Thank you . . .’ Dee looked up. ‘Is it okay if I call you Abby?’

‘Yes. Yes, of course.’

‘Can you tell me what happened, Abby?’

She took a breath. ‘I’d dug up an old rose. When I found the bones, I assumed it was a pet. But then I found the skull.’

CHAPTER TWO

Dee looked over to where the tower and crenellated roof of Linton Lodge were just visible over the top of the trees.

'I remember passing this place on my way to primary school,' she said. 'It was like one of the pictures in my book of fairy tales, the castle where the giant in "Jack and the Beanstalk" lived. I used to run past, absolutely terrified he'd get me.'

'The tower is a touch Brothers Grimm,' Abby agreed. 'Although, with the garden so overgrown, I might have gone for "Sleeping Beauty". Ruth's gardener retired a couple of years ago,' she explained. 'He was pretty much past it for years before that. My husband cut the lawn, but that was about it.'

'He didn't make it this far,' said Dee, looking around at the dead winter stalks sticking through the lush new growth.

'No. No one's been down here for years. I had to cut back the bushes to clear the path.'

'You mentioned Ruth. Who is she?'

'Ruth Finch. My husband's great-aunt by marriage. She'd lived here all her married life. She died a few months ago, which is when my husband inherited the house.'

'She was living here on her own?'

'Howard wanted her to move into a care home, but she wouldn't budge. She did have live-in help.'

'I'll need her name.'

'Is that necessary? Pam's only been working here for the last three or four years. The bones must have been there for much longer.'

'I'll need the name of anyone with access to the house and grounds.'

'But . . .' Abby shrugged and let it go. 'Pamela Lewis.'

'Where is she now?'

'She lives in Spencer Court. Number three.'

Dee made a note. 'And where was she before she worked here?'

'She'd spent years in St Catherine's. She was only released into the community when it was closed down.'

'The old mental institution? She was capable of caring for your aunt?'

'She and Ruth managed very well together.'

'And she's living in Spencer Court? Those places are expensive. Did your aunt leave her a legacy?'

'Five thousand pounds and a few personal items.'

That was something else she had to do. The solicitors had dealt with the money, but Howard, ridiculously irritated with the bequest, was being petulant about handing over the small items she had been left, and Pam had asked her to help.

'Five thousand pounds wouldn't buy her a doormat in Spencer Court,' Dee pointed out.

Abby frowned. 'I assumed the local authority had rehoused her.'

'The local authority can barely run to a hostel these days.'

'I suppose not. Ruth's late husband was on the county council for years and they both did a lot of charity work. Maybe, when she knew she was dying, Ruth called in some favours.'

Dee nodded. 'Why was Pamela Lewis in St Catherine's, do you know?'

About to ask if it was relevant, Abby decided that the line of least resistance would get this over with more quickly.

'My daughter has been doing a social science project on St Catherine's and Pam's been helping her. According to the records she was shut away for something called "moral delinquency".'

Dee frowned. 'Moral delinquency?'

'Back in the good old days, unmarried girls who'd had a baby, or even just casual sex, could be shut away in places like St Catherine's. Lucy's project has been quite an eye-opener.'

'How old is she?'

'Lucy? Sixteen.'

'Pamela Lewis.'

'Oh, sorry. I don't know. Is it important?'

'Did she work here as a girl?'

'You're thinking the baby could be hers?' Abby shook her head. 'No. They met through church after they closed St Catherine's.'

Dee checked her notes. 'Ruth Finch left this property to your husband?'

'Howard is technically still my husband, but we're separated and in the process of a divorce.'

Dee gave her an odd look. 'So you won't be living here?'

'No.'

'Forgive me, but if that's the case can I ask why you're working here?'

'It's business,' she lied, indicating the logo on her overalls. Her husband's arm-twisting was no one's business but her own. 'Earthly Designs.'

'Of course. I've seen your van. Very colourful. I didn't notice it when we drove in.'

'Someone rear-ended me at the Bridge Road traffic lights a couple of days ago. I'm using the family car.'

'The Volvo estate parked at the front of the house? The front offside tyre is a bit low on tread.'

Oh joy. You do your public duty and get a warning about your tyres —which, since the family car was, for the moment, Howard's responsibility, would involve another opportunity for Natalie Grant to humiliate her.

'It's on my to-do list.'

'At the top would be my advice.' The tone was friendly enough, but the warning was clear. 'But what I need now are your husband's details, and anything else you can tell me about who's lived here in the past,' she said.

'I called his office to let him know what I'd found but he wasn't there. According to his PA he's away at a conference and won't be back until Monday.'

Even as she said it, she frowned.

Conferences tended to be bun fights. Lots of drinking and a fair bit of bed-hopping. Hardly the kind of event that couldn't be disturbed.

'Is something wrong?'

'What? Oh, no. It's just that he promised Sophie, our youngest daughter, that he'd be at her dance show on Saturday.'

He might be furious with her, making her pay for trying to outwit him. Right now — distracted by Izzy, their coming baby and his political ambitions — he wasn't exactly knocking it out of the park in the fatherhood stakes, but Sophie had always been special . . .

Realising that Dee was looking at her, she said, 'He's got a lot on his mind. He's the CEO of Finch Developments,' she added.

'Isn't that the company demolishing St Catherine's?'

Abby nodded. 'Howard took over from his great-uncle George when he retired and then inherited his share of the business when he died a few years ago. They'll be using the site to build affordable housing.'

Dee pulled a face. 'Is there such a thing in Maybridge?'

'Probably not,' Abby agreed. Situated on the edge of the Cotswolds, Maybridge might be small, but it was one of the most expensive towns in the country. She'd been fortunate to inherit her mother's house, but didn't know how young people managed.

'His aunt didn't have any children of her own?'

'No, but Howard's father died when he was very young, so George and Ruth brought him up.'

'What happened to his mother?'

'Is that relevant?' Abby asked.

'We'll need as much information about the house and its occupants as possible if we're to find out who gave birth to, and possibly buried, this baby.'

'You're going to investigate something that happened decades ago?'

'It's an unexplained death,' she said, 'but it'll be up to the coroner how far we take it once we've gathered all the relevant information.' She looked thoughtful. 'What makes you think it was buried that long ago?'

'The rose was already well established when I first came here with Howard before we were married. The summer-house was in much better condition then.'

'That's helpful, and presumably he'll be able to tell us who was living here before then.'

Oh, God . . . The bones were bad enough. Digging into his family history would not improve Howard's temper.

'You think it might have been one of the family?'

'A DNA sample will settle that.'

'Is that necessary?' Abby, heart sinking, knew who he'd blame for that indignity. 'I'd have said a servant girl in trouble. Except . . .'

'Yes?' Dee asked when she hesitated.

'Nothing. It's just that the box the baby was buried in would have been expensive.'

'Stolen, perhaps?'

'It's possible, but a servant couldn't have planted the rose.'

'Maybe the father was one of the gardeners. I imagine there are records of the staff employed here? Would they be in the house?'

'You'll have to ask Howard,' she said, getting to her feet. 'Is that all, only I have to do a supermarket dash before the children get home.'

Dee closed her notebook, tucked it away in her breast pocket and took out a card. 'We're done for the moment, but we will need you to make a formal statement for the coroner.'

Abby nodded. 'Of course.'

'And if anything useful should come to mind, family gossip, that sort of thing,' she continued, 'you can call me on this number.'

'Ruth never gossiped,' she said, taking the card and slipping it into her pocket.

Not with her.

She might have talked to Pam, but she didn't want her bothered so kept that thought to herself.

'I'm afraid you can't do any more work here for the moment, Abby,' Dee said as she stood up. 'And if, as a result of this, you need any counselling—'

'I'll be fine.'

She nodded. 'You won't forget about that tyre?'

'*Top of the list*,' she muttered under her breath, as Dee paused to exchange a word with Shiv before striding away.

Abby crossed to where he was working. He'd taken photographs and, having excavated the hole, held out an evidence bag containing a plain silver cross for her to see.

'I found this,' he said. 'It's hallmarked, so it will give me a date to work with. Any ideas?'

It looked very like the kind of cross that thousands of girls would own. Ruth had given them to her girls as Christening gifts and had worn one very like it herself.

'It was the mother's?' she suggested, imagining the distraught woman taking it off and putting it into her dead baby's hand.

'Maybe,' he said. 'I won't be able to tell if death was due to natural causes until I take a closer look. Maybe not even then.'

'No!' Horrified, Abby took a step back, her hand to her mouth.

There had been love here.

This wasn't a hurried scratching at the soil. The infant had been tenderly wrapped in a blanket, placed in a beautiful box, before being buried deep in this secluded corner of the garden.

'Are you all right, ma'am?'

'I've been better,' she said, blinking away the tears that had welled up. 'Was there any sign of a note? Anything that might help to identify the infant or its mother? Or to tell us what happened?'

'I'll keep looking, but paper would have rotted once the roots broke through the box.'

Abby shivered. The image of roots smashing through the box, through the bones, wasn't something she wanted in her head.

'Someone will give you a call to let you know when you can pick up your things. You can take the toolbox if you didn't use anything in there.'

'No. Just the spade, the hand fork and the trowel.'

'Is there anything else?' he asked, when she didn't grab it and go.

'No . . .' But walking away felt like abandoning this infant and, on an impulse, she took her secateurs from her pocket and cut a white rose from a nearby climber.

'When you've finished, will you leave this in the grave?' she asked.

'We will treat the remains with respect,' he assured her.

She laid the rose on the grass and picked up her toolbox.

'Don't refill the hole when you've finished.' He gave her an odd look. The thought had probably never occurred to him. 'I'll be planting a replacement rose.'

'Oh, right. I'll let you know when you can do that,' he said, 'but in the meantime you should probably give yourself a few minutes before you drive.'

She nodded and, after one last look, she walked up through the garden to her car, peeled off her overalls, flung them in the car boot along with her toolbox and slid behind the wheel.

Shiv was right. It took her three jabs to get the seatbelt fastened and her hand was shaking as she reached for the ignition key.

She sat back, wishing she could bypass the supermarket, go home, have a cup of tea, a soak in a warm bath. All the soothing things you did when you'd had a shock.

The things she'd done the day that Izzy Hamilton had knocked on her door and calmly informed her that she was pregnant with Howard's baby.

Not that his affair came as any great surprise.

In the past the women had been anonymous, brief flings, and afterwards he'd been full of remorse, promising that it would never happen again.

There had been a time when she'd believed him. A time when she had wanted to believe him. By the time she'd realised she was fooling herself, she hadn't cared enough to divorce him and deprive her children of their father.

It was the baby that had changed everything.

Howard had married her seventeen years ago because she was pregnant with Lucy, and with history about to repeat itself, and selected as his party's candidate for one of the safest parliamentary seats in the country, he wanted a suitable setting for his new career as an MP.

For his beautiful, young trophy wife.

Izzy Hamilton was going to be let loose on the house, but he had turned to her to transform the sadly neglected garden of Linton Lodge into a picturesque backdrop for social gatherings.

Her stuff-it-up-your-arse response had backfired badly.

Despite what she'd told Dee Newcombe, this wasn't business. She had no choice but to fit the work around her paying contracts. Which was why she'd been here in her lunchtime, uncovering the bones of a long-dead infant.

CHAPTER THREE

Abby looked up at the house. The family archives would have details of everyone who'd ever worked at the Lodge.

Ruth had kept garden diaries too, dating back to when, as an eighteen-year-old bride, she'd moved into the Lodge with George. If the rose hadn't gone through the household accounts, it was possible that was where she could find out exactly when it had been planted.

But since she'd never had a key to the house, the archives were out of reach. And, thankfully, none of her business.

The supermarket in the new business park on the edge of town was busy. Abby was given the finger by a man who thought she was going to pinch his parking space — she was, but only because she hadn't noticed him.

Jolted into paying closer attention, she was more alert when a woman with a small child on board pulled out without looking, but by the time she had found a place to park, grabbed a couple of bags from the boot and tossed them into a trolley, she was physically shaking.

Food. Concentrate on the food . . .

She piled in veg, fruit, mince, chicken, sausages — the amount three growing children could eat was terrifying.

Milk, cheese, yogurt, eggs. She'd done this so often that she didn't have to think about it. Bread . . .

She swung around the aisle to grab loaves from the bakery and ran into the back of a man checking out an endcap display of expensive chocolates.

'*Ohmigod*, I'm so sorry,' she began as he turned. And then she froze.

'Abby . . . ?'

Jake . . . For a moment her mouth worked, shaped the name, but no sound emerged. Then it did: 'You've grown . . .' And once in action it didn't know when to stop. 'Or I've shrunk.'

He shook his head, laughing. 'Oh no, Abby Lawrence, you are exactly how I remember you.' He reached out, thumbed a smear of dirt off her face and held it up for her to see. 'Foot in your mouth and up to your neck in compost.'

'I wish.' Abby rubbed self-consciously at her cheek. 'But you could be right about the compost.'

'Earthly Designs,' he said, taking in the name emblazoned across her T-shirt. 'I've looked for you every year at Chelsea, hoping to see you holding up a gold medal card.'

She swallowed, remembering how she'd once shared not only her sandwiches with him, but her ambitions.

'Life, and three children, got in the way. I can't believe you're back in Maybridge,' she said, turning the conversation away from her failure, wanting to know about him. 'Where have you been all this time?'

'Here and there.'

'Surely you mean there?' she said. 'Is this a flying visit?'

'No. I'm back for good. No one, not even your husband, is going to drive me away this time.'

'Oh . . .' And just like that, she was the one on the defensive. 'Why? I can't imagine you have good memories of Maybridge.'

'No?' He lifted an eyebrow and she felt herself blushing. 'There's nothing wrong with the town, Abby. It might be small but it has ambitions. There are good transport links, and it has the beauty of the Cotswolds to recommend it.'

'That sounds like a pitch from the Chamber of Commerce,' she said.

'It is, but I didn't need the Chamber of Commerce to convince me that it's the right place to relocate my company. Why don't we go and have a coffee,' he suggested, 'and I'll tell you all about it.'

Jake's invitation was tempting, if only for the chance to sit down . . .

'I wish I could.'

'You're turning me down?'

'It's not you . . .' She wanted to sit with him, hear everything he'd done since he'd disappeared but, clinging to reality, she shook her head. 'The children will be home from school any minute, desperate to be fed.'

Worse, if Howard heard that she'd been seen cosying up over coffee with a man, he'd do his utmost to toss an affair into the divorce settlement. Especially if he discovered the man was Jake Sullivan.

'They'll appreciate your cooking all the more if they have to wait,' Jake said. 'They might even manage to work the toaster.'

'Believe me, they all know how,' she said, moving out of the way as someone, muttering irritably, pushed past her. 'It's why there's never any bread.'

She added three loaves to her trolley.

'You can spare half an hour after all these years.' Not waiting for an answer, he put the bottle of champagne he was holding into her trolley, seized the handle and headed in the direction of the café, leaving her with little option but to follow.

Not that it was a hardship. The years that had added heavy-duty moisturiser to her nightly routine had been kinder to Jake Sullivan.

No longer the skinny, badly dressed kid in foster care whose brains had been a threat to Howard and his fellow jocks at high school, his hair was still curling around his neck, but these days was cut by someone who knew what they were doing.

Jeans were jeans, and his clung to him like a second skin, but the leather bomber jacket he was wearing had the butter-soft look that surely came with a heavy price tag.

He parked the trolley beside a table half hidden by a potted palm — he couldn't have made it look more clandestine. 'What can I get you? Coffee, tea?' He paused. 'Hot chocolate?'

Hot chocolate had been the comfort he'd offered when, shaking and tearful, he'd rescued her from humiliation at the school prom.

'Just tea,' she said, quickly, hoping that he'd put the pinkness in her cheeks down to the heat. The supermarket crush.

He was right about the children, they were perfectly capable of managing without her for half an hour, but while he was gone, she took the chance to call Lucy, who, judging from the background noise, was still on the school bus.

'Hi, Mum. What's up?'

'Nothing. I'm in the supermarket. I just wanted to let you know that I'm running a bit late.'

'There's no need to rush. Tom's got cricket nets so he's still at school, and I'll sort out a snack for Sophie.'

'Thanks, sweetheart. Talking of snacks, can you stop by at Aunt Molly's on the way home? She's made a cake—'

'Do I have to? I've got a ton of homework and she'll keep me ages.'

'Tell her you have to get back for Sophie, although you might want to take a peek at Mabel's kittens.'

'*Mabel's had kittens?*' Now she was interested. 'Can Sophie have one? She's been so sad since Dad left.'

'Possibly, but don't say anything to her until I've thought about it. Did you have a good day?'

'I've been at school, Mum. I have exams in front of me that will define my entire future . . .'

'You'll ace them, and even if you don't—'

'Mum!'

'—it won't be the end of the world, so don't be such a drama queen.'

'You don't understand!'

She did, only too well. Exam pressure, peer pressure, was relentless at that age, and Howard's abandonment had hit her hard too. It wasn't just Sophie who could do with a kitten.

That's if it *was* schoolwork that was bothering her, rather than mean girls giving her a rough time about her father getting Izzy Hamilton up the duff.

Or a boy . . .

'Checking in?' Jake asked, as he set down a tray containing a pot of tea for two and a couple of slices of cake.

'Just asking Lucy to pick something up on her way home.'

'It looked heavier than that.'

'She's rising seventeen. Exams, boys . . .' She found herself blushing.

'You said three children?'

She nodded. 'Tom is fourteen next month and Sophie is ten. Is that lemon drizzle cake?'

'You look as if you could do with a treat.'

'Well spotted. I've had a horrible afternoon.'

'Do you want to talk about it?'

'I don't even want to think about it. I want to hear about you. You disappeared without a word, Jake. What happened to you? Where did you go? And what's this about a company?'

'IT security is big business.'

She grinned. 'The nerd strikes back?'

'How is Howard?' he asked. 'Still playing rugby?'

For a moment he held her gaze as they remembered the night of the prom. What had happened after she'd slapped Howard and he'd rescued her.

'No. He picked up a knee injury.'

'Painful, I hope.'

'How badly did he hurt you, Jake?'

'It was worth it.'

It took Abby a moment to deal with the lump in her throat.

Jake put his hand over hers. 'It wasn't your fault.'

'I embarrassed Howard in front of everyone at the prom and then ran off with you. He was never going to let it go.'

'Unlike you, it would seem. I can't believe you married him, although I hear that he's moved on,' he said. 'That he's about to become a father again. That must be tough.'

'Our marriage was scraping along the bottom long before Izzy Hamilton caught his eye, but the children love their dad and it's hard on them.'

'Then I'm sorry for them but you always deserved better.'

Abby shook her head. 'Old news. What happened to you? Did Howard and his friends run you out of Maybridge?'

'They didn't have to. I was eighteen, school was over and, as far as the system was concerned, I was an adult. I needed a job until I started at Bristol in the autumn, so I did what all hopeful youths do and went to London.'

'How was it?'

'A real eye-opener. There was a big demand for what I could do so I decided the three expensive years at uni would be better spent earning the money to start my own company.'

Which would explain why the letters she'd written had been returned undelivered. But not why he'd never got in touch with her. Never picked up the phone, sent a "wish you were here" postcard. Not that she could have left her mother.

'I meant how was university, but obviously you had bigger ideas.'

He shrugged. 'There were long hours and some seriously hairy moments in the early days, but it was worth it. I just wish you'd dumped Howard and found someone who deserved you.'

She'd thought, for one sweet moment, that she had . . .

'I didn't see Howard again until after I'd graduated and came home for good.'

'I don't understand. Why were you still in Maybridge? You were going to get a job at Kew, or some great stately home.'

Abby shrugged. 'I was offered a job with the National Trust in Norfolk, but Mum never really got over Dad's death. When I realised just how fragile she was, I knew I couldn't leave her.'

'So instead of tending a grand garden, you started your own company.'

'Not then. I got a job at the nursery out at Longbourne. I'd been there a few months when Howard came in looking for a plant for his great-aunt's birthday. There was an awkward moment, but then he said he'd heard my mother was unwell . . .'

'That's all it took?'

'Most of my friends had moved on, had careers. I was a carer, Jake, and I was lonely.'

'That's a long way from marriage.'

'You remember what they used to tell us in those awkward sex ed sessions in school about no contraceptive being a hundred per cent safe?'

'So? No one cares if you're not married these days.'

'True, but Howard's great-uncle George threatened to disinherit him if he didn't do his duty to his unborn child.'

'Really? That's a bit . . . Victorian. If he'd been a girl and got pregnant would they have sent her out into the snow?'

Abby shivered as she thought about the baby buried in the garden . . .

'There were no girls. None that survived beyond infancy. But you're right, Linton Lodge was stuck in the nineteen fifties.'

'So you made the ultimate sacrifice to save him from having to stand on his own two feet?'

'It wasn't like that.' She pulled a face. 'We might not have been love's young dream, but adding single-parenthood to living with my Mum's depression . . .'

The memory of it still sent a lump into her throat, and when Jake's hand tightened over hers, she looked up.

'I felt as if the walls were closing in on me,' Abby said, 'and Howard was always kind to Mum and happy for us to live with her.'

At the time it had felt as if a huge weight had been lifted from her shoulders, and for quite a long time it had been okay.

CHAPTER FOUR

'Failed marriage, failed career . . . You must think me utterly pathetic,' Abby said.

'No . . .'

She managed a smile. 'That could have been more convincing.'

'I was thinking about the time you entered the competition run by the local paper to design a sensory garden for the Memorial Park. I walked past it today and there were people sitting on the bench, enjoying the scent from the roses and lavender.'

'You offered to help with that,' she reminded him. 'How long did you stay?'

'I was only ever in it for the sandwiches.'

She laughed. 'That's a fact.'

His hand was dangerously comforting, and she pulled away, reaching for her tea. It was too hot, the cup burning into her fingers, but she hung onto it.

'We can't all have storybook endings, Jake. He may have become an accidental father, but Howard loves his children. Our youngest, Sophie, was born with a heart murmur, and he used to sit up all night with her when she was a baby.'

'I'm sorry to hear that.'

'She's okay now. It's not that uncommon and, in the end, it settled down by itself.'

'Releasing him to play away.'

Abby frowned. 'Have you been checking up on us?'

'I was talking to someone in the council offices. Howard's name cropped up and I mentioned that our paths had crossed at high school.'

'Why would you do that?'

'People like to gossip.'

She shrugged. 'I never mixed with the County Hall crowd and what Howard referred to as his "little diversions" never lasted for long.'

'And that excuses him? Whatever happened to the Abby Lawrence who punched him out at the prom? She wouldn't have put up with that kind of behaviour.'

'She didn't have three children whose lives would be shattered by divorce.'

'So?' Jake raised an eyebrow. 'What's different now?'

'Izzy Hamilton is pregnant, and marriage is, once more, the only answer.'

The fact that she was not only young and beautiful but politically connected had nothing to do with it. At all.

Was being dumped for his political ambitions better or worse than because the wrinkles were beginning to show?

'You've heard that he's the party's candidate for the next election?'

'I know that Howard's future father-in-law is chair of the local party and this is a safe seat,' he said. 'And these days adultery is no bar to high office.'

'And none of that puts you off bringing your company here?'

'On the contrary. Parliament will get Howard out of local politics and off the Planning Committee doing favours for his cronies. He'll spend most of his time in London, completely neutralised by the party whip.'

'No,' Abby said, 'he never did that. He loves this town, and he takes his responsibilities seriously.'

'You're defending him? Doesn't it rankle that, having supported him for all these years, he's chosen a younger model to be the wife of Howard Finch MP?'

'Oh, please! Can you see me hosting high-power cocktail parties? Politics is in the Hamilton DNA. Izzy was bred for the role.'

'A family in which the men lead and the women serve.'

'It was ever thus . . .' She pulled a face as a thought struck her rather forcibly.

'What?'

She shook her head. 'Nothing . . .' Only that she'd assumed Howard had slipped up, got caught, but she'd been kidding herself. He'd found a replacement who not only looked the part but had all the right connections.

A replacement who had amply demonstrated her qualification for the job by relieving him of the task of informing wife number one that her time was up.

The wife who had been determinedly looking the other way. Ignoring the gossip, assuming that Izzy, like her predecessors, would go away.

Clinging to the imaginary security of a hollow marriage.

Which of them, she wondered, had slipped up with the contraceptive? If it was an accident?

Had Izzy gambled that a baby would make Howard a permanent fix?

Or could it have been the other way around?

Marriage to her had given Howard freedom from his dominating and strait-laced family, the comfort of free bed and board . . .

Marriage to Izzy gave him an open door into national politics.

Could he have been that calculating?

'You're putting on a brave face, but I can see that it hurts,' Jake said, as she bit into the cake with unnecessary savagery and then, as the sugar and lemon filled her mouth, felt sick.

'Enough of Howard,' she said, abandoning the cake. 'Tell me what you've been doing, apart from becoming important,' she said. 'Are you married?'

'Married, divorced, no kids.'

'I'm sorry.'

'Rachael was a mistake. She reminded me of someone I'd carelessly lost.'

Within the bustle of the supermarket café, they were encompassed by a zone of silence as Jake looked at her and she looked back, remembering a night that she had never forgotten.

Abby's heart gave a ridiculous little flutter that was echoed in parts of her body which had lain dormant for far too long. There was no saying how long the moment would have lasted, but every bit of her jumped as her phone, lying on the table by her hand, began to shout at her.

'*This is Lucy. Answer immediately.*'

She rolled her eyes. 'Tom got hold of my phone and gave them all individual ring tones,' she said, picking it up. 'Lucy? Is there a problem?'

'Your office phone rang. I couldn't get to it before the machine kicked in. It was someone from the *Observer* wanting to talk to you about the bones of some baby that you found?' Her voice was shaking. 'What bones, Mum? What's he talking about?'

She didn't believe it. It had been no more than a couple of hours . . .

'It's okay, sweetheart,' she said, already on her feet but doing her best to keep her voice calm, when she wanted to scream her outrage for the entire supermarket to hear. 'It's nothing to worry about, but don't answer the phone or the door. I'll be home as soon as I've got through the checkout.'

She should have been home. This is what happened when you took a self-indulgent half hour dwelling on what might have been, instead of concentrating on your real life.

Jake had risen to his feet. 'What's the problem?'

'Nothing. Family drama. I've got to go. Good luck with everything . . .'

She grabbed her trolley. The supermarket was crowded but she dodged through the shoppers, shouting her apologies as she raced to the checkout, only to come crashing to a halt as she saw the long queues. Harassed mothers who'd picked their younger children up from school, infants demanding sweets from displays handily placed to catch their eyes . . .

'Shit!' She got a warning glance from a woman with two small children. 'Sorry . . .'

'Abby . . .' She turned to find Jake at her elbow. 'You've got my champagne.'

She looked in the trolley and saw the bottle lying among her shopping, a darkly expensive counterpoint to the budget chicken and sausages.

'Oh, sorry . . .'

He didn't take it.

'Is there anything I can do?'

'No . . . Damn journalists. You'll read all about in the *Maybridge Observer* in the morning.'

She looked around the woman in front of her, trying to see what was holding things up.

'Go,' he urged. 'I'll take care of this and drop it off.'

'I can't ask you to do that!'

'Howard might think a supermarket queue beneath him, but I can assure you that I've done it before. From both ends. Where are you living now?'

'Same place.'

The queue was stationary as someone waited for a price.

'You're still living in your mother's house?'

'Yes.' She hadn't wanted to move, and Howard had been content to stay there. She had been a very cheap wife. No wonder he'd kept coming back . . .

'Okay,' Jake said, 'I need a couple of things, but I'll drop your shopping off as soon as I'm done.'

'I haven't got any cash. Let me give you my card,' she said, reaching into her bag.

'For heaven's sake, Abby, I've got this. Just go.'

She looked at him for a moment, then turned and ran.

* * *

'Mum . . .'

Abby dropped her bag and car keys on the kitchen island and wrapped her arms around Lucy, who clung to her like the little girl she had been what felt like just weeks ago.

'It's okay, sweetheart. It's okay.'

'Okay?' She wrenched herself away. 'You found the bones of a baby! In what world is that okay?'

'Where's Sophie? Did she hear the message?'

'No. She grabbed some cake and took it upstairs. She said she's doing her homework, but she'll be playing *Minecraft*.'

'Ask her to come down, will you? And I'll tell you both what happened today, but first I have to make a phone call.' Lucy didn't move. 'Please, sweetheart.'

She ran up the stairs shouting for her sister while Abby took out the card that Dee Newcombe had given her.

'Abby . . . You sound upset. Have you thought of something?'

'No, I haven't thought of anything, and yes, I'm very upset. Did you inform the local press about what I found at Linton Lodge?' she asked. 'Only someone from the *Observer* called and left a message on my office answering machine that my daughter overheard.'

'That's . . . unfortunate.'

'Unfortunate?'

'My inspector thought that the local press might help us discover who buried the baby.'

'Really? Can you imagine what the poor woman will be going through if she sees the headlines?'

'It's not my decision, Abby, and there will have to be an inquest, so it can't be kept secret. But I am sorry that your daughter heard about it that way. I've no idea how they could have found out that it was you who discovered them.'

'It's just possible that they rang around all the gardeners in Maybridge,' she replied sharply, 'or perhaps it was the fact that the Lodge belongs to my husband, and I run a gardening service — might that have invited an educated guess?'

'Yes . . . Yes, of course. I'm sorry,' she repeated. 'I will pass your complaint up the line.'

And with that Abby's anger seeped away. This wasn't about Dee Newcombe, this was her guilt for dallying in the supermarket with Jake when she should have been at home.

'No, I'm sorry for being so bad-tempered . . . You've got a job to do.'

'And you've had a bad day. When do you think you can come in to make a statement?'

'How long will it take? I'm going to be playing catch-up with the jobs I missed today.'

'Can you come in early tomorrow morning? Eight thirty? It shouldn't take too long.'

'Can we make it nine? I do the morning school run.' It would still take a chunk out of her day, but she wanted it over with.

About to ask when she could go back to the Lodge, she realised that she had the perfect excuse to stay away for a few days and catch up with the paying jobs.

Before she could compose herself to tell her girls what had happened, the office phone began to ring. The number flashed up "unknown" but she was pretty sure who it was going to be.

'Earthly Designs.'

'Mrs Finch? Gary Jackson at the *Maybridge Observer*. I left a message? We've had a report from the police about the bones you found at Linton Lodge. Is there any chance of a quick interview so that we can make tomorrow's paper?'

'Your less than discreet message was overheard by one of my children, Mr Jackson, so I'm sure you'll understand that I'm a little busy right now. I suggest you contact my husband at his office. Finch Developments.' And hung up.

Who knew, Natalie might consider a call from the press enough of an emergency to risk contacting Howard. The whiff of scandal, in a family that had been the model of moral rectitude until he'd started playing around, would certainly get editorial juices flowing. Especially with an election in the offing.

She would have liked to think that now they were separated it was none of her business, but there were the children to consider and, taking a deep breath, she headed for the kitchen to give Sophie a hug.

'Did Lucy tell you about the message?'

'No . . .' She glared at her sister.

'You said you were doing your homework.'

Sophie flushed. 'I was!'

'Girls! This is important.' Once she had silence, she said, 'I'd rather have told you all together, but Tom won't be home for a while—'

'What?' Sophie demanded. 'Has something happened to Daddy?'

'No, sweetheart, he's absolutely fine,' she said. Sophie had always been Daddy's little girl and had been displaying anxiety issues since his departure. 'As you know, I'm doing some work for him at the Lodge, but today, when I was digging out the roots of an old rose, I found some bones. They were very old,' she added, quickly.

'How old?'

'It's impossible to say, but certainly more than twenty years. Probably a lot older.'

'Whose bones?' Lucy asked.

Good question. And she wouldn't be the only one asking that. Or want to know who had buried the infant.

CHAPTER FIVE

News of her discovery was going to be on the front page of the local rag in the morning, and it was better Sophie heard the full story from her.

'They were the bones of a baby,' she explained. 'It had probably been stillborn.'

'That means it never breathed,' Lucy said before Sophie could ask.

'Never?'

'It happens sometimes,' Abby said, 'when something is wrong with the baby.'

'Oh . . .' She thought for a moment. 'But why was it buried in the garden instead of the churchyard?'

'I don't know, but it had been done with love,' she said, hoping to mitigate the horror a little. 'It was wrapped in a hand-knitted blanket, placed in a beautiful box and left with a little silver cross.'

'A cross? Was it Great-Aunt Ruth's baby? She always wore a cross, and she would have wanted to have her baby close.'

'You can't bury people in your garden, Sophie. It's not allowed,' Lucy said. 'And if Aunt Ruth'd had a baby that died it would have been buried in the family vault at St Michael's.

Besides, she was wearing her cross the last time we saw her in the hospital.'

'She could have bought a new one.'

Dragging her mind from the image of the dry, humourless Ruth and George doing anything as unrestrained and fun as having sex, Abby said, 'Lucy's right, sweetheart, but the thing is, if you find human bones, you have to call the police, so it's going to be in the paper tomorrow.'

And probably on the local news tonight, although hopefully without her name being mentioned.

'Your friends might ask you about it at school.'

'Will they use DNA to find out who the mother was?' Lucy asked.

'Possibly.'

'If you could find out when the rose was planted, that would give you a date.'

'It was very old,' she said.

'That doesn't matter. After Uncle George died and Daddy was going through some paperwork for Aunt Ruth, I asked him when the house was built—'

'Somewhere in the middle of the nineteenth century?'

'It was in eighteen sixty-eight,' Lucy said. 'He showed me the Land Registry documents. They're in a room on the top floor with all the ledgers and household accounts going back to when the house was built. The rose is bound to be there.'

'Among thousands of entries. It would take forever to find it. It might even have been a gift,' she said. 'People knew that Aunt Ruth loved her garden and gave her plants for birthdays. That's how I met up with Daddy again, after uni. When he was buying her a plant.'

'Don't you want to find out?' Lucy demanded.

'Of course, but it's a job for the police.'

'Oh, please! They aren't going to lock up anyone for an illegal burial after all these years, so why would they bother looking?'

'Lucy—'

'And what will happen to the bones when the police have finished with them? They'll be left in a cardboard box gathering dust unless someone claims them. No name,' she added, passionately, 'just a case number.'

'Does Daddy know about the baby?' Sophie asked.

'Not yet,' she said, turning with relief to her youngest. 'I rang his office, but he's away at a conference.'

'I could call him.'

'He'll be in meetings, sweetheart, and there's nothing he can do while he's away.'

'Oh . . .' Her face fell. Clearly, she'd hoped that this news would bring him to the house.

Lucy, seeing her distress, said, 'Mabel's had kittens, Soph. I saw them when I picked up the cake from Aunt Molly's.'

'Kittens?'

'And she gave me a flyer about the church summer fete,' Lucy said, turning away, pretending she hadn't heard. 'She's hoping you'll run your usual plant stall.'

'How many kittens?' Sophie demanded.

'When is it?' asked Abby, catching on to the teasing.

'June, I think. She's written a note on it. I've pinned it to the notice board.'

'Let me see . . .' She made a performance of hunting among thank you notes, a card for a dental appointment that had happened months ago, several party invitations for Sophie, notices from window cleaners who only came once . . .

'Lucy!' Sophie looked as if she was about to explode. 'Tell me about the kittens! How many are there? What colour are they? Can we have one?'

Lucy raised her eyebrows at her mother, who returned an imperceptible nod.

'There are five of them, Soph. There's a ginger tabby, one white with ginger tabby patches, two white ones with ginger and black patches and one very fluffy black-and-white kitten.'

'Oh . . .'

'Aunt Molly said that if Mum agreed, you could have one.'

With all thought of everything else swept from her mind, she said, 'Can I, Mum? Can I? Please, please, please . . .'

It was so rare for her to be the good parent, the one giving treats for once, instead of the endless nagging about homework, messy rooms, screen time . . .

She made a mental note of the date of the summer fete and gave Lucy a discreet thumbs-up for first-class distraction technique.

To hell with thinking about it.

'I think a kitten is exactly what we need.'

Her warning that it wouldn't be able to leave its mother until it was eight weeks old was drowned out by the excited squeals as Sophie jumped around the kitchen.

'But—' she began, when she could finally make herself heard.

'No! No horrible buts!'

'But,' she repeated, remembering what Molly had said, 'we'll be out most of the day and one kitten would be lonely by itself.'

Lucy grinned, but it took Sophie a moment longer . . .

'Are you saying that we can have *two* kittens?'

She nodded and was almost knocked over by a ten-year-old flinging herself at her and wrapping her arms around her in a bear hug.

'Thank you, thank you, thank you!'

'Come on, let's get the shopping out of the car and then we can go and choose them,' Lucy said, too cool to hug but unable to hide the kind of smile that had been missing since her father had moved out.

'Ah . . . Slight problem. I don't have the shopping.'

Lucy turned in the doorway. 'But you were in the supermarket when I called you.'

'Yes, but I wanted to get home before anyone turned up on the doorstep asking about the bones I found, and the queue was horrendous—'

'Don't say you abandoned it! We'll starve!'

'Don't worry, you'll be fed. I was talking to an old friend when you rang, and he offered to put it through the checkout for me.'

'He?' Lucy was on it instantly.

'Jake.' Just saying his name churned up such a mix of emotions, mostly guilt, and she felt her cheeks heat up. 'We were all in the same year at high school.' There was a crunch of tyres on the gravel. 'That's probably him now.'

There was the thump of a boot lid, the click of the side gate and then Jake was at the kitchen door, a bag of shopping in either hand. One hessian, with the words "Crazy Gardening Lady" on the side, the other pink, proclaiming the bearer to be the "World's Coolest Mum".

'Sorry I was so long,' he said. 'There was a minor collision in the entrance to the car park. No real damage, but the exit was blocked while hot air and insurance details were exchanged.' He placed the bags on the kitchen island then said, 'Hello, Lucinda.'

'Jake? What are you doing here? How do you know my mother?'

'I told you. Jake was in the same year as Daddy and I at high school,' Abby said, feeling like a teenager caught out by her mother as Lucy turned and stared at her. 'What I'm wondering is how you've come to be on first-name terms with him.'

'Jake came to school this afternoon to talk about internet safety.'

'And you told me you'd had a boring day.' Abby turned to Jake, eyebrows raised. 'You never mentioned that you'd been back to school when we were reminiscing in the bread aisle.'

'I'd just come from there when you nearly ran me down with your trolley,' he said, picking up on the hint not to mention that they'd been having a cosy one-to-one over tea and cake when Lucy had called.

'Come on, Luce! Let's go!'

'The child panting with impatience is Sophie. The girls have an urgent appointment with some kittens,' she explained. 'Say hello to Jake, Sophie.'

'Hello, Jake.'

'Hello, Sophie.'

'We have to put away the groceries before we go,' Lucy said, clearly wanting to stay and see just what kind of friends they were.

'I'll let you off this once, but I'm relying on you to choose a pretty kitten for me. And tell Aunt Molly I'll be along later to cut her grass.'

Lucy gave her a look that suggested she was just putting off the interrogation. 'Maybe we should have a kitten each.'

'Two's company, three's a crowd.'

'In that case you should find another home for Tom,' she suggested.

'No need. You'll be away at university soon enough.'

She shrugged. 'It was worth a try. Goodbye, Jake.'

'Goodbye, Lucinda.'

Neither of them spoke until the sound of their feet running down the drive had died away.

'You've had the kitchen extended,' Jake said, looking around.

'We needed more room,' she said. 'I twisted Howard's arm when he was grovelling for forgiveness after one of his dalliances.'

'The expense must have clipped his wings for a while. Although not as expensive as a divorce.'

'There was no question of him coming back this time, even if he'd wanted to,' she said, concentrating on unpacking the bags, putting the meat and vegetables in the fridge.

Taking the hint to drop the subject, he said, 'I take it the drama that brought you racing home has been sorted?'

'Not really. It'll be on the front page of the *Observer* tomorrow, no doubt with all kinds of sordid speculation. Howard is going to be furious.'

'Will it help to talk about it?'

'No . . . Yes . . . I don't know.'

'Why don't you give it a try?'

Abby closed the fridge door. It was ridiculous to feel as if she were somehow betraying Howard by telling Jake what she'd found when the news would be public property in the morning.

'Howard's great-aunt died a few months ago,' she said. 'He's finally got his hands on Linton Lodge.'

'The gothic monstrosity at the top of Huntsman's Hill? Was that the inheritance that required his name on a marriage certificate?'

'That and Finch Developments.'

'The family firm? I can see the incentive.'

She looked up. 'That's just a little bit insulting, Jake.'

'I didn't mean—'

'He was excited about the baby. He was excited about all of them,' she said. 'He wanted a big family.'

'So much so that he's starting again, but not until his aunt was dead.'

'The house was going to come to him on Ruth's death no matter what,' she said, 'and she adored him. She might not have approved of divorce, but Izzy Hamilton is exactly the kind of woman she would have chosen for him.'

'I'm sensing you weren't a fan.'

'The feeling was mutual. I'm sure Ruth's refusal to move into a nursing home was to prevent me from moving into her precious house,' she said, as she unloaded the rest of the shopping and tucked it away in the cupboards.

'She didn't approve of Howard's choice?'

'Less a choice, more an inconvenient mistake. I hoped we might bond over our mutual love for gardening but, as far as she was concerned, I was a town girl, no better than she ought to be, who'd seduced her darling boy when he had been meant for the daughter of some well-connected county family. Worse, our unfortunate moral lapse failed to produce a son.'

'Which meant you had to lapse again. Twice. And you still failed to provide a spare.'

He was so serious that it took her a moment, then she laughed, really laughed for the first time in what felt like months.

'She needn't have worried. I might have had my eye on the kitchen garden as a base for Earthly Designs, but the house always gave me the shivers. I not only championed her cause to stay put,' she said, 'I was willing her on to a century.'

'The divorce was perfectly timed to save you from that, at least.'

CHAPTER SIX

Abby gave Jake a look and he held up his hands.

'I'm sorry. That was insensitive.'

'No, you're right. I'd been dreading it.' She picked up a tin of biscuits. 'You've put this in my bag by mistake.'

'No mistake. I was tossing up between flowers and chocolates for Zaida, but the first is a nuisance when you're in the middle of preparing dinner and the second is lazy and probably unwelcome.'

Zaida?

'And chocolate biscuits are better?' she asked.

'They're for her children. Was it a stupid idea?'

'For her children or mine?'

'They don't grow out of them when they get older, do they?'

Zaida has young children . . .

'I seem to remember that you liked them,' she said, 'and my three will be delighted. I'm sorry they've gone, or the girls could have thanked you themselves.'

'There's no need to tell them it was from me if it would be awkward.'

'No . . . Well, maybe,' she said, wondering if the mother of the younger children who was, she assumed, going to share the champagne, had a husband. Which was none of her business. 'I need to pay you for my groceries.'

'You don't have any cash,' he reminded her, 'but it's not a problem since it means that we'll have to meet tomorrow. For lunch?'

'It's a working day for me, Jake.' And it was going to be a long one.

'You don't stop to eat?' he asked.

She had until Howard had arm-twisted her into working at the Lodge.

'A sandwich on the go.' Hot, sweaty and in her overalls.

'I could bring a picnic. Payback for all the times you shared your sandwiches — and chocolate biscuits — with me when we worked in the school garden.'

'Worked? You never worked. You were only there to avoid the sports field and help yourself to the contents of my lunchbox.' It hadn't taken her long to realise how much he'd needed the food and she'd always made extra on gardening days.

'The food was welcome,' he said, 'but the company was better. So? Are you up for it? We could take out a boat and make an afternoon of it.'

'Sadly, tomorrow I will be working twice as hard to catch up on the jobs I missed today. I could drop the money off at your office.'

'Is that a hint that you don't want my company?'

'No . . .' She couldn't think of anything she'd enjoy more than a repeat of those innocent lunch hours. Innocence that had been lost on the night of the prom. 'But it's probably not a good idea.'

'Howard is bunked up with Izzy Hamilton,' he reminded her. 'He can't possibly object to you meeting up with an old friend.'

'You're not just any old friend,' she reminded him, 'but we never had that cup of tea. Have you got time?'

'Have you?'

'The girls have stemmed their hunger with cake,' she said, 'and Tom's at cricket nets.'

'He takes after his father, then.'

'In looks and sport,' she said. And, like his father, he was going to be a girl magnet. She'd have said that Tom had a gentler soul. She hoped so, but she had no idea what he was like at school. 'The next few years are going to be . . . interesting.' She pulled a face. 'As are the next few days,' she said, switching on the kettle and taking down a couple of mugs as Jake slid onto a stool at the breakfast bar.

'This is about the drama?'

'As I said, Howard has inherited the Lodge. I'm doing some work in the garden—'

'You're kidding,' he said.

She waved a hand. 'It's complicated. Anyway, this afternoon I uncovered the bones of a baby.'

'Good God, Abby. No wonder you looked so shaky when I saw you.'

'I thought it was a cat, which was bad enough, but then I found the skull . . .'

As the horror of it came back to her, the mug she was holding slipped through her fingers and shattered on the floor.

In a heartbeat Jake was on his feet, his arms around her, pulling her close. She didn't resist the comfort.

'They were very old bones,' she said, leaning into his chest.

'I don't care how old they were, Abs, that's got to be a shock to the system.'

'I'm okay. Really,' she said, forcing herself to pull away. 'But a reporter from the *Observer* rang here and Lucy heard him blurt it all out on the answering machine.'

'Why call here? Surely the first place to contact would be Howard's office . . .'

'Oh . . .'

'What?'

She shook her head. 'That's how they knew it was me. They called there first, but as Howard is away, Natalie, his very helpful personal assistant, suggested they try me.'

'You're kidding. If my PA had done that his feet wouldn't have touched the floor.'

'Not going to happen . . .' She pulled a face. 'The poor cow has been mooning after Howard since he took her on ten years ago. She's made herself indispensable. Covering for him when he was playing away, hoping that one day it would be her turn.'

He shook his head. 'Well, that's not about to happen.'

'No, and since she can't take out her frustration on Howard, I'm her punchbag.'

'Does he know?'

'How she feels? Of course he does. He's been keeping her hopes alive for years with little gifts and that sad "if only I wasn't married" smile . . .'

'That's a dangerous game. If he's not careful, one of these days she'll put more than sugar in his coffee.'

'Jake!'

'Sorry . . .' He pulled a face. 'My little fantasy.'

'Hardly. If you wanted to hurt him, you'd hack into his bank accounts and give all his money to charity.'

'Don't give me ideas,' he said, but then lost the smile. 'Is Lucinda okay?'

'A bit shaken,' she said, then realising what he'd said, 'Everyone calls her Lucy. How did you know that her name is Lucinda?'

'I asked the kids to write their names on sticky labels for the talk this afternoon,' he said, 'and that's what she wrote.'

'Oh . . . And you noticed her? Among how many students?'

'Just years eleven and twelve, but I'd have picked her out of a packed hall.'

'Really?'

'Come on, Abby, she's tall, with almost white-blonde hair. She looks just like you at that age. And like you, there were boys a lot more interested in looking at her than listening to me.'

Abby pushed back a loose strand of hair, still fair but these days with a helping hand from the hairdresser.

'How many boys?' She shook her head, not wanting to know. 'There is no way I'm letting her go to the prom.'

'Good luck with that,' Jake said. 'So? What next?'

'I have to go to the police station and make a statement for the coroner, but they can't seriously think they're going to find the mother after all this time.'

'It's got to have been someone connected with the house. I imagine there will be records?'

'Of every penny spent since the day they dug the foundations of the house. And Ruth kept a gardening journal, which is another source of information.'

'Did you mention them to the police?'

She shook her head. 'I suggested they ask Howard, but I imagine he'll deny any knowledge of them. He's going to be absolutely furious with me.'

'Why? You didn't bury the bones.'

'No, but if I hadn't been so determined to clear out all the roots of that old rose, I wouldn't have gone deep enough to find them.'

'I don't understand why you were there in the first place.'

'Tom is going on a field trip to Iceland this summer.'

'So?'

'Howard wants the garden put straight before he moves in with Izzy, so we came to an agreement.'

'Are you saying that he's applying emotional blackmail to get you to work for him before he'd pay up?'

'Mum . . . ?'

Tom was standing in the doorway, sports bag slung over his shoulder. If Lucinda was like her, then Tom was the image of his father. Tall for his age, with lumberjack shoulders and a mess of fair hair that in his case was in dire need of a cut.

'Is that true?' he demanded. 'Is Dad making you clear up his garden before he'll pay for my trip?'

'No! No, of course not, Tom. Your trip is paid for,' she said, which was true. 'The deal is that we would go halves on this kind of thing, but Dad offered to pay for the whole trip if I did some work in the garden.'

Tom looked at her for a moment, as if trying to judge whether she was telling him the truth. Then he turned to Jake. 'Is that your car in the drive?'

'It is.'

'I saw it outside school today. You gave a talk on the internet to the sixth form.'

'I'm giving another one for years nine and ten next week.' He stepped forward and put out his hand. 'Jake Sullivan. I was in the same year as your mum and dad in high school.'

Tom grinned. 'Tom Finch. Can I do my work experience with you?'

'Tom! You're going to be doing that with your dad. You said you were looking forward to it.'

'I am. He's going to let me have a go on a digger, but I don't want to be a builder. IT is the future.'

'It's a growth industry,' Jake agreed. 'I'm still in the process of moving to Maybridge so can't offer work experience yet, but once we're set up, I'll see if I can sort something out with the school.' Jake turned back to her. 'I'll have to take a rain check on the tea, Abby, Zaida's expecting me. It was good catching up.'

'Yes . . . Enjoy your evening.'

Neither she nor Tom spoke for a moment, almost as if they were holding their breath until they heard his tyres crunching over the gravel.

'It's very quiet. What is it?' Abby asked. 'The car.'

'A Tesla.'

'Nice.'

Tom laughed, breaking the tension. 'Understatement of the year.'

'That good?'

'Come on, Mum, it's all electric. The future . . .'

She grinned.

'Oh, you're kidding.'

'Sorry, I shouldn't tease. Grab me a bag of oven chips from the freezer, will you?' Food never failed to distract him.

'I can't see any chips,' he said. 'There are some hash browns.'

'They'll do.'

'Mum . . .' he said, as he handed them over. 'I could give you a hand at the weekend. I don't know much about plants, but I could cut the grass.'

'That would have nothing to do with the fact that there's a ride-on mower at the Lodge?'

He grinned. 'I could handle it.'

'Thanks, kiddo. I'll bank that offer, but the garden is out of bounds for the moment.' She ran through the events of the afternoon, warning him about the newspaper. 'Be careful of people asking you questions about what I found.' She'd have to warn the girls about that too. 'Just say you don't know anything.'

'That's easy. I don't. How long until tea? I'm starving.'

CHAPTER SEVEN

'Aunt Molly said you'd want the white kitten with little patches of black and orange,' Lucy said, as she picked at her sausage. 'We chose the black-and-white one. She's going to have long hair, like Mabel.'

'They sound perfect. Have you thought of any names?'

'Patch and Princess,' Sophie said.

'Princess!' Tom made a pretence of sticking his fingers down his throat. 'Why can't we have a dog?'

'Because I'm out all day.'

'You could take it with you.'

'My clients expect me to keep their gardens looking neat and tidy, not take along a four-legged digging and pooping machine. Now, I'm going to leave you to clear up while I go and cut Aunt Molly's lawn.'

'Oh, but— Ow!'

'Sophie?'

'Nothing.' Abby looked at Lucy, who looked back, the picture of innocence despite the fact that she had clearly just kicked her sister under the table.

'Why do you cut Aunt Molly's grass?' Tom asked. 'She doesn't pay you.'

'I do it because she was a friend of your great-grandma's and I've known her all my life. She's family.'

'But you've had a horrible day. I could go and cut it for you.'

Abby, warmed, said, 'That's very kind of you, Tom, but she has a favour to ask, so I'll let you get on with your homework.'

'I'd rather be cutting grass.'

'Save your enthusiasm for the Lodge. Oh, and Tom, when I say you clear up, I do mean all three of you.'

'I know. Clearing the table and stacking the dishwasher is not girl's work,' he said parrot-fashion, having heard it a hundred times before.

'Believe it, because this is an equal-opportunities household and I'm perfectly happy to let Lucinda loose on the ride-on mower if you're in any doubt.'

'Lucinda?' Tom grinned. 'Can I have that sausage if you're not going to eat it, Looocinda?'

She rolled her eyes. 'Help yourself. I've decided to become a vegetarian.'

'Hold it right there!' Abby took a breath. 'I have no problem with any of you deciding to become vegetarian, but I need notice of any change of diet, so you're going to have to eat what's on your plate tonight.'

'Have you any idea—?'

'If the kitchen is clean and tidy when I get back,' she said, not in the mood for a discussion about the contents of sausages, 'I'll break out the tin of chocolate biscuits that somehow fell into my trolley today. Although I can't promise they'll be vegetarian.'

She left them to it, in no doubt that Tom would eat all of Lucy's sausages, but too tired to care as she pushed open Aunt Molly's gate.

She stopped as she was hit by the scent of freshly cut grass. The patch of lawn at the front had been cut, the edges neatly trimmed. It was the same around the back, where she found Molly sitting on her garden bench, a youth sprawled out in a chair beside her, with a can of soda in his hand.

'Abby!' she said. 'Come and meet Cal. He's my sister's grandson.'

'Hello, Cal. Is this your work?' she asked, looking at the lawn.

'Hasn't he done a good job?' Molly said.

'Excellent,' Abby agreed, wondering why no one had mentioned that the grass had been cut so that right now she could be lying in the bath. Then she remembered the kick Lucy had given her sister under the table. Molly had obviously asked them not to tell.

The favour she wanted had to be important.

'Go and fetch Abby a can of pop, Cal.'

'No, I'm good—'

'Coffee, then. No sugar.'

He unfolded himself like a marionette — skinny, slightly disjointed, not yet quite grown into his limbs — put down the can and disappeared into the house.

'He's a good boy,' Molly said.

'I'm sure he is.'

'Penny thinks I'm losing my marbles, so she's sent him to stay with me.'

Abby frowned. 'Why would she think that?'

'You've met my sister. Penny is the smart one who had a job in a . . .' She trailed off, waved a hand. 'She wore a white coat.'

'She's a bit bossy?' Abby recalled.

'A bit, but she took care of me when I was young. I forgot her birthday. I never forget birthdays . . .'

'It happens to all of us.' Abby hadn't noticed anything amiss, but she visited once a week at the most and, just lately, she'd been too busy to sit down for a chat after she'd cut the grass. But maybe Penny was right . . . 'Cal will be company for you,' she said.

'Cal? Oh, yes, but he's going to be bored rigid stuck around me all day. What he really needs is a job. The girls tell me that you're working all hours. Not even time for lunch. You wouldn't have to pay him much.'

Oh, right.

It wasn't Molly whose marbles had got loose. Her own brain was fogged with an overload of emotional crap, or she'd have caught on sooner.

She could certainly do with an extra pair of hands if she was going to get through the next month or so, but against that was the paperwork involved, not to mention the cost.

'If I took him on,' she said, cautiously, 'I'd have to pay him the minimum wage. It's the law.'

'Couldn't you just pay him cash in hand?'

'You know I can't.'

Molly shrugged, clearly thinking that she was being a bit of a jobsworth. 'Just a suggestion.'

'One that could get me into all kinds of trouble. Has he ever done garden work before?' she asked. 'Apart from cutting your lawn?'

'No, but he's stronger than he looks and despite that slightly dozy exterior, he's quite bright. He could do the basic lawn cutting and you could get through it all much more quickly. Take on more jobs. And he's good with engines.'

'You do a good job selling him, Molly. Do you want to tell me the real reason he's here?'

She shrugged, sighed. 'He's been in a bit of trouble. His mum wanted him out of the way for a while.'

'What kind of trouble? I go into people's gardens, Molly. They trust me around their homes.'

'He's been going on demos. You've seen the kind of thing that's been happening in Bristol. His mum thought he was at school and had no idea until he got arrested and cautioned after a scuffle with the police. There's no dad to keep him on the straight and narrow and Penny suggested he come here to keep an eye on me.'

'It sounds to me more like the other way around. You said he should have been at school. How old is he?'

'He's nearly eighteen and good with his hands. He had a part-time job in a garage for a while, but he said that Black Lives Matter is more important.'

'He's got a point,' she said. If that's all it was. 'How long is he staying?'

'For the summer . . .' It sounded more like a question.

Cal arrived carrying a mug of coffee. 'No sugar,' he said, putting it down on the table. Clearly a boy of few words, which would be restful.

Abby needed to be sure. 'Cal, can you go around the lawn again with the edging shears. Trim it a touch closer.'

'Again?' he repeated, affronted. 'It's perfect.'

She made no comment, just waited, and after a moment he shrugged and fetched the long-handled shears from the shed.

Abby watched as he went around the edge, taking off another millimetre with a lazy economy of movement that made it look easy.

'Close enough?' he asked when he was done, looking at her with just a glint of humour in a pair of very dark eyes.

'Close enough,' she said, doing her best not to betray her true thoughts and afraid that she wasn't quite making it.

She was torn. He was a natural if ever she'd seen one and Molly was right, she could do with the help. She was equally sure that there was more to his arrival than a skirmish with the police at a demonstration.

'Okay. I've got some work that needs doing. Nothing fancy. Lawns, edging, cutting back shrubs. I'll show you what to do.' It would take a bite out of her profits but while he was doing the heavy work at the Lodge, she wouldn't be getting behind and upsetting paying customers. 'Minimum wage,' she warned, 'and I won't take any nonsense. Are you up for it?'

'I've got nothing else to do.'

'Give me your phone number and I'll send you a text when I need you, but for now clean off the shears and put them away. Oh, and Cal . . .'

He raised his eyebrows.

'From now on, you'll be cutting your aunt's lawn.'

'Will I get paid for that?' he asked.

'The same way I do,' she said. 'In cakes and kittens.'

He grinned at that, and she realised with something of a shock that with his olive skin and lost-boy demeanour, he'd be dangerous around her more vulnerable ladies.

Around Lucy.

Not a problem. He was going to be safely out of the way at Linton Lodge and she'd be the one picking up cakes from now on.

'Thanks, Abby,' Molly said, when he'd loped off, 'I really appreciate you doing this for me. It'll be such a relief to have him occupied.'

'With luck it will be good for all of us,' she said. 'Apart from taking on extra work for Howard, something rather unsettling happened today that has set me back. I wouldn't mention it, but you'll read all about in the paper tomorrow.'

'The paper? What happened?'

'I uncovered the bones of an infant.'

'I . . .'

For a moment Molly couldn't speak and Abby, aware that she hadn't been able to have children of her own, took her hand. 'I'm sorry. I didn't mean to upset you.'

'No, it's just the shock. For you.'

'It was,' she admitted, 'and of course the police had to be called. It's why I'm so behind today.'

For a moment neither of them spoke, then Molly said, 'Did Lucy give you my note about the summer fete? Your plant stall is always so popular.'

'She did, and of course I'll do it. Now, has Mabel been through enough today or can I take a peek at the kittens?'

* * *

Abby's find made headlines in the *Observer*, which came as no surprise. What she hadn't anticipated was seeing her face peering back at her from the front page.

Not the neutral head-and-shoulders shot she used for Earthly Designs' social media pages, but the picture of her in her overalls, foot on a spade, that they'd lifted from her website.

The idea had been to show that, just because she was a woman, she wasn't afraid of getting stuck into the hard work of creating and maintaining a garden.

The *Observer* had contrived to make it look as if she'd posed for the photograph in the act of digging up the bones.

Bad enough, but it carried on inside with pictures of Howard with Izzy, mention of his runaway mother and the tragic death of his father in a shooting accident. They hadn't put the last phrase in inverted commas, but they might as well have done. There was even a photograph of Howard's great-uncle Stephen, who'd died at Dunkirk.

The story was a gift of an excuse to rake through old history and they hadn't missed a thing.

The first call was from Megan West, with whom she'd developed an unlikely friendship.

'Abby! What the hell?'

'Meg . . . How was your holiday?'

'Forget my holiday. I go away for a few days and come back to find you on the front page of the *Observer*.'

'A few days? You've been lying on a beach in the West Indies for the last two weeks. I'm in the wrong business.'

'You're not in the wrong business, sweetie. You're just doing it wrong. You need to employ two or three hefty lads on whatever scheme the government is using to keep them off the streets these days and charge your customers the going the rate for garden maintenance.'

'And you wonder why estate agents have a bad name.'

'Apprenticeships,' she said, totally unabashed. 'That's the thing. You'll be teaching them valuable skills, setting them up for the future, but we can talk about that another time. What's all this about you finding bones at Linton Lodge?'

'The *Observer* hasn't left anything out.'

'I've read all the gory details and the ghastly innuendo,' she said, 'but there's nothing about how you're feeling.'

'That's because I wouldn't talk to them.'

'I don't blame you, but it must have been a shock to the system.'

'I'm okay, really, but I'm in the middle of the pre-school rush. I'll call you this evening.'

'Wait! I've got some news for you.'

'You've met someone?' she asked. 'A handsome millionaire who happened to be lounging by the pool—'

'Sadly, no, but I came in early this morning to get ahead before we open. Did you know that Howard has instructed us to put Linton Lodge on the rental market?'

'What? Hold on, I can't hear myself think.' She left the chaos of the kitchen, where the local radio was giving out traffic reports and the children were bickering over breakfast, and headed for the quiet of the room — little bigger than a cupboard — that she'd converted into her office. 'Now,' she said, 'say that again.'

'Howard has put Linton Lodge on the rental market.'

'That's what I thought you said, but I still can't believe I'm hearing it.'

'It was on the lettings list that went out yesterday and Steve left a message asking me to arrange an inventory of the place as a matter of urgency. I take it Howard hasn't said anything to you?'

'The last I heard, Izzy was all set to rip the place apart. I'm reliably informed that she's been talking to an architect and a seriously upmarket interior designer.'

'There are always people who can't wait to tell you what your ex is doing with the new woman in his life,' she said. 'There's a reason I have tissues on my desk.'

'Believe me, I couldn't be less interested, but what on earth is he thinking? Izzy is going to make his life hell if he's thrown a giant spanner in her works.'

'There's an upside to everything,' Meg said. 'He's going to have to come up with a really convincing reason for the delay. Something to do with the divorce settlement would be my bet, bearing in mind his recent disappointment over the marital home.'

Abby sighed.

She'd met Meg, a partner at estate agents Marshall & West, when she'd found her, key in hand, about to let herself into her house.

Howard, assuming that she'd be at work, had instructed them to value the house as part of the divorce settlement.

Abby had invited her in and explained why that was not going to happen.

It was true that, when she'd inherited the house from her mother, Howard had suggested that she add his name to the deeds 'for tax purposes'. He'd even offered to have his own solicitor do it for her, but when she'd mentioned it to Freddie Jennings, who'd drawn up her mother's will, he'd informed her that a spouse did not have to pay inheritance tax on the family home.

He'd also pointed out that if she added Howard's name to the deeds and they later divorced, he would have claim to half the property, and then left her to make her own mind up whether she would be happy with that.

Until then, Howard had always chosen to return to home comforts after what he referred to as his little "indiscretions", but there was no guarantee that would always be the case.

With Freddie's help, she'd made a will leaving the house in trust to the children and, later, when Howard had, oh-so-casually, asked her if she'd seen her lawyer about adding his name to the deeds, she was able to assure him, with perfect honesty, that she had.

She hadn't bothered to explain the result.

Meg, who'd been through a nasty divorce herself, and was no fan of Howard, had congratulated her on a lucky escape and called out a locksmith to replace all the locks while they'd bonded over lunch.

They had since become firm friends, a fact they'd kept from Howard and his buddy — and Meg's business partner — Steve Marshall.

It had been left to his solicitor to explain the true situation once he'd begun dealing with the divorce settlement.

To say that Howard had not been amused was a classic of British understatement.

CHAPTER EIGHT

Meg's call was swiftly followed by half a dozen calls from friends and clients who wanted to know what had happened, and one that was just plain nasty.

Out of time, she switched her phone to silent, leaving the kind, the curious and the obnoxious to leave a voicemail if they felt so inclined.

She saw the older children on their way to school, then she stopped for Cara, Sophie's best friend who she drove to school in the morning. A favour that Emma, her mother, returned in the evening.

Cara normally ran out to the car but today Emma came with her and leaned down to the open window.

'I saw the paper, Abs. What a shock. Are you okay?'

'Yes, I'm fine, although I could have done without my face on the front page,' she said.

'Give yourself a break and take the day off.'

'I can't. Yesterday put me behind, and I'll be better working anyway.'

'If you say so.'

'I do. I'll see you at rehearsal this evening.'

Having dropped the girls at school, she picked up her van from the garage, leaving the elderly Volvo to have a new tyre fitted and headed for the police station rather later than she'd planned.

Dee met her, brushed aside her apology, and ushered her through to a bare interview room.

They went through what had happened, Dee stopping every now and then to clarify details.

'Have you thought of anything else that might help the coroner?' she asked. 'Is there anyone you can remember working at the house? You mentioned a gardener? Can you remember his name?'

'Warren? No, Warrender. I'm sorry, I don't know his first name.'

'We can check that with your husband.'

Abby nodded but thought it likely that Howard would have a convenient memory lapse.

'There was a cross,' she remembered. 'Shiv suggested that the hallmark might help to date the burial. Has he checked that?'

Dee shook her head. 'The forensics lab are busy and since this isn't an urgent case, it'll be a while before we get anything back from them,' she said. 'Including your tools, I'm afraid. Can you manage? Do you have spares?'

Abby nodded. 'Is that it?'

'Just a few more details . . .' She glanced at the open file in front of her. 'You told me that your husband was raised by his great-uncle and aunt after the death of his father from a gunshot wound.' She looked up. 'The verdict was accidental death.'

'You've been reading the local paper.'

Dee managed a wry smile. 'We take the more lurid details with a pinch of salt,' she said, 'although the implication was that it was suicide.'

'Yes, I'm surprised they didn't put the word accidental in quotes, but Howard never talks about his parents.'

'We haven't been able to contact your husband yet. Do you have any idea where his mother is living?'

'His mother?'

'From what you said about the age of the rose, it's possible she was around at the time. Apart from her, and any staff we can find, everyone else is dead.'

'Sarah Finch left her husband, abandoning Howard when he was very young. I've never met her,' Abby explained. 'I don't even know if she's still alive. Your best bet would be the family solicitor. Presumably they got in touch with her when her husband died.'

'And they are?'

'The family use a London firm. His office will have the details.'

Dee looked up. 'They don't act for you?'

'I chose to remain with the local firm of solicitors who handled my family's affairs. Freddie Jennings at Jennings, Jennings and Partners,' she added, before she was asked.

'Okay, well, I think that's it for the present. I'll get this typed up for you to sign. Would you like tea or coffee while you're waiting?'

Abby shook her head and, once Dee had gone, checked her voicemails. Most of them she could ignore, but Natalie had left two, sounding so frantic that, taking pity on the wretched woman, she called her back.

'Abby, I've been trying to get hold of you all morning.'

'It's only just gone nine, Natalie, and right now I'm at the police station.'

'Have they arrested you?'

'What? No, of course not. Why on earth would they arrest me? I'm just making a statement for the coroner.'

'Oh, I thought . . .' She didn't disguise her disappointment. The woman was clearly losing it. 'How could you tell them all that stuff? They've implied all sorts about his family. His father . . . Howard is going to be livid.'

'Maybe you should have thought of that before you gave the *Observer* my name. Lucy was alone in the house when she heard the message they left.'

'Well, if you'd told me what you'd found—'

'Which I would have done if you hadn't been so hostile. I am not your enemy, Natalie. And I didn't tell them anything. The *Observer* dug up all that information from their archives.'

The only answer was a loud sniff.

'Clearly you haven't spoken to Howard yet,' she said, sharply hoping to distract her from tears. 'Do you want me to call him?'

'You can't. His phone is switched off.'

'So much for an emergency number,' Abby said, annoyed.

'Why would he leave a number? He doesn't care about you or your children. He's in Paris with Izzy.'

'Paris?'

'It's so unfair! Howard promised that one day, when he was free, he'd take *me* there.'

Abby doubted that he'd promised anything of the sort. He might indulge the poor woman's fantasies, agree with her that it would be lovely to go there one day, but he wasn't stupid.

'Now he's met that woman, it's never going to happen . . .' This time her voice broke on a sob.

'Natalie—'

'Don't! Don't patronise me with your pity. I know it's over. We're in the same boat and it's sinking, but he'll be sorry.'

'No doubt, but maybe you should think about . . .' Before she could advise her to look for another job, Abby realised that she was talking to herself.

Hopefully Natalie's resignation was already on his desk, although she probably thought — hoped — that Howard would beg her to stay.

'Okay, all done,' Dee said, appearing a few minutes later. 'If you could read this carefully and then sign it for me . . .'

Abby read her statement and was relieved to see that it was just a bare statement of facts.

'Is there anything else?' she asked, once she'd signed it.

'That's all for now. I'll check with forensics and let you know when you can continue working at the Lodge.'

'Thank you.' While she was in no hurry to return, she still had a lot of work to do there and the fact that Howard intended to let the place didn't change that.

It was probably why he was pressuring her to get it tidied up.

'How are you now?' Dee asked, walking her out. 'And your daughter?'

'Lucy's okay, although I imagine the children will be bombarded with questions at school today. I left messages for their heads.'

'There's been nothing from your husband?'

'His personal assistant has now admitted that his conference is in fact a mini break in Paris with the future Mrs Finch. Which explains the lack of communication.'

'Why would she lie about that?'

'Natalie has always been unshakeably discreet, but the piece in the newspaper shook her sufficiently to admit where he was.'

'In that case it's unlikely that he's surfing the net for the latest news of what's happening in Maybridge,' Dee said, her face unreadable, 'but there's no urgency. We'll catch up with him when he gets home.'

* * *

All Abby's clients had seen the paper and wanted to talk about what had happened. Finally, in desperation, she texted Cal, asking him to join her so that he could handle the mowing. He was quick, did a good job, and she could see that he was going to be really useful.

Dee called just after lunch to let her know that she could go back to Linton Lodge whenever she liked.

Like wasn't the word she'd have chosen, but she arranged to pick up Cal in the morning. She'd take Tom with her too and let him loose on the mower. If they all got stuck in over the weekend, she could begin to make some serious inroads on the overgrown parts of the garden.

With the last job done, she dropped Cal in town and drove out to the garden centre in Longbourne to pick up the replacement rose she'd ordered when she had a call from an unknown number.

She was tempted to let it go to voicemail, but it could be someone who'd seen her in the paper and wanted some work done. No publicity is bad publicity . . .

'Earthly Designs.'

'Abby . . .'

'Jake.' She sank onto a chair in a display of garden furniture.

'I've just seen the paper,' he said. 'Are you okay?'

'I could have done without the endless questions everywhere I went today.'

'It'll have all died down by Monday.'

'Tomorrow's chip paper,' she agreed. But by then Howard would have returned from Paris and be on the warpath. 'Can this wait?' she asked. 'It's been a tough day and I have to get back for the kids.'

'I'll only be a minute. I heard what you said about how things are right now, but I'm going back to London tomorrow, a business thing I can't get out of, and I wondered if you were free for dinner tonight. You deserve a break after what happened, and I imagine Lucinda will babysit if suitably bribed?'

'Believe me, sitting down to a meal that I haven't had to cook would be bliss, but Sophie has a dress rehearsal for a show with her dance school this evening and I'm helping with costume changes.'

He laughed. 'You're definitely going to need a treat after that. I could stay on for lunch tomorrow?'

'I'm working this weekend,' she said. 'Howard's put the Lodge on the rental market, so I need to get cracking on putting the garden straight.'

'So the rumours are true?'

'What rumours?'

'I heard there's a problem with the St Catherine's site. Contamination. Asbestos . . .'

'That would be a rumour put about by the same gossip who filled you in on Howard's indiscretions. Only this time talking through his hat.'

'Are you sure about that?'

'The hat?' Jake didn't owe Howard any favours, but repeating dangerous gossip was beneath him and could lose people their jobs. 'He has his faults, but he knows his business. That kind of problem would have been picked up on the site survey and remedial costs set against the purchase price,' she said icily as she got to her feet. 'Good luck with the move.'

* * *

Tom had Scouts and Lucy was going to spend the evening with a friend. Once at rehearsal, everyone was too busy getting children in and out of a variety of costumes to grill her about the bones she'd found. A few offered "what a shock" and "how sad" remarks.

Once it was all over, Emma, who was taking Sophie home for a sleepover with her own little dancer, said, 'You look as if you could do with a large drink, Abs. Are you okay?'

'I've had better days,' she admitted.

'There was no comment from Howard, I notice.'

'He's away, which is why I'm the one on the front page of the *Observer* today.'

Sophie, who was settling herself into the back of the car with Cara, said, 'He'll be back tomorrow because he promised to be at the show.'

Abby threw a desperate look at Emma, who said, 'Buckle up quick-smart, girls. I've got hot chocolate and marshmallows waiting at home.' She shut the door. 'I take it from your expression that's not going to happen,' she said, quietly.

'He's in Paris with Izzy.'

She shook her head. 'Words fail me . . .'

Abby had the words, but this was not the moment and, as Emma climbed into the car, she said, 'Be good, Soph. Don't stay up all night giggling, or you'll be too tired to dance tomorrow.'

Once she was safely home, Abby poured herself a large glass of wine, curled up on the sofa and called Meg.

'That's tragic,' she said, when she'd heard the whole story. 'Have you any idea who the mother might be?'

'Not a clue, but Lucy is in a bit of a state about the fact that there's no one to care. She thinks that the bones will end up in a box gathering dust on a shelf, just a case number.'

'She's probably right.'

'If I could take a look in the Lodge archives, find a name . . .'

'Sleuthing? I like it, but you're going to need a hat.'

'Don't be silly.'

'All the best female detectives have a hat. Will you go for a felt fedora? Or do you favour a practical weatherproof like Vera?'

'I should probably go for something with a large brim to protect my skin from turning to leather,' she said, 'but what I really need is to get into Linton Lodge and I'm hoping that you have a key.'

CHAPTER NINE

'A key?' Meg repeated. 'But you're sorting out the Lodge gardens. Surely Howard doesn't expect you to pee in the woods.'

'There's a washroom for staff in the kitchen garden.'

'Dear God, Abs. Spiders, cobwebs . . .' Her shudder was audible.

'No spiders. Ruth was very fussy about dirt being tracked in, and Howard had to use it when he came to cut the grass, so he made poor Pam give it a thorough scrubbing before he'd use it.'

'I suppose you should be grateful he didn't foist that job on you.'

'Small mercies,' she agreed, 'but he's in Paris with Izzy this weekend and, since I'm unlikely to get another chance to go through the archives, I'm hoping you can do the open sesame bit.'

'And if you do come up with a name, what then?'

'I'll worry about that if it happens. I do know that Howard won't want the police digging around in the family files.'

'You think he'll conveniently lose them?'

'Don't you? That baby had a father, and who knows what they'll uncover if they track down the women who worked there all those years ago. He has a political career to protect.'

'You could tell the police where they are,' Meg pointed out.

'I'm in enough trouble already.' She waited for a moment. 'He'll be back on Monday so there isn't a lot of time.'

'Can you be there in the morning?'

'I'm going to be working there all day.'

'Okay. I have an appointment to view at ten o'clock. I'll let you in then.'

'Thanks—'

'Hold on. I'm not done.'

'Oh?'

'I had a rather dishy guy in the office this morning looking for a house with river frontage.'

'Pricey.'

'He's moving his business out of London. He saw the artist's impression of the proposed Finch development of St Catherine's, and he mentioned that he knew you and Howard. Jake Sullivan?'

Well, obviously . . .

'We were all in the same year at high school,' she said.

'That's what he said.'

'What else did he say?'

'Nothing. But he had a look when he said your name that made me think there was a lot more than old schoolmates to the story.'

'He could have told you that back in the day, when he was a skinny foster kid, a bit of a nerd, he avoided being bullied on the sports field by volunteering to help in the school garden.'

'A shared interest is always a good start.'

'His only interest was the contents of my packed lunch.'

'You shared your sandwiches with him? That's so sweet.'

'In return for fixing my laptop when it was playing up.'

'That's it?'

'What else would there be? I was going to the prom with the hottest boy in the school, Meg. Rugby captain of rugby, cricket captain, a head taller than the rest of them.'

'You're talking about Howard, aren't you?'

'I was the envy of the sixth form.'

'Girls are so stupid,' she said, 'but how come you got so lucky? Lovely as you are, I can't see you as a natural for prom queen.'

'Blonde enough, but not thin enough?'

'Let's just say that I don't see you as a fashion-obsessed airhead.'

'I asked him why he'd chosen me when we met again, a few years later. He said I was tall, I was blonde, I didn't giggle inanely like most of the girls in the sixth form, and because I didn't live on lettuce leaves, I had the biggest tits.'

'Girls are stupid and boys are shallow. Knowing Howard, and you, I'm guessing it didn't end well.'

'One of the girls told me she'd overheard him talking to his mates about what he had planned for my deflowering.'

'Shallow and entitled.'

'He was my date, Meg, and I had protection in my bag. There was no way I was going to college a virgin, but she told me that he'd set up a video cam and was taking orders for downloads.'

'Oh, yuk.'

'I was so angry that I didn't stop to think. I slapped him in front of everyone and told him that he was a pig.'

'And?'

'To be honest, what followed is a bit of a blur. All I know is that in the shocked silence that followed, Jake appeared from nowhere and hauled me out of there.'

'What a hero!'

'Yes . . . He offered to call a cab, which I knew he couldn't afford, and anyway it was still early. Mum would have wanted to know what had happened and I wasn't about to tell her.'

'So?'

'So, it was a warm evening. I took off my shoes and we walked back to town along the riverbank.'

'Please tell me this is going where I hope it's going!'

'I was upset, he was sweet and, no, I didn't go to college a virgin. But guess who was on hand to soothe Howard's ruffled ego and make his night?'

'The girl who told you . . . She made it up, didn't she?'

'She just laughed when I challenged her.'

'And Jake?'

'Howard made sure I knew that he'd been dealt with. I tried to find him afterwards, but he'd left Maybridge and I didn't see him again until yesterday, when I bumped into him at the supermarket.'

'Just as your divorce is about to be finalised. Excellent timing.'

'Come off it, Meg. The children are my only concern right now. And the mother of the baby whose bones I found.'

'Why don't you leave it to the police?'

'They won't do anything.'

'I suppose not, but what the hell are you doing working for your ex anyway? I hope he's paying you the going rate.'

Tired, decidedly emotional and with a couple of glasses of very expensive Pouilly-Fuissé, that Howard had overlooked, inside her, she said, 'He's not paying me at all.'

'What? I don't understand . . .'

She topped up her glass. 'Tom is going on a very expensive trip to Iceland this summer and his dad has refused to pay for it unless I sort out the garden.'

'I would have told him what to do with his garden.'

'I did a lot better than that. I pawned the heirloom Linton engagement ring, worth approximately £750,000 at the last insurance valuation, for the exact amount of the trip. Then I gave him the ticket so that he could redeem it for Izzy.'

'Oh . . . My . . . God, Abs. That's the most ballsy thing I've ever heard.'

'Unfortunately, my triumph was short-lived. His response was to refuse to sign Tom's permission slip to leave the country.

The last thing I wanted was for Tom to find out, so I'm working for nothing for as long as he wants me—' She stopped as the back slammed shut. 'That's Tom now. I'll see you tomorrow.'

* * *

'Are you okay, Tom?'

Normally when he came home from Scouts he was ravenous, but last night he'd said he was tired and had gone straight to bed. Now he was toying with his breakfast.

'Let me take your temperature.'

'There's nothing wrong with me,' he snapped, sliding out of the chair. 'I'm just not hungry. I'll go and start the van.'

Something was up, but she knew from experience that there was no point in pushing. He'd tell her when he was ready.

'I'm picking up Cal, so it'll have to be the Volvo. Can you move the tools and overalls?'

'The overalls are for him, right? You don't expect me to wear them?'

'Cal is on the Earthly Designs books, so I'll be paying him. And he's skinny enough to fit into a pair of my overalls. You, my overgrown beloved, won't.'

'I could come and give you a hand, Mum,' Lucy offered.

Abby's heart sank.

Cal was a very good-looking boy, and her daughter — fair hair loose about her shoulders instead of tied back in a scrunchy, wearing just a little too much make-up and her nails gleaming with newly applied polish — was not dressed for gardening.

'I think I've got all the help I can handle in the garden,' she said, 'but if you could run the vacuum around the hall and living room, and maybe prep some veg for dinner, that would be brilliant.'

Abby had anticipated a protest, but Lucy managed to swallow down her disappointment.

'What are we having?'

'Something that you'll eat?' she suggested.

'If I made a veggie pasta bake, you could ask Cal.' The suggestion, casual enough on the surface, was belied by the tinge of pink that rose to her cheeks. 'He's vegetarian and Aunt Molly keeps forgetting and giving him sausages.'

'I'll ask but he may have other plans.'

'I'll text him . . .' Lucy began, then stopped, realising that she'd betrayed the fact that she had his number. 'What about Sophie?' she asked, quickly changing the subject.

'Cara's mum is dropping her back at about four, but I'll be home by then,' she said, picking up the cold box containing sandwiches and drinks. 'Are you going out?'

'Maybe,' she said, with a lift of her shoulders.

'Okay, but remember,' Abby warned, 'if your friends want to talk about the bones, anything you say can, and probably will, end up on social media.'

* * *

Tom, who'd been monosyllabic in the car, brightened a little at the sight of the mower. He checked the fuel, then set to work on the half acre of lawn that had once been an immaculate, weed-free sward, but was now a sea of dandelions and daisies.

'It's running a bit rough,' Cal said.

'It's probably due a service. Molly told me that you're good with engines,' she said. 'That will be useful.'

He shrugged. 'Do you want me to take a look?'

'Maybe later, when Tom's finished. Can you drive?' she asked.

'I'd do a better job than that,' he said, as Tom turned a fraction too late, went wide and took out a slice of the border, sending earth and stones rattling against the blade.

Abby winced. 'Slow down!'

'Sorry! Just getting the hang of it.' Tom stopped, but only to fish out his earbuds and plug them into his phone.

'Give me a ring when Meg arrives, will you?'

He raised a hand to indicate that he'd heard, causing a slight wobble. Once she was sure he was in control, she turned back to Cal.

'Do you have a driving licence?'

'I passed my basic for a motorbike. But I haven't passed my test.'

'Well, that's a start. There's an old motorbike here that you could fix up, but you're going to need a full licence for this job. I'll need you to be able to drive the van.'

'That costs money.'

'Well, this is your chance to earn some.' Abby handed him a pair of overalls and pulled hers over her shorts and T-shirt. 'Come on, I'll show you where everything is.'

She headed down the garden, telling him what needed to be done, but then, realising that she was on her own, turned to see him standing by the small, lily-covered lake.

'How do people get to have all this?' he asked. 'All this land? A lake in their garden?'

'The Finch family owned a farm way back,' she explained. 'The land was poor and there was a lot of stone. In desperation they stopped trying to grow stuff and started selling the stone.'

'Luck, then.'

'Not luck. They used what they had to survive, Cal, and it was desperately hard work. This didn't happen overnight.'

He shrugged and followed her to the walled kitchen garden.

It had been too much for one gardener to manage and had been left to nature since George died. It was heart-breaking to see the beds thick with weeds, the espalier fruit trees throwing out untidy shoots.

Even the range of stone-built workshops were in need of repair. Roof tiles had slipped, the paint on the doors had blistered and cracked, and the gutters were stuffed with debris.

Not her problem, Abby reminded herself as she opened the nearest door and turned on the light to reveal a cobweb-draped potting shed.

There was a bench on one side, stacks of pots and seed trays, and racks of hand tools along one wall.

'This is fucking amazing . . .'

'If you're going to work with me, you're going to have to drop the adjectives,' Abby said, sharply.

'What?' Then the penny dropped. 'Oh, right. Sorry. But this place . . .'

'You're impressed?'

'If I had somewhere like this . . .' He stopped.

'What would you do with it, Cal?'

'I'd build a sleeping platform up there,' he said, waving up at the cobweb-hung rafters, 'and set up a shop where I could fix bikes.'

'There's one at the far end, where the machines were serviced,' she said, smiling at this first evidence of enthusiasm.

She'd once dreamed of turning this range of workshops into offices and a studio for Earthly Designs. Using the walled garden to grow plants and, maybe, living the dream she'd shared with Jake of designing a garden that would win gold at Chelsea.

There was access down here from the road, so she wouldn't have had to go near the house and, in the early days of their marriage, Howard had been encouraging.

His great-uncle George might have gone for it, but Ruth cut him off before he could agree, informing Howard, rather sharply, that his wife should be at home taking care of her baby.

Like Cal's great-aunt Molly, she had never had a child of her own and clearly thought Abby should be grateful for the blessings she had.

'As I said, there's an old bike that my husband used to ride to school. It may be rusted up and beyond saving but you're welcome to take a look.'

Cal's eyes lit up. 'Now?'

'Work first, fun later,' she said, taking down shears and secateurs and wiping off the dust before testing them against her thumb for sharpness. 'I regret that none of these tools have engines, but they are valuable,' she said. 'Don't drop them or leave them lying on wet grass. You'll find oil to clean them on that shelf when you're done.'

'I know about looking after tools.'

'In that case,' she said, 'grab a wheelbarrow and a rake from next door and follow me.'

CHAPTER TEN

'This isn't the best time of year to cut back some of these shrubs,' Abby explained, as she showed Cal what needed doing and where to cut, 'but they're blocking the path.'

'It would be quicker with a chainsaw.'

'No doubt, but this isn't about speed. It's about care. You need to be aware of nesting birds, so work quietly and keep your eyes open. If you see any nests give them a wide berth.' She handed him the shears. 'Let me see you have a go.'

He might have yearned for a chainsaw, but he demonstrated his ability to listen and learn and, at this rate, would be an asset.

'What do I do with the cuttings?' he asked.

'Take them into the kitchen garden. We'll have a bonfire later.'

Leaving him to it, she returned to the car for her border spade and the cardboard box containing the rose.

The garden centre where she'd once worked had a good range of climbers from one of the foremost rose growers in the area, but the Blush Noisette was a very old variety.

She wouldn't have normally replaced one rose with another, but she wasn't about to argue about it. Howard wanted it replaced, so replaced it would be and — as roses went — it was a good choice.

It would take extra work to protect it from replacement disease, which was why she'd dug so deep but, once established, it would bloom throughout the summer and fill the air with its musky clove fragrance.

The secluded corner of the garden where she'd found the bones was much as she'd left it apart from the hole, which was deeper and wider, and some of the perennials had been trampled.

She stuck her spade in the soil heaped up beside the hole, trimmed broken stems and, having added the trimmings and a few weeds to the remains of the dead rose piled up on the wheelbarrow, took it around to the kitchen garden and dumped it out for the boys to make a bonfire later.

She had filled a watering can and had just placed it by the rose when her phone buzzed.

It was Tom. '*Meg's here.*'

Glancing at her watch, she realised that it had taken longer than she thought to set up Tom and then Cal, but she had to go back to the car to fetch a bag of compost before she could plant the rose.

'*Tell her I'll be right there.*'

Grabbing the handles of the wheelbarrow — something else that could do with a little oil — she headed for the house.

There was no sign of Meg, but Jake was sitting on the front step, a striped navy-and-white polo shirt stretched across his shoulders, jeans worn soft with age splitting at the knees and straining against his thighs.

'Jake,' she said as he rose to his feet. 'How fortunate. I wasn't sure when I'd see you again, but I've been to the cash machine.'

'No,' he protested, but she went to the car, took some notes from her wallet and offered them to him. 'I didn't come here for your money, Abby.'

Well no, she didn't imagine he had.

'I missed you at the house and Lucy told me you'd be here.' She waited. 'I offended you yesterday. I didn't want to go away without making things right.'

She shook her head. 'I shouldn't have hung up on you, but I don't like gossip.'

'I'm sure you've had your fill of it in the last few months.'

'I have, but nothing so unfounded and malicious.'

'Are you sure it's unfounded?'

'You don't get to Howard's position without making enemies,' she said.

'You're very defensive of him in the circumstances. I assumed you would have heard the rumour, but it's not only Howard who'll be hurt if the company is in trouble. You might want to check it out.'

'Oh, I will, believe me. And I'll tell Howard. He should at least know what's being said, and by whom?' She raised an eyebrow inviting him to give her the name.

'It was Councillor Crawford.'

'What a surprise. For your information, Bryan Crawford is a poisonous little oik who Howard had removed from the planning committee last year. He wouldn't tell me why, but the man had clearly been up to no good. He made some pretty nasty threats at the time about getting even.'

'And he's still on the council?'

'He's a member of the same party, and you don't rock the party boat.' She pulled a face. 'He must have thought he'd found a soulmate when he met you.'

'I only mentioned that we'd been at school at the same time.'

'And your tone would have told him the rest.'

'Probably,' he admitted. 'I'll give him a wide berth in future.'

'Good decision.' She held out the cash, and with a sigh of resignation he took it.

'This is too much.'

'Pennies. Don't even think of counting out the change. The kids fell on the chocolate biscuits like the half-starved waifs they are,' she said before he could argue.

'I believe they went down well with Zaida's kids too.' He stood there for a moment, but then put the money in his back pocket.

'Who's Zaida?' The words slipped out.

'She's the woman who makes my company run like clockwork. She and her husband moved down here early so that she can project manage the fitting out of the offices.'

'Does he work for you too?'

'No. He's an academic. He's going to be lecturing at Bristol when the new year starts. Meanwhile, he's taking care of things at home.' He raised an eyebrow. 'So? Are we okay now?'

She nodded.

'In that case, since I'm in the market for a rental, will you give me the tour?'

'You're not interested in the Lodge. You're just being nosey.'

'I am,' he admitted, 'but I'm told riverside properties are in short supply and it's going to take time to find exactly what I'm looking for.'

'Even so, this is a little on the large size for one person.'

Tom, who'd finished mowing and had wandered over to join them, said, 'You don't want to live in this dump. You should go for one of those cool warehouse conversions on the Quays.'

'I have one of those in London,' Jake said. 'If I'm going to live in the country, I want a garden with a lawn that runs down to the river. And a boathouse. I imagine this place has one?'

'It does, but it hasn't been used in years and it's in a dangerous state. It should have been demolished years ago.'

'Oh, well, I don't have a boat anyway, so I can live without it. Shall we?'

'I'm sorry, Jake, I don't have time to show you around. You'll have to make an appointment with Meg.'

'Mum wants to take a look at the family records,' Tom said. 'She's hoping to find out who might have buried the baby, but I'll show you around if you like.'

'You're here to work,' Abby reminded him, 'and the lawn edges are in a shocking state. You'll find the edger in the tool store.'

'If would be much quicker if you got one of those battery jobs.'

'The old-fashioned kind don't break down or go flat in the middle of a job, and I'm paying you minimum wage for your time, the same as Cal. You'll need the money for those walking boots you want for Iceland.'

'You don't have the money to pay me,' he said, 'and I don't need walking boots because I'm not going to Iceland.'

And with that he stomped off before she could say anything.

'Iceland?' Jake asked.

'It's a joint schools geographic study tour.'

'Is that his subject?'

'No, he's sport and IT all the way, but it's hiking on a glacier, lava tube caving, snorkelling in the Silfra fissure . . .' She shook her head. 'He's been in an odd mood all morning.'

'Girl trouble?'

'Oh, please. Not yet . . . I've already got Lucy mooning over Cal.'

'Who's Cal?' Jake asked.

'My new helper. He's one of those skinny boys with large soulful eyes.'

And she knew from experience just how dangerous they could be.

'I don't imagine there'll be a rush to take this place, Jake. If you're really interested, give Meg a ring and she'll show you everything on your next visit.'

'Okay, forget the tour. I'll help you search through the paperwork, and afterwards, by way of thanks, we'll pretend we're eighteen again and you can share your sandwiches with me. You did bring sandwiches?'

'I thought you had to get back to London.'

'This evening is early enough.'

Abby hesitated for a moment, but he was right, two pairs of eyes would be better than one.

'Come on, then,' she said, kicking off her boots in the porch and stepping over the threshold.

The hall was large, with an imposing oak staircase rising to a half landing where a window looked out over woodland and, below it, the river.

'Christ, Abby, who's that?'

She swung around, guilt rendering her certain that she'd been found out, but Jake was staring at a portrait that dominated the hall.

'That's Howard Finch, Senior. Howard's grandfather. The likeness is a bit unsettling,' she admitted.

'Unsettling? It's Howard with a beard.'

'Howard has grown one just like it. Izzy told him it would give him gravitas,' she said, heading towards the back of the house just as a woman erupted from the kitchen.

'A total waste of my time,' she declared, heading for the door. 'I'll be in the car, Miss West.'

'Not impressed?' Jake asked, when Meg followed a moment later.

'It's like the curate's egg. Good in parts. She wants all the old-world charm of an English country house but with a designer kitchen and the latest in bathroom technology.'

'There's not a lot of charm here,' Abby said.

'Oh, she adored the tower, the fake Tudor panelling and the crenellations. It was the plumbing that let it down. I don't suppose I could tempt you to take it while I find you something suitable, Jake? It has all the river frontage you could desire.'

'I was just suggesting to Abby that she should show me around,' he said.

Abby glared at Meg, daring her to encourage him.

'Go for it!' And Meg was grinning as she tossed her the keys and followed her disappointed viewer. 'Set the alarm and lock up when you leave, Abs. You can tell me how it went when you drop them off.'

'Well, there you are,' Jake said. 'Permission to view granted.'

'Not before I've done what I've come for,' she said, sliding her hand through her overalls to put the keys in her shorts pocket and then opening the door to Ruth's sitting room.

No one had been in here since Ruth's death, and dust shimmered in the sunlight that was pouring in through the French windows.

Unlike the rest of the house with its dark panelling, heavy furniture and smoke-filmed oil paintings, the walls of this room had been stripped, plastered and painted in the palest peach.

The soft furnishings were cream with a dark green and peach floral design. The simple table that Ruth had used as a desk, and the shelving with a low range of cupboards that took up an entire wall, were painted in cream chalk paint.

'This is different,' Jake said, as Abby crossed to the French windows, throwing them open onto a sunken garden where roses and lavender were beginning to come into their own.

'This was Ruth's private sanctuary.'

The shelves were stacked with gardening books in all shapes and sizes, but the diaries were kept in one of the cupboards beneath the bookshelves.

She'd occasionally caught a glimpse of them and knew that they were identical, bound in dark green leather with the year embossed in gold on the spine.

The door was locked and there was no key.

She looked around, but it wasn't in the small celadon dish on the shelf, or in the matching pot containing coloured pencils, sitting on the writing table beside the silver-framed portrait of Howard as a curly-haired infant.

She tried the drawer, but it contained nothing but Ruth's personal writing paper, envelopes and a Mont Blanc pen case.

'What are you looking for?' Jake asked.

'A key . . .'

She opened the pen case and caught a glimpse of silver, half hidden in the folds of black velvet that were cradling the vintage fountain pen.

'What on earth was she writing in her garden diaries that had to be kept under lock and key?' Jake asked.

She shook her head. The idea of family secrets sent a frisson of alarm and excitement shooting up her spine as she slid the key into the lock and opened the door to reveal the packed shelves.

'That's a lot of diaries,' Jake said.

'There were a lot of years,' she said, taking one of the earlier diaries from the shelf, 'but I can discount anything after 2006.' Which didn't mean that she wouldn't want to read them later.

'That's very specific.'

'The rose was already well-established when Howard went down on one knee in front of it.' She shivered now at the thought of the baby buried beneath it. 'When I said yes, he picked a bud from it as a placeholder for the Finch engagement ring, which was kept in a safety deposit box at the bank.'

Ruth hadn't been pleased about that. Maybe she'd suspected what they'd been up to in the summerhouse in what Howard had referred to as the secret garden. And that's how it had appeared. Overgrown, forgotten . . .

In the event she'd confined herself to giving him a stern lecture about cutting roses with a clean knife rather than snapping them off roughly, allowing disease to get in.

Pretty much what she'd told him herself.

'He actually went down on one knee?' Jake sounded sceptical. 'I can't imagine Howard being that romantic.'

She pulled a face. 'I was speaking metaphorically, although I think he would have done if I'd insisted. It's hard to believe now, but he really did want to marry me.'

'That's not hard to believe, Abby. The big question is whether, if you hadn't been pregnant, you would have said yes.'

'If I hadn't been pregnant, he wouldn't have asked me.' And there it was again. The suspicion that he may have seen marriage as an escape from the control of his great-aunt and -uncle.

'He always was a fool. How long do roses survive?'

'It was in a sheltered spot. It could have lived for years, but it had been neglected. There were long shoots that hadn't been tied down and it was in full leaf when it was caught by the storm that blew through here last month and torn from the wall.'

She opened the volume she was holding and discovered that although the year was embossed on the spine, it wasn't a diary, but a journal. The dates were written in by hand and there were gaps of days, weeks . . .

There were alternate lined and plain pages on which Ruth had sketched ideas for borders, drawn plants and flowers. She'd stuck in seed packets and written notes about how they'd performed, and made notes about gardens she'd visited.

And then, at the back, Abby discovered a pocket for receipts.

All this one contained was an old black-and-white photograph of a young girl in a maid's uniform, smiling shyly at the camera.

'She was quite an artist . . .'

Jake, who had been casually leafing through another of the journals, held it out so that she could see an exquisite watercolour of a yellow rambling rose.

'That's *Rosa banksiae* "Lutea",' Abby said, pushing the photograph back into the pocket and closing the volume she was holding.

'You can tell just by looking at this?'

'That's the south wall of the house. It's in flower now, if you want to see the real thing.'

'I'll take your word for it.' He glanced up. 'Did you find anything?'

She shook her head, not quite sure what she'd found and needing time to think about it.

'It's going to take a lot more than a couple of hours to go through them all,' he pointed out.

'Yes . . .' And there was something about that photograph that made reading them a matter of urgency.

CHAPTER ELEVEN

Jake took out his phone. 'I'll rent the house. That'll give you all the time you need.'

'What? No!' Abby protested. 'What on earth would you do with a huge place like this?'

'It won't be just for me,' he said, putting a number into his phone and hitting dial.

'Oh?'

'I'll be coming and going until the company move is complete, and while Meg is doing a good job of finding potential property for my staff to rent or buy, quite a few of them are young and single. This place would give them a base, time to look around and find their feet.'

'You can't use Linton Lodge like student digs,' she said, doing her best to ignore the treacherous little rollercoaster ride her heart had just taken. 'Howard will have a fit.'

He grinned. 'And just like that the idea has become irresistible . . . Meg,' he said as his call was picked up. 'I've decided to take Linton Lodge. You have all the company details so if you'll get the process started straight away . . .' He listened for a moment, then said, 'Yes, full housekeeping, and will you organise a contract with Earthly Designs for the garden maintenance . . . ?' He laughed at something Meg said, then thanked her and ended the call. 'All done. You've got all the time you need.'

'I can't believe you just did that.'

'I once read that if you practice,' he said, 'you can believe six impossible things before breakfast.'

'We're not in Wonderland,' she snapped. 'This is real life.'

'So much the better. And Meg is delighted.'

'Meg . . .' She rolled her eyes. 'Has she any idea what she's just done?'

'Let a house that she thought would be impossible to shift? If I was her client, I'd be thrilled.'

'This might be a joke to you, but Howard is one of Marshall & West's biggest clients. They handle the sale of all Finch Developments properties. If he finds out that they've let his precious house to you, he'll never use them again.'

'The lease will be in the company's name,' he said. 'He need never know. It will be our private joke.'

'You think? A new company moving into a small town like Maybridge is news, and Steve Marshall plays golf with Howard.'

'In that case you might advise Meg not to mention my name.'

'The only thing I'll be telling her is to rip up the lease along with anything involving me. I want nothing to do with it.'

'Someone will have to keep the daisies in check.'

She opened her mouth to protest, but clearly there was no reasoning with him, so she closed it again.

'Now that's settled, have you brought sandwiches, or do I have to send out for pizza?'

'Hullo!'

Jake turned at the sound of a plaintive voice calling from the front door.

'Abby? Are you there?'

'Oh . . .'

'Problem?' Jake asked.

'No. It's Pam Lewis.' She put the journal back on the shelf and closed the cupboard door. 'She'll have come to pick up some things Ruth left her.'

'Then I'll leave you to sort that out while I take a look around upstairs.'

'I'd rather you called Meg to say that you've changed your mind.'

'Don't be such a spoilsport,' he said, grinning as he turned to head up the stairs.

'Men,' she muttered. 'They never grow up.'

Pam was standing in the porch, shifting nervously from foot to foot and clutching a crumpled envelope.

'I called to see if you'd got my things and Lucy said you were here.'

'Good timing.' She could at least get one thing crossed off her to-do list. 'Come on in.'

'Are you on your own? I thought I heard a man,' she said. 'Mr H-Howard isn't here?'

'No, he's away.' Since she seemed reluctant to come in, Abby stepped down into the porch. 'Is that your letter?'

Pam handed her the envelope, which contained the solicitor's letter informing her of her legacy, with a list of other small bequests including a Tiffany lamp.

'Is that the lamp from the drawing room?'

'Yes. I remember Mrs Ruth coming home with it,' Pam said. 'I'd never seen anything so beautiful . . .' She stopped, flushing pink.

'How lovely that she remembered.' She ran through the list, then looked up. 'She left you a silver cross?'

'I've already got that,' Pam said, smiling as she lifted the chain to show her.

Abby put her hand beneath it and let it lie across her palm. 'Isn't this the one Ruth wore?' she asked.

The one that Howard had searched high and low for so that his aunt could be buried with it. A cross very like the one buried with the baby.

'Mrs Ruth wanted me to have it,' she said, but wouldn't meet her eyes. 'She gave it to me when she was in the hospital.'

It sounded unlikely, and Howard had made a fearful fuss when it hadn't been with her things after she died.

She'd assumed that it had eventually been found, but she'd had nothing to do with the funeral arrangements.

She'd attended the service and come back to the house with the children, but her only role had been to take them home once condolences had been offered and the real business of political networking could begin.

It had been Izzy who'd organised the caterers and filled the house with flowers, and Izzy, in designer black, who had played the perfect hostess.

Abby would have liked to believe that Ruth was turning in her grave. The truth of the matter was that Isobel Hamilton was exactly the kind of woman she'd have lined up for her precious boy but for his carelessness with a condom.

'Come in, Pam,' she said. 'You'll have to show me where to find this stuff.'

'It's all in a box in the cleaning cupboard.'

'What?'

'I had it all ready to take home after the funeral tea, but when M-Mr Howard saw me at the church he told me I wasn't to come to the house.'

'Oh, Pam, I'm sorry.' She'd been so embarrassed by the awkwardness of it all, feeling like a leftover spare part, that she hadn't noticed. 'Ruth would have wanted you there.'

The sad truth was that Howard had been furious that his aunt, without consulting him, had summoned her solicitor and added a codicil to her will leaving Pam a substantial sum of money.

'You must stand up for yourself, Pam,' she urged. But, honestly, was she any better? She'd almost certainly have added Howard's name to the deeds of her house if Freddie Jennings — who probably knew more about Howard's dalliances than she did — hadn't pointed out the downside.

And her attempt to thwart his arm-twisting had backfired so badly that she was now doing exactly what he wanted.

At least she could put this one thing right.

The box contained the Tiffany lamp, a small painting, a cairngorm brooch and a pair of silver-backed hairbrushes, nestled in newspaper.

'We need some more paper to keep them safe,' Abby said.

'I can manage,' Pam said, clearly anxious to be off.

'Are you sure?' The box wasn't light, and it would be awkward to carry. 'If you put it in the back of my car, I'll drop—'

Her offer to drop it off on her way home was cut short by Pam's squawk of alarm as Howard's silver BMW swept in through the gate.

'Oh, sugar . . .'

Forget Pam's forbidden presence, the spray of gravel as he skidded to a halt at the front door warned her that he was already at the end of a very short fuse.

'What the fuck have you been doing?' he demanded as he climbed out of the car. Then, spotting Pam, 'And you can bugger off. You've had everything you're getting from my family.'

'Howard!'

'Don't *Howard* me! You have no idea . . .' He caught himself. 'What's in that box?' he demanded.

'Ruth left Pam some keepsakes.' She was still holding the letter and she held it up for him to see.

He snatched the letter from her hand and without looking at it tore it once, twice, three times and let the pieces fall to the ground before turning on Pam.

'Damn it, she's wearing Ruth's cross! Did you take it from her in the hospital?' he demanded. 'Sitting there for hours, holding her hand, pouring your lies into her ears . . .'

He reached out as if to snatch it from her, and Pam, who until then had been frozen, let out of a shriek of near terror and, as she stumbled back, lost her grip on the box.

As it hit the stone flags of the porch floor, there was the unmistakable sound of breaking glass.

'Nooooo!'

Pam fell to her knees, but Howard kicked the box out of her reach, knocking it over so that shards of red glass spilled across the porch like a splatter of fresh blood.

'Get out!' he said. 'If I ever see you here again, I'll call the police—'

Pam whimpering and clearly terrified, took to her heels, but before Abby could go after her, Howard had turned on her, blocking her way.

'And on the subject of the police, what the fuck did you think you were you doing calling them about some old bones you found?'

'I didn't have a choice,' she said, making a deliberate effort to lower her voice. Calm things down. 'It's the law.'

'Law my arse!'

Already wound up for a row, the business with Ruth's cross hadn't helped. He'd never been violent, at least not to her, but she'd never seen him this angry and she took a step back.

'If you'd covered them up, no one would have been the wiser,' he said, matching her step and right in her face, 'but you couldn't resist the chance of embarrassing me, could you?'

'It was a dead baby, Howard.'

'Dead, buried, forgotten and it should have stayed that way!'

'And would have done if you hadn't twisted my arm over the garden,' she said, snapping at the injustice of it. 'Who else would have taken the same trouble when replanting a rose? It's because I actually care about what I do that you want me here at your beck and call—'

'Abby? Are you okay?'

She was very far from okay.

She had known that Howard would be unhappy with hints of a scandal involving his family splashed all over the *Maybridge Observer.* It was not the sort of publicity anyone about to step up to the national political stage would welcome, but she'd banked on this being a row she could put off until after the weekend.

She should have ignored Natalie's vitriolic outburst and listened to her youngest child.

He may have moved in with Izzy Hamilton, but despite the way he was using Tom to spite her, he loved his kids and Sophie was special to him. If he'd promised Sophie that he'd be at her dance show, he'd get there come hell or high water.

But Howard's attention was no longer on her. He was glaring at Jake, whose appearance was not about to improve the situation.

'Who the devil are you?' he demanded. 'And what are you doing in my house?'

Abby had hoped that, safely out of the way checking the bedrooms, Jake wouldn't hear or, if he did, would have the good sense to stay out of sight.

'I'm moving in,' he replied.

Oh, great.

'Moving . . . What on earth are you talking about?'

'I've agreed terms on this place with the agent, but I've asked for Earthly Designs to continue to take care of the garden,' he added. 'In case that's a concern.'

'What? No. I've changed my mind.'

'Too late. The contract has been agreed,' Jake said, 'so if you'll excuse me, I'm checking out the bedrooms, although I can't see anything to beat the one with the four-poster.'

Abby's heart sank.

So much for their "private joke".

Face-to-face, Jake was unable to resist twisting Howard's nose, and the sacred four-poster did it.

'Not in a hundred years!'

'I doubt either of us will be around in a hundred years. It's just six months . . .'

Howard dismissed this with an angry gesture then, about to say more, frowned. 'Have we met?'

'We have,' Jake confirmed, 'but it's been a while.'

CHAPTER TWELVE

Abby saw the moment when recognition dawned and caught her breath, waiting for the explosion. She didn't have to wait long.

'Jake Sullivan! What the hell are you doing back in Maybridge?'

'Like you, Finch, I was born here.'

'You're nothing like me.' He took a step towards him. 'Get out! Get out of my house now!'

Jake didn't move. 'Your house? Surely the woman you've been married to for seventeen years will get part of it? That's the way it usually works in a divorce.'

'That's none of your damn business.'

'None at all,' he agreed, 'but it did occur to me that the rental ploy might be a delaying tactic. Holding off the planned renovations to keep the valuation down? Unless the rumours about the St Catherine's site are true and you need the money.'

Nooooo!

Howard looked as if he were about to explode.

'What rumours?'

Jake, thoroughly enjoying himself, turned to her and said, 'I know a lawyer who'll make sure you get everything you're entitled to, Abby. She's an absolute terrier when it comes to mendacious men.'

'Oh, it's like that, is it? So much for the affronted virtue. How long has this been going on?'

Abby sighed. 'Don't be ridiculous, Howard.'

'Ridiculous? Do you think I didn't know about the two of you sneaking off and having a little fuck party at the prom? Well, you know how that ended,' he said, poking Jake hard in the chest before turning on her. 'And as for you—'

Finger extended, he was on the point of repeating the gesture when Jake hit him.

For one shocked moment the world stood still while Howard rocked a little on his heels. Blood spurted from his nose, ran into his beard and splashed onto the front of his pale blue, fresh-from-the-laundry shirt.

He wiped the back of his hand across his nose, looked at the blood, looked at Jake. And then he hit him back.

Jake had filled out over the years, but with several inches and a lot more weight behind his fist, Howard knocked him off his feet.

That done, he pulled a handkerchief from his pocket, mopped the blood from his face and beard and then, as if nothing had happened, turned to her.

'Where's Tom?' he demanded.

'Tom?' It took Abby a moment to catch her breath.

'Lucy told me he's here.'

'He went to fetch a lawn edger,' she said and, thankfully, was taking his time about it. 'Just be grateful he wasn't around to witness you bullying an old lady—'

'That old lady can take care of herself, so you can drop the sanctimonious tone. You swore you'd never tell Tom about our agreement.'

'An agreement suggests that both parties had a choice in the matter,' Abby replied. 'The only reason I'm here today, working in your garden, is to prevent your son from finding out just how petty and vindictive you can be.'

'Don't lie to me. I know you've told them. You're determined to poison them against me.'

Stung by the injustice of his accusation, she was the one stepping forward.

'You think? How about having to put up with taunts about their father's sex life at school? You know how that goes, Howard. Back in the day you would have been first in line with the mockery.'

For a moment he stood his ground. 'I'm not done with this. And Sullivan had better be gone when I get back.'

With that, he turned and walked away.

Furious with him, furious with herself, she turned to Jake, who was sitting up and testing his jaw.

'Idiot,' she said.

Satisfied that his jaw was in one piece, he flexed his hand and winced. 'You're right. Next time I'll hit him with something harder than my fist.'

'Oh, for heaven's sake . . .' She let it go. 'Are you okay? Tell me if you're seeing double and I'll take you to A&E.'

'I'm okay.'

'Your knuckles are bleeding.'

He glanced at his hand. 'It's not my blood,' he said, getting to his feet.

'Are you sure?'

He grinned. 'Quite sure.'

'It's not funny.'

'No, ma'am.'

'You'd better put some ice on it.'

'Yes, ma'am.' Then he saw the broken glass. 'What happened here?'

She sighed. 'Did you happen to notice which way Pam went?'

He shook his head, but from his expression clearly wished he hadn't. 'Ice . . .'

Abby watched him walk towards the rear of the house to find the kitchen. He appeared to be okay and, after a moment, she stooped to set the box upright and gather up the broken glass.

She'd just finished when a dark blue Mercedes sports coupe with the hood down swept up the drive and came to a halt alongside Howard's BMW.

'Oh, great,' she muttered as Izzy Hamilton pulled off her headscarf, shook out long, shampoo-glossy chestnut hair and stepped out of her car, her pregnancy bump emphasised by her clinging dress. 'Could my day get any worse?'

'Abby,' she said sweetly, although whether her smile went higher than her mouth, it was impossible to tell through her dark glasses. 'I didn't expect to see you here.'

No, there was definitely an edge to that.

'Didn't Howard tell you I'm working here?' she asked.

'On a Saturday?'

'I'm playing catch-up after a disrupted week.'

'Of course.' The smile remained but it had all the sincerity of a crocodile viewing lunch. 'It must have been such a shock finding those nasty bones.'

'The bones weren't nasty,' Abby said. 'How they got there is another story. How was Paris?'

'Wonderful. Since you've sold the Finch ruby, Howard insisted on taking me to Cartier.' She extended her left hand to display a stunningly modern band of diamonds on her ring finger.

'Howard told you that I'd sold the Finch ring?'

'You've got some nerve, I'll give you that. It was a family heirloom.'

'The fact that was it on loan for the duration was made very clear to me when it was placed on my finger for the engagement photograph and the wedding.'

Since then, it had remained in the bank except for big occasions.

'Don't get me wrong, I don't blame you. I just didn't think you had the guts.'

'It wasn't a question of guts. Despite what Howard may have told you, I gave it back to him a couple of weeks ago.'

Okay, not the actual ring, but the pawn ticket so that he could reclaim it, and he'd got off very cheaply.

Izzy raised a pair of beautifully sculptured eyebrows. 'Why would he lie?'

'Who knows? Maybe he thought you'd want something of your own rather than the ring with which he promised till death us do part to his first wife.'

Izzy flushed an angry pink and any pretence at friendly condescension evaporated.

'He was right about that. Rubies would be totally wrong with my colouring.'

'That must be it,' Abby agreed, but wondered if Jake was right about St Catherine's after all. Had Howard needed some fast cash?

'He's absolutely furious with you about the story in the newspaper.' Izzy made no attempt to disguise how happy that made her. 'What on earth were you thinking?'

'I was thinking that the law is very specific on the subject.'

'Really? They were very old bones.'

'Old or not, it was still someone's baby,' she said, looking pointedly at Izzy's bump.

'Why are you here, Abby? It's just a waste of time clearing the place up when the landscape designer I've engaged is going to rip it all out.'

Abby might resent being forced to work at the Lodge, but that gave her an unpleasant jolt.

'Rip what out?'

'Those dreary old trees and shrubs are going for a start.' Izzy's smile was back as she swept her arm in a broad gesture. 'I'm going to open up the view and then I'm going for prairie planting. And I've been sourcing sculptures,' she said. 'Can you imagine how it will look with the breeze rippling through golden grasses and wildflowers?'

Abby, who thought that high above the town, without the windbreak of mature trees and shrubs, the breeze would do rather more than ripple, raised her eyebrows.

'Does Howard know what you have in mind?'

'He said I could do whatever I liked.' Izzy's smile was patronising. 'I can see that my vision is a little radical for you, Abby. I imagine you're out of touch with modern garden design.'

'All I'm envisioning is mass habitat destruction,' she said. 'Although I think you'll find that quite a few of the trees will have preservation orders on them.'

'Howard's chair of the Planning Committee. He can get around all that red tape.'

'No doubt, but he's never used that power for his own benefit and I very much doubt that he's about to start before an election. As I'm sure that your father will warn you, felling mature trees on a whim never goes down well with the voters. Even in a safe seat.'

Izzy had no comeback to that.

'Actually,' Abby, wounded by the suggestion that she was out of touch, continued, 'when Howard talked to me, he told me that he wanted to restore the garden to its original design as a memorial to his aunt. So, before you invest too heavily in sculpture, it might be a good idea to discuss your plans with him. He went that way,' she added, helpfully.

'A memorial . . . ? Oh, for heaven's sake. I've never heard of anything so ridiculous. I'll catch up with him when I've taken a few measurements.'

'Measurements?' Jake, who had clearly learned nothing from his confrontation with Howard, chose this moment to make himself known.

Izzy turned at the sound of his voice and lowered her dark glasses so that, as she looked up at him, he got the full impact of her dazzling smile and eyes of such a luminous green that Abby suspected the involvement of contact lenses.

But she was probably just being a bitch.

'For my interior designer. Izzy Hamilton,' she said, extending her hand. 'And you are?'

'Jake Sullivan,' he said, ignoring the hand. 'I'm afraid you're going to have to put away your tape measure and call off your designers for the time being, Miss Hamilton.'

'Excuse me?'

'I've agreed to a six-month tenancy on the Lodge. Twelve if I take up the option to renew the lease.'

Izzy's smile faltered. 'What? No. That's impossible. Howard promised . . .'

'Promised?' Jake raised one eyebrow a millimetre. 'You'd trust the word of a man who'd cheat on his wife?'

On top of Howard's lie about the Finch heirloom ring and the fact that he'd discussed the garden with her, this was clearly too much, and Izzy expelled a hiss of fury.

'I'll kill him . . .'

She turned and stormed off in the direction she'd indicated, pausing only to take off the ridiculously high heels that were sinking into the lawn and fling them into the nearest shrub.

'Damn . . .' Abby drew in a slightly shaky breath. 'I shouldn't have done that. If the pair of them hadn't made me so angry . . .'

'What did you do?'

'Behaved like a spiteful cow.'

He grinned. 'I'm sure she made it very easy for you.'

'That's no excuse.'

'Anyone would think you felt sorry for her.'

'Not sorry, but I know Howard. Right now he's letting her play with her designers because he's all for an easy life—'

'Play?'

'He'll keep finding excuses to put off making a decision about anything until the baby arrives. After that she'll have that big Christmas wedding to plan, an election to campaign for and then a London flat to decorate. And Linton Lodge will remain exactly as it is. Just the way Howard likes it.'

'Really?'

'It's in his bones, Jake. Family history. The stone came from his great-great-grandfather's quarry and every part of it has the Finch hand on it.'

'What about the prehistoric kitchen?'

'Country house condition. He spent his childhood at the kitchen table being fed treats by the cook.'

'Why here?' Jake asked. 'Where were his parents?'

'If you'd read more than the headline . . .' She sighed. 'His mother ran away with her lover when he was little more than a toddler and his father died in a firearm accident not much later.'

'A firearm accident? Is that what they call it when the upper classes blow their brains out?'

Jake didn't sound particularly sympathetic, but then he'd been abandoned as a child and there had been no caring family to take him in. No one to feed him treats. He'd been thrown on the pity of overstretched social services at an age when he was too angry, too difficult, to appeal to adoptive parents.

'So what happened to Howard?'

'George and Ruth, with no children of their own, raised Howard's father when his invalid mother was moved into a nursing home, and then, after Howard lost both his parents, they raised him.'

'Your baby's bones wouldn't have made the front page back then.'

'No chance,' Abby agreed. 'The Finch family were part of the Maybridge establishment. Magistrates, businessmen, benefactors of charities, with reputations that it was in everyone's interests to protect.'

'The establishment closing ranks. Not much has changed.'

'Maybe not, but it was the world that Howard had been brought up in and he married me rather than risk losing it.' She sighed. 'There's no way he's going to cut down trees planted by his family more than a hundred years ago.'

'Izzy must know all this.'

'I doubt it. The emotional trauma is buried deep and he never talks about his parents. It's as if he's wiped them from his memory.'

'Then I do feel just a little sorry for her, but it's not all bad news. She's about to make Howard's difficult day a whole lot worse.'

'All because you saw an opportunity to tweak his nose.'

'Nose, jaw . . . I think we're equal on that score.'

'I hope the bruises are worth it.'

Jake raised his eyebrows. 'I'm not sensing much sympathy.'

'I might be kinder if you assured me that you were joking about taking a lease on the house.'

'Why would I be joking?'

She let out a huff of exasperation. 'Seriously, do not make this into a pissing contest over me.'

His face hardened. 'Believe me, Abby, I'm doing this entirely for my own pleasure.' He turned to go back into the house. 'Forget Howard. You want to look at those journals.'

'No.'

He stopped, looked back and realised that she hadn't moved. 'Shit . . . You really are angry with me.'

'Don't take it personally. Right now, I'm angry with just about everyone.'

Most of all with herself for taking it out on Izzy. And for wanting, rather desperately, to forget about everything and walk down to the river with Jake. Share a picnic. Share good memories and, if she were being totally honest, be that eighteen-year-old girl again, if just for an hour or two.

It was not going to happen . . .

'I'm sorry,' he said.

'On the contrary, you're enjoying yourself. I don't blame you for wanting payback, but this is my life.'

And she knew, as sure as God made little green apples, that today's ugly scene would come back to bite her.

CHAPTER THIRTEEN

'What about the journals?' Jake asked.

Tempting as it was to spend time with him while she scoured them for clues as to the mother of the baby, she couldn't risk getting involved.

The divorce was proving stressful enough and the children needed her undivided attention.

'I'm going to put them in the car before Howard comes back and then, when I've planted the rose, I'm going home to soak in a lavender-scented bath until the urge to scream leaves me.'

In the meantime, with any luck, Izzy would extract a promise from Howard to bar her from the house and garden and she'd never have to come here again.

'Won't he miss them?'

'I doubt he knows they exist and, if he does come after me for them, I'll say I was concerned that Izzy might throw them in a skip.'

'Okay . . . And lunch?'

'I've lost my appetite,' she said, 'and you should leave before Howard comes back.'

'It was your company I wanted . . .' Realising he wasn't helping himself, he let it go. 'What about the boys?'

'I'll leave them the cold box and they can walk home.'

About to say something, he changed his mind. 'Let me help you shift the journals, at least.'

'I think you've done more than enough for one day,' she said, then relented a little. 'If you want to make yourself useful you can grab that bag of compost from the back of the car and stick it the wheelbarrow.'

'Where do you want it?'

She wanted him to leave, but he was clearly determined to help and there was no sign of Howard, who had taken the path through the wood away from where she was working.

Hopefully, he'd washed the blood out of his beard at one of the garden standpipes and was now sitting somewhere quiet having a heart-to-heart with Tom.

'Keep to the left of the shrubbery, carry on through a little grove of silver birches and you'll come to a secluded part of the garden with a summerhouse—'

'A summerhouse?' He clutched his fist to his chest. 'This is too cruel. I always dreamed that one day I'd have a summerhouse.'

'—and a large hole,' she said, refusing to be amused by his attempt at clowning. 'Don't think of doing anything helpful like filling it in. I have to line it with cardboard first.'

'Yes, ma'am.'

'And don't call me ma'am!' she retaliated, but despite everything, she was struggling to keep a straight face as she picked up Pam's box and put it in the back of the Volvo to drop off on her way home.

The ruin of the lamp dealt with any desire to laugh. Poor Pam . . . Ruth had been a difficult woman, but there had undoubtedly been a bond between the two of them.

Howard had been irritated that he couldn't talk his aunt into a nursing home, and he blamed Pam's presence for that, but there was no excuse for the way he'd behaved.

The box safely stowed, she grabbed a couple of large hessian shopping bags from the mud room and wasted no time in loading the journals.

Jake hadn't returned by the time she'd put them in the car, so she headed down the garden, assuming that he'd stayed to take a look at the summerhouse.

Or maybe not, she thought, as she heard someone pushing through the thick shrubs in this overgrown part of the garden.

'Jake?'

There was no answer and she stopped to listen. It was eerily quiet.

There was no sound of Cal's shears attacking the shrubs, no raised voices as Izzy berated Howard. Even the birds seem to have dozed off in the heat.

All she could hear was the rustling as someone, or something, in a hurry disturbed the leaf litter on the woodland floor.

'Pam?' she called. 'It's Abby.'

There was no response and she sighed. The poor woman had fled and who could blame her?

As she ducked under a branch, she could see the rose in the box where she'd left it, along with the watering can.

Jake had left the wheelbarrow with its bag of compost beside it but her little border spade was lying on the grass as if it had been tossed aside, presumably by Howard, who was on his knees, peering into the hole she'd excavated.

She had hoped to avoid him, but she took a breath and composed herself. 'There's nothing to see. The police took everything away.'

He said nothing, didn't move.

'Howard?'

When there was still no response, she went closer and, concerned, laid a hand on his back.

'Howard? Are you okay?'

Instead of turning to her, he began to slowly topple sideways, and she instinctively grasped a handful of shirt, but he was a lot heavier than her and, as he fell, she overbalanced and went down with him.

She lay there for a moment, too shocked to move. 'Howard, this is no time for joking around . . .'

There was no answer and, concerned now, Abby pulled herself to her feet. She was already reaching for her phone where it had fallen when she saw the blood.

Not just the splashes of blood from the nosebleed when Jake had hit him. His shirt was soaked with it.

Had he had a heart attack, hitting his nose again as he went down?

He wasn't breathing.

CPR . . .

No, phone first . . .

'Emergency, which service do you require?'

'Ambulance. Linton Lodge, Huntsman Hill, bottom of the garden. I think he's had a heart attack.'

'Is the patient breathing?'

But there was no time to talk. She dropped the phone and, using all her strength, managed to push him onto his back so that she could start chest compressions.

She'd done a basic first aid course years before. They'd pumped the dummy's chest to "Stayin' Alive".

She knew you had to go in hard, but Howard wasn't a dummy. The blood on his shirt front was warm and sticky and she had to fight down the nausea as she pumped at his chest, one-two, one-two . . .

Clear his airway, the distant voice of the first-aid instructor prompted. Soil clung thickly to the blood on his face and neck. She grabbed a tissue from her pocket, wiped it around his nose and mouth, then tilted his head back to try mouth to mouth . . . .

That was when she saw the gaping wound at his throat.

CHAPTER FOURTEEN

Abby reached for her phone, but her hands, red and slippery with Howard's blood, were shaking so much that she couldn't hold it.

Overcome with a confusion of feelings — revulsion, guilt, grief for her children, anger that anyone could do this — she rubbed her hands down the sides of her bloodied overalls. Rubbed them over and over in an attempt to get them clean, but the iron scent of warm blood filled her nostrils.

Unable to bear it, she struggled out of them, flinging them away from her before, fingers shaking, she jabbed at Dee's number.

'Newcombe.'

'Help me, Dee . . .'

'Abby? What's wrong?'

'It's Howard,' she said. 'He's dead. And it's my fault.'

'Have you called an ambulance?' she asked.

'I . . . I . . .' Abby, struggling to breath, couldn't get the words out.

'Abby!' Dee said, sharply enough to cut through her rising panic.

'Y-yes . . . I d-did that before I realised . . . I can hear a siren . . .'

'Good. Well done. Where are you?'

'In the garden. Where I found the b-bones.' The sun was beating down, burning into the back of her neck, but she felt like ice. 'I started CPR but then I saw his throat . . .'

'Stay on the line, Abby . . .' The phone went silent. Alone with Howard's body she began to shiver and she crushed the phone hard against her ear so that she wouldn't drop it.

'Abby? Are you still there?'

'Y-yes.'

'Can you tell me what happened?'

'He was so angry,' she said, 'b-but he was right.'

'Right? Right about what?'

'I should have left them. The bones. Covered them back up. If I'd done that, he'd still be alive.'

'Is anyone with you, Abby?'

'No . . . Yes . . . Tom and Cal are somewhere in the garden . . . Oh, God, Tom! He mustn't see this . . .' A crow flapped down, and she ran at it, waving her arms and shrieking.

'Abby? What's happening? Talk to me!'

'It was a crow . . . And flies . . . There's so much blood . . .'

'We'll be with you very soon, but I want you to walk away.'

'I can't leave him!'

Their marriage might be over, but they'd been together for a long time. He'd been there when their children were born, his face alight with joy as he'd held them. He'd been at her side, holding her, comforting her, when her mother died . . .

'Hello?'

Startled, she spun in the direction of the voice.

'Paramedics . . .'

'Through here!' she called out, almost faint with relief as two men in green overalls pushed their way through the shrubs.

'What's happening now?' Dee asked.

'The p-paramedics have arrived.'

'Let me talk to them.'

'It's the police,' she said, holding out her phone. 'They want to talk to you.'

One of them looked at the phone then pulled on a pair of latex gloves and gave it a quick once over with a wet wipe before taking it and carrying it to where Howard lay, talking to Dee as he checked for signs of life.

The other took her arm, ushering her away from the scene.

'I'm Matthew,' he said. 'What can I call you?'

'Abby. Abby Finch. That's Howard. My husband . . . at least he was my husband.'

'We've got it, Abby. Look at me,' he said, standing so that he blocked out the sight of Howard's body. 'Concentrate on your breathing. In one, two, three . . .'

He counted her through them until she regained control, then he led her to the bench. 'Do you know what happened?'

She shook her head. All she knew was that someone had lashed out at Howard with her spade, but she didn't want to think about it. Or who might have done it.

The second paramedic joined them. 'Mrs Finch? Abby? Is it okay if I call you that?'

'Yes . . .'

'I'm Raj, Abby. I'm very sorry to have to tell you that there's nothing we can do for your husband.'

She nodded. She hadn't needed anyone to tell her that Howard was dead.

'I'm going to stay here with him until the police arrive,' he said. 'Matthew will take you up to the house and make you a cup of tea.'

'My son is somewhere in the garden. I don't want him to see . . .'

The breath stopped in her body. How on earth was she going to tell the children that their father was dead? Watch as their world shattered, the way hers had done when, six years old, she had been told that her father would not be coming home.

But her father had been a hero. Killed in the line of duty.

To die like this . . .

'Why don't you give him a call and ask him to meet you at the house?' Raj suggested.

'Yes . . .' She took her phone, relieved to be handing over the responsibility for Howard to someone else. To leave the horror of it.

She tried calling Tom as Matthew escorted her back to the house, but it went straight to voicemail.

'No luck?' he said.

'He's supposed to be trimming the lawn.' But there was no sign of him as they approached the house.

'I'm sure he'll have heard the siren and come to see what's happening.'

'He'll have his earbuds in, listening to music,' she said, shivering as they left the bright sunshine and entered the shade of the house. About to send him a text, she caught sight of the blood around her nails, felt it drying in the creases of her fingers.

Horrified, she fled to the cloakroom, turned on the tap and watched as the water ran red.

'Abby?'

Dee's voice jerked her out of the repetitive soaping and rinsing long after the blood had gone and for a moment she clung to the edge of the basin.

Dee tapped on the door. 'Abby? Are you okay?'

'I'll just be a minute,' she managed, making the effort to pull herself upright, dry her hands and open the door.

'I'm so sorry.'

Abby swallowed, opened her mouth but couldn't think of a thing to say.

'Where's the paramedic?' Dee asked.

'I don't know. I saw my hands . . . The blood . . .' Then, seeing Dee's face, 'I shouldn't have washed them, should I?'

'Don't worry about it. Come and sit down.'

'No . . . I sent Tom to the kitchen garden for an edge trimmer. I need to find him.'

She took a step towards to the door, but Dee caught her arm, restraining her.

'My partner will find him,' she said, speaking into her radio as Matthew appeared with a tray containing a teapot, cups and saucers, milk and sugar.

'I couldn't find any mugs,' Matthew said, putting the tray on a low table in front of the sofa in the morning room. 'Or teabags.'

'Ruth wouldn't have them in the house.'

'Oh, right. Well, it's my first time with a teapot. I hope it's okay.'

'It'll be fine,' Dee assured him. 'Could you wait for my DI and direct him to the scene?'

He nodded, closing the door as he left.

'I know that you've had a terrible shock, Abby,' Dee said, 'but the sooner we know what happened . . . Are you able to answer a few questions?'

She made a helpless gesture and sank down onto the sofa, where Dee joined her.

'I assume you were working in the garden?'

'I was catching up after Thursday. I was going to plant the new rose . . .'

'And you brought your son with you?'

'Tom wanted to help. He was cutting the grass. And I've taken on a lad, Cal Henderson, the young relative of a family friend.'

Dee took out her notebook. 'What's his address?'

'There's no way Cal is involved with this. He's never met Howard . . .'

'But he might have heard or seen something.'

Dee made a note of Molly's address. 'There are quite a few cars outside. I know the Volvo is yours, but who else is here?'

'The BMW belongs to Howard . . .' Abby stifled a moan, burying her head in her arms as she was caught by the sideswipe of memory.

He'd been like a kid at Christmas the day he'd come home with his first Beemer. He couldn't wait to take her and Lucy out for a ride.

The last few years had been difficult, but there were a lot of good memories.

'He's done nothing to deserve this,' she said, tears stinging the back of her eyes. No one deserved to die so brutally, and she wrapped her arms around herself, rocking to stop herself from shaking.

Dee poured tea into one of the cups, added a splash of milk, a large spoonful of sugar and, having stirred it, put the cup in front of her. 'I know it's a cliché, but it does help.'

'This is going to take more than a cup of tea.'

'Take your time.'

Abby took a sip of the tea to show willing, wincing at the sweetness.

'There's a blue Mercedes?' Dee prompted, after a moment.

'That's Izzy's. Izzy Hamilton. Howard's new partner. She came to do some measuring up but when she realised she couldn't do that, she went to look for Howard. She said . . .'

'What did she say?'

In the heat of the moment, she'd said she'd kill him, but she hadn't meant it.

Abby shook her head. 'She's pregnant. If she's confronted by a police officer . . .'

'She'll have heard the ambulance arrive and come to see what was happening.'

'The garden goes right down to the river and there's the wood. If she'd heard the siren, she'd probably think it was going past.'

Dee nodded, spoke into her radio again, warning the officer to look out for a pregnant woman. 'Try not to alarm her,' she added before glancing at her notebook. 'Who owns the Tesla?'

Her mouth dried and she took another sip of the over-sweet tea. 'Jake . . . Jake Sullivan.'

'Who is he and what's he doing here?' Dee waited, pen poised over her notebook.

'Howard put the house on the rental market. With Marshall & West. On Bridge Street.'

'And he was interested?'

'Yes . . .' Her phone pinged with a text. Jake? She ignored it.

'Is there someone from the agency showing him around?' Dee asked.

'Megan West was here showing someone else around but she had to leave. We know one another so she was happy to leave me with the keys.' Aware that was going to raise questions, she said, 'We were all at school together. Jake, Howard and me.'

'So you know him?'

'Jake and I were fairly close at school, but I hadn't seen him for years. Not until we bumped into one another the other day. In the supermarket. Quite by chance,' she added.

Her phone began to shout out the "pick up the phone" message from Lucy and this time she grabbed it.

'Lucy?'

'Mum, Tom's here. He's had a row with Dad . . .'

'He's at home? Take care of him. I'll be right there,' she said, on her feet and out of the door before Dee could react.

She caught up with her in the hall. 'Abby? What's happened?'

'It's Tom. He . . .' She stopped. 'I have to go . . .'

Dee didn't argue. 'You're in no state to drive and it'll be quicker if I take you.'

'Not a police car. Please. They're children . . .'

After a moment, she nodded. 'Okay. Give me your keys. We'll take yours.'

Outside, the sweep of the drive and the parking area in front of the house was now filled with vehicles. Scene of crime scene officers had arrived and were climbing into overalls.

Dee spoke to a plain-clothes officer explaining what she was about to do. The man gave Abby a long look.

'Stay with her until I can get there,' he said.

'Yes, sir.'

They had just reached the Volvo when Jake wandered up from the path that led up from the river. He was walking casually, hands in his pockets, head down, apparently lost in thought.

A smear of blood on his polo shirt stood out like a red stop sign.

'Jake!'

He looked up, took in the scene before him and straightened, instantly alert.

'Has there been an accident? Has something happened to Tom?'

'No. It's Howard,' she said. 'He's dead.'

'Dead?' His shock was palpable. 'Christ, how hard did I hit him?'

CHAPTER FIFTEEN

Abby heard Dee's intake of breath and she shook her head. 'No! That's not . . .' But she couldn't meet Jake's eye. 'I have to go.'

'I'll take you,' he said.

Dee stepped forward. 'I'm afraid you'll have to stay here until Detective Inspector Glover has had a word with you, sir.'

'Can't it wait?'

'No, Jake,' Abby said, sliding into the passenger seat. 'I need you to stay here and take care of Izzy and Cal. See they get home safely. Please . . .'

He looked at her for a long moment then nodded.

Then she shut the door, cutting herself off from the house, the garden, from Jake . . .

Dee said nothing, concentrating on getting her through the Saturday morning traffic as quickly as possible.

'Sophie . . .'

Dee glanced at her.

'She's at a sleepover with a friend,' Abby said. 'I need to pick her up.'

'Of course. You'll want to tell them all together.'

She didn't want to tell them at all, but she gave Dee the address and called Emma to warn her that there was a family crisis.

They'd known one another from baby group and had been firm friends ever since, so when Emma saw a uniformed officer sitting in her car, she didn't ask awkward questions, but simply whispered, 'I'm here. Call me if I can do anything.'

* * *

Abby was afraid that Dee would question Tom, ask him why he'd left the garden and come home, but she took herself off into the kitchen to make more tea, giving her space to break the news to the children.

Her mother had fallen apart when her father was killed, leaving her confused, not knowing what had happened. She must not do that . . .

'I need you all to sit down,' she said, looking at each of them as, aware that this could not be good, they sat on the sofa. 'I have some very sad news about Daddy.'

'What?' Tom demanded.

'Something happened to him when he was in the garden this morning—'

'He's hurt?' Lucy asked.

'Is he in hospital?' Sophie demanded.

'No, Sophie.' She was on her knees in front of them. 'I'm so sorry, sweetheart, but Daddy has died.'

'Died?' Her little face crumpled up in a frown. 'Like Aunt Ruth?'

'Yes, sweetheart. He's with Aunt Ruth and Uncle George.'

'He won't see me dancing tonight?'

'Not tonight.'

Not ever.

'Daddy is dead?' The colour had drained from Lucy's face. 'Is it my fault? I was so angry with him this morning but I shouldn't have yelled at him. I thought he was going to have a heart attack . . .'

'No!' Abby reached for her hand, grasping it in her own. 'No, Lucy.'

'But why didn't you go to the hospital with him?'

'Why are the police here?' Tom demanded.

No ducking this question.

It wasn't just Dee's presence. The DI would come to ask questions. They'd be polite, but she knew she had to be high on their list of suspects.

Soon the phone would start ringing and it wouldn't just be Gary Jackson from the *Observer*. When a parliamentary candidate died it was national news. When he was murdered . . .

'It wasn't a heart attack, Lucy. It had nothing to do with what you said to him this morning.'

'Then what?' she demanded.

'The police are here because someone attacked him. They'll be coming here to ask me some questions.'

Tom looked sick. Clearly Howard had found him, but what had happened then? What had made him leave the garden and come home?

The thought sent icy fingers through her, but she gathered everyone up in a hug.

Tom, embarrassed, shook her off as Dee brought in a tray with tea and a plate piled up with the remainder of the chocolate biscuits.

'I didn't know what the children would like.'

'I don't want anything.' Sophie tore herself away. 'And if Daddy's not going to be there, I'm not going to dance. Not tonight. Not ever again!' Before Abby could stop her, she rushed out of the room, her feet pounding on the stairs before her bedroom door was slammed shut.

Abby started after her but Lucy said, 'I'll go.'

'Are you sure?'

'We're sisters,' she said. 'I know how she's feeling.'

'She thinks I don't understand,' Abby said, when Lucy had gone, 'but I lost my Dad when I was six years old.'

'I'm sorry . . .' Dee's phone rang. 'I need to take this.'

'Use my office. It's across the hall,' she said. 'You will tell me what's happening?'

Tom was staring out of the window and jumped when she touched his arm.

'Was it her?' he asked.

'Her?'

'Izzy Hamilton. I heard her shouting at him.'

Tension drained from Abby, leaving her so weak that she had to lean against the wall.

'What was she saying?'

'That he couldn't let go. That dad was tied to your apron strings. That was why he wanted you to take care of the garden. Why he hadn't given her some ring. She told him he could keep the cheap one he'd palmed off on her. I heard a splash,' he said. 'I think she threw it in the lake.'

They'd fought because she couldn't keep her mouth shut. Because she'd wanted to score a point off Izzy and she'd got exactly the result she'd wanted.

Now he was dead, it felt mean, cheap . . .

'She was wrong, Tom. I was there because your dad trusted me to do a good job, but Izzy's hormones are all over the place right now. It's not surprising that she feels insecure.' Then, she had to ask: 'Did you see Cal before you left?'

'He was in the kitchen garden when I went to fetch the edger.'

Abby frowned. There was no way he could have finished cutting back the shrubs.

'Where exactly?'

'In the machinery store at the far end.'

Of course he was. She should have realised that he wouldn't have been able to resist taking a look at the motorcycle.

'He didn't see me and I didn't hang around because I wanted to get done. I was on my way back when Dad found me.'

'What happened, Tom? With Dad?'

'He wanted to give me the permission form for the school trip. I told him I wasn't going to Iceland, so he could forget about making you work for him.'

'Oh, love . . .'

'I told him to stuff his damn form and to forget about me because I didn't want him to be my dad anymore . . .'

Tom choked on the words and there were tears streaming down his face. Heart breaking for him, she tried to hug him.

He shook her off. 'Don't.'

Feeling utterly helpless she said, 'What did he do?'

'Nothing. He just stood there for a moment, then he turned and walked away. I was so angry with him . . .' He looked wretched, guilty. 'I overheard you talking to Meg.'

When she'd had a couple of glasses of wine and her mouth had run away with her.

'I'm so sorry you found out like that. I wish you'd come and talked to me about it.'

'Why? It was between him and me.'

Oh, dear lord . . .

'It was the last thing I said to him, Mum. I'll never be able to take it back.'

'He knew you didn't mean it.'

'How?'

'Because he was your dad.' Confronted with this boy, so like him in looks and temper, hurt and beyond angry with him, it must have been like looking in a mirror. 'Because he loved you. He walked away to give you time to calm down. And you did the right thing. You came home.'

'No.' He shook his head. 'It was Lucy. She found me.'

'Lucy? She was there?'

'I'd told her what I'd heard. He came here this morning, saying horrible things about you getting him in the paper, and she totally lost it. She told him that we knew exactly how he was forcing you to work for him and that we thought he was . . . Well, she didn't hold back.'

That explained why he'd been in such a foul temper . . .

'She tried ringing me to warn me, but when I didn't answer she guessed I had my headphones in. She ran all the way up through the woods, but she was too late.'

'I'm so, so sorry. None of this was about you, Tom.' She put her arms around him, but he was still stiff and unresponsive. 'I should have agreed to do what he wanted when he first asked me,' she said, the tears now streaming down her own face. 'If I hadn't been so furious with him, none of this would have happened.'

'It's not your fault,' he said. 'He was the one who cheated, left us . . .'

'He left me, he didn't leave you. You must never doubt that he loved you.'

And somehow it was Tom wrapping her in a bear hug now, and for a long moment, neither of them moved until her phone buzzed, warning her that she had a text.

Tom, suddenly embarrassed, peeled away, saying that he needed a drink.

She hesitated for a moment, wondering whether to follow him, but realising he probably needed a few moments, she looked at the text.

It was from Jake.

'*I told the police everything that happened this morning. They've taken samples from every orifice and, since I have his blood on me, I'm clearly high on their suspect list.*'

She texted back, '*You and me both. Are you still at the police station?*'

'*They've let me leave for now, although I'll have to give a formal statement. I don't think they've found Izzy or Cal.*'

Izzy?

She wasn't surprised that Cal might have legged it at the sight of a uniform, especially since he'd sloped off to look at the motorbike. But why would Izzy?

No. It was impossible.

She'd been angry, but the thought of her grabbing a spade and swinging it . . .

Her phone buzzed again.

'*I've called Megan and told her what's happened. Is there anything I can do?*'

'*No. The children need all my attention right now.*' Then she added, '*Is Izzy's car still there?*'

'*Yes. They were widening the search when I left.*'

'*That's not good.*'

'You need to concentrate on yourself, Abby. I have a legal body on fast dial if you want someone with you when you're summoned to make a formal statement.'

'*No!*' Could anything make her look more guilty? '*I have to go.*'

'*I'm here for you.*'

'*You've done enough . . .*' She thumbed in the words, then deleted them. She couldn't blame him for this, although, as she re-read his texts, it was almost, she thought, as if he suspected that she, or maybe Tom, was responsible . . .

The phone buzzed again. Meg.

'I'll be with you as soon as I can get away. xxx'

'It's your busiest day, there's nothing you can do.'

'I can give you a hug. xxx'

She looked up as Dee re-joined them. 'DI Glover is on his way to ask you some questions.'

She nodded. 'Can I phone Aunt Molly and let her know what's happened before she hears it from someone else?'

'Aunt Molly?'

'Molly Taylor. Cal's great-aunt. He's going to be in a state when he gets home. He's not eighteen yet . . .'

'Okay. But no details,' she warned.

The phone rang for a while before Molly picked up. 'Yes?'

'Aunt Molly, it's Abby. Is Cal there?'

'Cal?'

Abby frowned. She hadn't noticed any serious deterioration in Molly's memory, but the last few months had been difficult and maybe she hadn't been paying sufficient attention.

'Penny's grandson.'

'Oh, Cal . . .'

'Are you okay, Molly?'

'A bit tired. I had a bad night . . . I went for a walk and then I talked to Gordon, but I sat down when I got home and must have nodded off. The phone woke me.'

Gordon, Molly's husband, had been dead for more than twenty years, but she still visited him. Still talked to him. She always said the dead were the best listeners.

'I'm sorry I woke you, but it's important. Is Cal there?'

'Isn't he with you?'

'He was . . .' She swallowed, still struggling with the words. 'I'm sorry, this is so hard, but I have to tell you that Howard is dead.'

'Yes, I know. I saw his picture in the paper. They said he fell down the stairs.'

What?

'No, Molly. That was Howard Senior, Howard's grandfather. He died more than thirty years ago.'

There was a long pause while she thought about it. 'I'm sorry dear, I seem to be in a bit of a muddle. Who's died?'

'Howard . . . My husband, Molly.'

In the silence that followed, Abby could almost hear the clogs meshing. 'I don't understand. He's so young. Was he in an accident? Your poor children. How are they? How are you?'

The words tumbled out in a rush.

'I'm not sure that any of us have taken it in, to be honest . . . But the thing is, Molly, the police couldn't find Cal.'

'The police? What do they want with Cal? Why are they involved?' she asked, her voice no longer wandering but suddenly sharp as a knife.

There was no point in holding anything back. It would be on the news that evening and the main topic of conversation when Molly went to church in the morning.

'They're involved because Howard's death wasn't an accident. Someone attacked him.'

'Not Cal!'

'No, but he was in the garden when it happened, and the police will want to know if he heard or saw anything.'

'Oh dear. If he saw them . . .' She let the sentence hang, but the meaning was clear enough. 'He would never hurt anyone.'

'I'm sure you're right and it's nothing for you to worry about,' Abby said, hoping to reassure her. 'He's not in any trouble.'

'Are you sure?'

'Quite sure.'

Of all the people in the garden that morning, Cal was the only one who had never met Howard. Unless, of course, he'd seen him looking at the motorbike and thought he was stealing . . .

'He's not in any trouble,' she repeated, with slightly less assurance, 'but the police do need to speak to him.'

'Oh, dear,' she repeated.

Oh dear, indeed.

She really should have pressed harder to find out what Cal's "bit of trouble" had actually involved, but it was too late now.

Abby left it at that, although she wasn't entirely convinced by Molly's assurance. Clear-headed, she might tell him to get back home to Bristol and keep his head down.

Right now though, the crunch of tyres on the drive heralded the arrival of the detective inspector and she needed to look out for herself.

While Dee went to let him in, Tom asked, 'Will they question me?'

She didn't have time to answer before Dee said, 'Abby. This is Detective Inspector Iain Glover. He's the officer in charge of this case.'

Tall, distinguished, with a touch of grey in his dark hair, he looked friendly enough, but Abby, a fan of TV crime drama, was aware that the spouse was always the main suspect.

Or failing that, the person who found the body.

She was it on both counts.

'Please, come in,' she said, indicating the roomy, if aged, leather armchair; the shine from which had been worn first by her father and then Howard.

'I'm sorry to meet you in these circumstances, Mrs Finch,' he said. 'My sympathies for your loss.'

'Thank you.'

'This is your son?'

'Tom,' she said. 'Do you want to speak to him now?'

'Not at the moment,' he said, with what looked like a genuine smile.

'I'll, um, go and join the girls,' he said, clearly relieved.

Once he'd gone, Abby quickly ran through her morning for the DI. What she was doing at the house. Setting the boys to work. Preparing to plant the rose.

He listened intently, despite the fact that he must have heard all this from Dee.

'So,' he said, when she'd finished, 'you found your husband's body in the same place as the baby's bones?'

CHAPTER SIXTEEN

The baby . . . It all started with the baby . . .

'Yes . . .' Abby cleared her throat. 'Yes,' she repeated, although he must know that.

'Why do you think he was there?'

'Howard was in Paris with his new partner until last night. He'd only seen the headlines in the *Observer* this morning.'

'No one had spoken to him? Warned him?'

'I called his office but Natalie Grant, Howard's PA, told me that he was at a conference and had put a *do not disturb* notice on his trip. It was only when she saw the newspaper that she admitted that he was in Paris with Izzy.'

'Why would Ms Grant lie about his whereabouts? It wasn't as if his relationship with Miss Hamilton was a secret.'

'The power gave her a buzz,' Abby said.

He gave her a thoughtful look, but said, 'So when he saw the paper, he came to Linton Lodge to check for himself?'

'I couldn't say. He'd come here earlier looking for me. Lucy, our oldest child, was here and she told him that we were at the Lodge.'

'Is she here now?'

'She's upstairs with her sister.' There was a thump as something hit the wall above them. 'Sophie's ten,' Abby said. 'She's taken it very hard.'

He nodded. 'Of course. And you need to be with her. I'll keep this as brief as I can.' He glanced at his notebook. 'I understand that you and your husband were in the process of a divorce.'

'Yes. He's planning . . .' She stopped, took a breath. 'He was planning to marry Isobel Hamilton at Christmas. She's expecting his child,' she added, although she was sure he knew that too.

'And when he arrived at the Lodge, he had an altercation with Mr Sullivan. When did he arrive?'

'Jake?' Since the DI had spoken to him, he already knew, but she said, 'Around ten. I'd put my new young assistant, Cal, to work and was preparing to plant the rose. Tom was near the house, cutting the lawn. He sent me a text to tell me that Megan West had arrived to show someone around the house.'

She found Tom's message on her phone and showed it to Dee, who made a note of the exact time.

'Why did he text you?' he asked. 'I was told that Megan West was there on business.'

For a moment Abby's mind went blank.

'Abby?'

'Yes, she was, but we're friends.' The family records had nothing to do with this. 'When I spoke to Meg yesterday evening she told me she was showing someone around the house this morning. She'd been on holiday. I wanted to say hello and arrange a date to meet. When I reached the house, Jake was already there.'

'You were expecting him?' the DI asked.

'No, but he knew I'd be there this morning. He was going back to London and just wanted to touch base before he left.'

'So you're friends with him too?'

'We were at school together.'

'I see. And he decided to take a look at the house?'

'Yes. Meg had to leave so she left me to show him around. He'd already decided it suited him and had called her to close the deal before Howard arrived.'

'Mr Sullivan said that your husband wasn't happy with the arrangement.'

'No, he wasn't,' Abby admitted.

'I'd have thought he would have been delighted. It can't be every day you find a tenant for a house of that size. What was the cause of the dispute?'

'It seems that while he was away, Howard had changed his mind about letting the Lodge.'

'Did he say why?'

'No. Perhaps Izzy, Ms Hamilton, can tell you more. I believe they discussed it while they were in Paris.'

He made another note then looked up. 'Clearly it was an awkward situation,' he said, 'but I don't understand why they came to blows.'

Afraid that whatever she said would look bad for Jake, she hesitated.

'Mrs Finch?'

'Howard was already angry when he arrived. With me,' she added, quickly. 'About the bones, the headlines in the newspaper. He thought I should have covered them up and forgotten about them.'

'Why didn't you?' he asked. 'You must have known it would embarrass your husband.'

'I knew he wouldn't be happy,' she admitted, 'but as I'm sure you know, it's a legal requirement to notify the police when you find human remains. No matter how old.'

The DI nodded. 'Of course. So, when he discovered that the house had been let, it added to his irritation.'

Irritation . . .

That was putting it mildly.

'It didn't help that he and Jake had history from their days at the high school. Howard became rude and physical, telling him to get out, but it was only when he turned on me that Jake hit him.'

'Did your husband have a history of violence towards you?'

'No!' Dee touched her arm, and Abby caught her breath. 'No,' she repeated. 'Never. But he was extremely angry.'

'Mr Sullivan was protecting you?'

'It was an instinctive reaction to provocation.'

'Would you say that your husband was out of control?'

'On the edge,' she admitted, 'but once he'd hit Jake he walked away.'

'I'm sorry, but I have to ask you this, Mrs Finch. Are you in a relationship with Jake Sullivan?'

A relationship? Did memories that sparked back over two decades count? Howard clearly thought so, but that wasn't what the DI was asking.

'The first time I'd seen Jake since the night of the school prom was on Thursday afternoon when, quite by chance, I bumped into him in the supermarket.'

DI Glover, smart enough to recognise that wasn't a flat no, asked, 'How many times have you seen him since?'

'While I was in the supermarket I had a panicked call from Lucy. The local newspaper had phoned, wanting to know about the bones I'd found.'

'I can confirm that, sir,' Dee said. 'Mrs Finch telephoned to make a complaint about the information being released to the press before she could tell her children what had happened.'

He nodded. 'Go on, Mrs Finch.'

'There were long queues at the checkout and Jake offered to put my trolley through the till and drop it off when he'd finished his own shopping.'

'So you'd kept in touch?'

'No.'

'But he knew where you lived?'

'I was born in this house. I was my mother's carer. Howard and I lived with her after we married, and I inherited the house when she died.'

'I'm surprised your husband didn't want to move into one of the luxury homes built by his company.'

'Oldfield Cottage has been in my family for several generations and I love it.' And Howard had been more than happy to stay in a house that cost him nothing.

'So, Mr Sullivan came here with your shopping.'

'He brought it into the kitchen, met the children. In fact, he'd already met Lucy earlier that day when he'd given a talk on internet safety at the high school.'

'You didn't make any plans to meet again?'

Abby, certain that Jake had already been asked that question, said, 'Jake asked me if I'd have lunch with him the next day so that we could catch up, but I was too busy.'

'And that was it?'

'He said he'd be in touch,' she explained, 'and then he phoned me on Friday afternoon to ask me out to dinner before he returned to London. I couldn't go because Sophie had a dance rehearsal.'

'Thank you, Mrs Finch. That's very clear. So, can you tell me what happened after the altercation?'

'Howard wanted to talk to Tom. I told him that he'd gone to the kitchen garden to pick up the edger, and he went to find him.'

'And then Ms Hamilton arrived?'

'Yes. She said she was going to measure up something for her interior designer . . .' She stopped.

'Mrs Finch?'

She shook her head. 'It's nothing. I'm just surprised that any interior designer important enough to have been commissioned by Izzy Hamilton would rely on a client for that kind of information. A wrong measurement could be disastrous.'

'That's true,' DI Glover said with feeling. 'I have a garage full of skirting board to prove it. But why else would she have been there? Did she know you'd be at the house?'

'Izzy said that she was surprised to see me.'

'Was it possible that she was checking up on Mr Finch? Did she have any reason to think that you might get back together?'

'None whatever, but she wasn't happy that I was working in the garden.'

'It seems an unlikely arrangement.'

'I'm trying to keep things friendly because of the children,' she said, shading the truth. She had enough points against her without admitting that Howard was using emotional blackmail. 'And he trusted me to get on with it.'

'Your husband hadn't told you that he was going to let the house?'

'No, but then it was none of my business.'

'But surely the property will be included in the calculation of the divorce settlement?'

'I've left all that in the capable hands of my solicitor. Dee has the details,' she added.

He made a note then looked up. 'So, did Ms Hamilton go inside and measure up?'

'No. Jake explained the situation and advised her to come back in six months.'

He glanced at his notebook. 'When, according to Mr Sullivan, she said, "I'll kill him"?'

For heaven's sake. When Jake said he'd told them *everything* . . .

'It seems a rather excessive reaction?' the DI prompted.

'She's pregnant.' Abby said, guilt at her own contribution forcing her to excuse Izzy's behaviour.

'There appears to have been a great deal of hot air flying about Linton Lodge this morning.'

'Enough to create its own microclimate,' Abby agreed. 'I'd had enough of it and decided to go home as soon as I'd planted the rose, and I asked Jake to take a bag of compost down the garden for me.'

'Was that entirely wise?'

'He wanted to help,' she said, 'and it was well away from the kitchen garden.'

'And what were you doing while he was taking the compost to the exact spot where your husband's body was found?'

'I was collecting some small items from the house that Howard's aunt had left to her carer. Pam Lewis. Dee has her details.'

'Mr Sullivan mentioned her. She was only there briefly, I understand.'

'Howard made her nervous. Pam left when he arrived.'

There was no need to repeat the things Howard had said to her.

'Without the items she'd come to collect?'

'Yes. I put them in my car to drop off later.'

'Then you went down the garden to plant the rose?'

'Yes.'

'And that's when you found your husband?'

She swallowed as she recalled the scene. The smell. The flies. 'Yes.'

He asked her to describe what she saw, which she did.

'Your spade had been moved?'

'I'd stuck it in the pile of soil, but it was lying on the grass some distance away. As if it had been flung there,' she added.

'Did you touch anything?'

'Only Howard. I spoke to him, but when he didn't answer, I touched his shoulder.'

'And that was when you realised something was wrong.'

'I was already concerned when he hadn't looked up or said anything, so I walked over to him and gave him a bit of a shake . . .' She stopped, reliving the horror of that moment.

'Take your time, Mrs Finch.'

She took a breath, knowing that he had to ask the questions and she had to answer them.

'He fell onto his side . . . I overbalanced and I went down with him.'

'That's when you got blood on your overalls?'

'I . . . yes . . .' For a moment she was like a goldfish, her mouth opening but no words making it out.

'Take your time, Abby,' Dee said.

'I took them off . . . It was the smell.'

'I'm sorry. I know this must be difficult.'

'Do you? Really?' she glared at him, sitting there in her father's chair, calm as you like. What did he know?

He said nothing, no doubt used to that kind of reaction, and she shook her head. He was just doing his job.

'Sorry . . . This is . . .'

'Can I get you some water?' Dee offered.

'No . . . Thank you.' She wanted this over as quickly as possible.

'You called an ambulance?' DI Glover prompted.

She nodded. 'Then I attempted CPR. It was when I tried to clear his nose that I saw . . . When I saw what had happened to him.'

'And that's when you called PC Newcombe, because you realised that he'd been attacked.' He glanced at his notebook. 'Can you confirm that you said, "It's Howard, he's dead, and it's my fault"?'

'Something like that,' she admitted.

'Why would you say that it was your fault?'

'Howard had made it clear that I should have reburied the bones I'd found instead of calling the police. If I had, he wouldn't have been there.'

'You believe the two incidents are linked?' he asked.

Did she?

'The discovery of the bones was in the newspaper,' he prompted. 'It could have provoked memories, and there's a public footpath through Linton Woods. Someone who knew the baby was buried there might have come to see what had happened.'

'It's possible,' she agreed, remembering the sound of someone in the woods. 'But why would they attack Howard?'

'Did he have any enemies?'

'No one who would kill him,' she said. 'Is this going to take much longer? I need to be with my children.'

'I just have a couple more questions.' He checked his notebook. 'Did you go into the summerhouse?'

'No. I wouldn't trust the floorboards.'

He looked up. 'Maybe the first time you went down the garden?'

'No.'

'You didn't notice that the door was open?'

'The first time?' She thought for a minute, trying to picture the scene, but then shook her head. 'No.'

'You didn't try the door?'

'No.'

'You didn't unlock it?' About to say that she didn't have a key, she felt the weight of them in her shorts pocket. 'Mrs Finch?'

'No, although I doubt it would have taken much of a push to open it. As I said, the wood was rotten. The door was open the second time I went there. Howard had been talking about demolishing it and he might have been checking to see how bad it was.'

'Did you see or hear anyone when you walked down the garden?'

'I thought I heard someone in the woods and called out, but there was no answer.'

'But you think there was someone there?'

She swallowed, remembering how spooked she'd been. 'Yes.'

'Thank you, Mrs Finch,' the DI said. 'Just one more thing.' She lifted a resigned hand and he said, 'Have you any idea why we found a receipt from a pawnbroker in your husband's wallet?'

'He still had it?'

'So you do know about it?'

'Yes. I borrowed some money against my engagement ring to pay for . . .' Before she could explain, Sophie hurtled into the room and flung herself into her arms.

'I'm sorry, Mummy. I'll dance if you want me to.'

She held her tight. 'Not today, sweetheart. I'll call Madame and tell her that you're feeling too sad. She'll understand.' She pulled her onto her lap, kissed her hair, then looked up as Lucy followed her into the room.

'We'll leave it there for now,' the DI said, getting to his feet. 'Maybe you could ask Tom if he saw or heard anything?'

'He heard Howard and Izzy having a row,' Lucy said. 'And I saw a car.'

CHAPTER SEVENTEEN

Inspector Glover glanced at Dee.

'I didn't know, sir,' she said.

'I haven't had a chance to tell anyone,' Lucy said. 'I-I had a message for Tom and when he didn't answer his phone I ran up to the Lodge. Through the woods.'

'That's quite a long way. It must have been very urgent,' the DI suggested.

'He was wanted for nets.'

'Nets?'

'Cricket nets.' Lucy, the world's worst liar, flushed pink.

Abby, aware that she was protecting Sophie from hearing what her father had done, said, 'Tom plays for the Maybridge Colts. He's their opening bat.' She'd tell Dee what had really happened later.

'And you saw a car?'

'There's an entrance down there. For the kitchen garden. I saw a car pulling out from there.'

'What time was that?'

'I'm not sure. Just before twelve?'

'Did you recognise it?'

She shook her head.

'Colour?' he asked, hopefully. 'Big? Small? Number plate?'

'Light coloured? It's overgrown there and I only noticed it because I heard a bang.'

'It hit something?'

'I don't know. It didn't stop . . .'

'Why don't you have a think about it?' Dee suggested. 'Take your time. Try and picture the scene. You probably saw more than you think.'

'You didn't see anyone?' the inspector asked. 'Or hear the row between your father and Miss Hamilton?'

She shook her head.

'Thank you, Lucy. You've been very helpful.'

'We'll do whatever we can to help,' Abby assured him.

'I'll need your fingerprints for elimination purposes. Has anyone apart from you handled the spade?'

'Tom put the tools in the car this morning.'

'Then we'll need his too.'

'Not today?'

'No, but the sooner the better. PC Newcombe will arrange a time. I'll leave you in peace for now, but if you think of anything—' he handed her a card — 'tell her or give me a call.'

Dee saw him out and they stood on the doorstep talking for a while.

'What do you think they're saying?' Tom asked, reappearing from upstairs.

'I have no idea.' Not true. She was pretty sure he was telling Dee to find out what Tom had heard and the real reason his sister had run all the way from home to speak to him, and get the whole story about the pawn ticket.

'Mum . . .'

'It's okay, Lucy. I'll explain—'

'No . . . Sophie, will you help Tom clear these cups away. Tom,' she added, pointedly, 'the tools need putting away.'

He opened his mouth, about to object to being ordered around by his sister, but catching the look she was giving him, he said, 'Come on Soph, Lucy can manage the cups. You can help me with the tools.' And not waiting for an argument, he swept her out the living room.

'Lucy?' Abby asked.

'You need to change your T-shirt, Mum.'

Abby looked down and saw the smear of blood where her hand had brushed against it.

For a moment she couldn't move and then she was running up the stairs, stripping off her clothes and flinging them out of sight in the laundry basket. Not that she'd wear any of them ever again.

Ten minutes later, hair washed, skin scrubbed until it tingled, she returned to the kitchen to find Tom emptying the contents of the cold box onto the island.

'I left the rest of the stuff in the mudroom.'

'Thank you, Tom.' There was a moment of silent understanding, then she said, 'Will you lay the table?'

He shrugged and got cutlery from the drawer. 'Plates, anyone?' he asked, looking at the girls. 'Or do I have to do it all myself?'

'It seems wrong to be eating,' Lucy said. 'It's just too normal.'

Having witnessed her mother slide into depression after the death of her father, not sleeping, forgetting to cook, never leaving the house, Abby was determined to keep things as routine as possible for the children.

'I know it's weird, but it's all about putting one foot in front of the other,' she said. 'Until we find a new normal.'

'I just wish—'

'I know.' Abby rubbed a comforting hand down Lucy's back. 'Try not to dwell on today. Think about all the good things we did together,' she said. 'The silly things. The holidays . . .'

Lucy sniffed. 'Dad really loved your cooking,' she said, then managed a smile. 'And your Scotch eggs.'

'And the tomatoes from the greenhouse,' chimed Tom.

'It's a bit early for those,' Abby replied. 'We'll have to make do with the ones from the supermarket. Will one of you go and ask PC Newcombe if she'd like something to eat?'

'Is she going to be here all day?' Sophie asked.

'They do that in television crime dramas,' Tom said. 'They leave someone to watch the family.'

'Not to watch,' Abby said. 'They're on hand to help. Deal with phone calls, that sort of thing.' And yes, talk to them, hoping to pick up information. Watch for tensions . . . 'Tell her she's welcome to come through to the kitchen.'

'Okay,' Lucy said, 'but be careful what you say because she'll be taking it all down and using it in evidence.'

'Are they going to question me?' Tom asked.

'Not today.' He was putting on a brave front but she could sense from his stiffness that he was barely holding it together, and he'd be mortified if he cried. 'We'll have to go to the police station to have our fingerprints taken,' she explained. 'They'll ask what you and Dad talked about and what else you saw and heard. Just tell them what you told me.'

'But suppose they give me the third degree?'

'We don't do that these days,' Dee said, following Lucy into the kitchen. 'We just need to know what you saw. And your mum will be with you.'

Tom blushed furiously. 'My mum? I'm not a kid.'

'Of course not. But it's the law. She'll be with Lucy when she gives her statement too.'

'Will you stay with me, Mum?' Sophie asked.

'They won't want to talk to you, Soph. You weren't there,' Tom's attempt at reassuring her did not go down well.

'But he was my daddy too. I could tell them all sorts of things about him.'

'Really?' Dee asked, smiling at her as she pulled out a chair and sat at the dining table, while Abby opened the bi-fold doors to let in the warmth and scent of the garden. 'Why don't you tell me about him?'

Abby shot her a warning look, but she gave the slightest shake of her head, listening intently as Sophie told her about her dear daddy.

For a while Lucy and Tom were quiet, but Dee gradually drew them out with gentle prompts until all three children were piling in.

Howard teaching them to swim, to ride their bikes, building sandcastles. How mad he'd been when Tom had flipped his skateboard and scratched his car.

Happy moments, the surprise treats, real memories to treasure before he'd been distracted by other demands on his time.

She needed to remember those too. Not just the bad times, the other women, the months since he'd moved out and their marriage had been reduced to negotiations about money.

Swallowing a lump in her throat, she mouthed a silent 'thank you' to Dee.

'Will Daddy have a funeral like Aunt Ruth's?' Sophie asked when they'd finished eating and the children had gone into automatic clearing-up mode. Stacking the dishwasher, wiping down surfaces.

She'd had to stop herself from telling them to leave it, that she'd do it. This was what they did every day, their normal routine, and they were going to need all the normal that was going in the next few weeks.

Abby, remembering the unremitting black and mournful scent of chrysanthemums at Ruth's funeral, silently vowed not, although she realised that she might not have a say in the arrangements.

Izzy had been at the helm of Ruth's funeral, and she might well demand the right to organise Howard's send-off.

What was the protocol when a couple were separated, and he'd moved in with another woman?

'It won't be for a while,' she said, silently promising the children that while she might be side-lined, they would be allowed to play their part.

'Are there going to be reporters outside the house?' Lucy asked.

'The locals will pick it up very quickly,' Dee said, then looked up from her phone. 'The *Observer* doesn't have enough staff to cover everything these days, and their first efforts will be trying to find out what happened.'

'But we can leave the house? Only, I was thinking I might take Sophie to visit our kittens.'

'That's a good idea,' Abby said. Once the news was out, they'd all be targets for anyone with a camera on their phone. Thankfully they'd broken up for half term and it would be a week before they were due back at school. She turned to Dee. 'That's okay?'

'We don't have to ask permission, do we?' Tom demanded. 'The club has a match tomorrow,' he said. 'We're playing Longbourne and Dad said . . .' He stopped.

'What did Dad say?' Abby asked.

He shook his head. 'It doesn't matter.'

'Try me.'

'He said he'd come to watch.' He swallowed. 'He promised if I made a half-century he'd take me to a test match at Lord's.'

She considered offering to take him herself, but Howard would probably have been offered box seats by a sponsor.

'I don't suppose a day at the Hampton Court Flower Show would do instead?' she asked.

He managed a smile. 'Nice try, Mum, but I'll pass.'

'That's probably a good thing. If I had a bag carrier, I'd go overboard buying plants and tools.'

'You always come back from those things with the car loaded,' he said. 'Dad rolls his eyes and says, "How many hoes does one woman need?"'

Tom did a very fair imitation of his father and for a moment they were all laughing until Lucy muttered, 'I'll bet he didn't buy Izzy Hamilton a spade for her birthday . . .' Her voice trailed off as she realised what she'd said. 'Was that it? Was that the one . . . ?'

'No. That's in the tool shed waiting for a new handle . . .' And even if it was returned to her, she'd never be able to use the one that killed Howard again.

'Let me check and see if there's anyone about,' Dee said, breaking the sudden awkward silence, but no one said anything until she returned. 'It's all clear out there. It'll take an hour or two for the media to get their act together and head down here, so you should be safe enough for the moment.'

'But if anyone approaches you in the street asking you questions,' Abby warned, 'or tries to take a photograph, ignore them and keep walking.'

'And call your mother straight away to let her know,' Dee added.

'I'd better go with them,' Tom said.

'Call me when you get there,' Abby called after them. 'Tom!'

'Don't fuss, Mum.'

'Lucy!'

'We'll call.'

'The reality hasn't sunk in yet,' Abby said when they'd gone. And she didn't just mean the children. She had to keep reminding herself that Howard was dead. 'How soon will it be before the press are on our doorstep?'

'The DI will do his best to keep a lid on it until he's ready to make a statement, and appeal for witnesses, but you can't have the kind of police activity there'll be at Linton Lodge without attracting attention.'

'And after yesterday's headlines, this is the first place they'll come,' Abby said.

'I'm afraid so.'

'Oh, God,' she said, sinking onto a chair. 'I was hoping Izzy would prove the sexier target . . .' She caught herself. 'Could I sound more callous?'

'Don't beat yourself up, Abby. We'll station an officer outside, but it's not going to be pleasant. I didn't want to say anything while the children were here, but I'd strongly advise you to close your front curtains.'

'Really?'

'Do you have any family you could go and stay with for a few days?'

'I don't have any brothers or sisters, neither did Howard. It's why Molly is so important. She's a link . . .'

'You're close?'

'She was my grandmother's best friend. They worked together in a hotel when they were young, and she was a huge support to my mother when she lost my Dad.'

'How old were you?'

'Six. He was in the army.'

'He was killed in action?'

'In the Balkans. Special Services.'

'I'm so sorry. There are no grandparents?'

'My grandmother sent my grandfather packing not long after my mother was born and then cancer took her far too young. My father never knew his dad. His mother got married when he was in his teens and he didn't get on with his stepdad. That's why he joined the army.'

'That's tough. Your Lucy seems a very competent and caring young woman . . .' Dee's phone rang and she excused herself to take the call.

Competent and caring but still a child herself, Abby thought. It wasn't just Sophie who needed to cuddle a kitten.

Meanwhile she had calls to make. First to Madame to tell her that she'd be missing a dancer that evening.

She didn't have much in the way of family, but Charlotte, a distant cousin and Lucy's godmother, had been her best friend since her childhood.

She wanted to call her, hear her voice, but she was on her way to France with her own brood and she didn't want to ruin her holiday. It was news that would keep until she was home.

She had just started to get in touch with her clients to let them know that she wouldn't be available for the following week, when Dee returned.

Abby looked up. 'Have they found Izzy or Cal?'

'Not yet,' she said. 'Were you aware that Cal has been in trouble?'

'Molly said he'd got involved in protests of some kind. That there was a scuffle and he'd got a warning.'

'I don't know about that, but he was cautioned for an incident involving a motorcycle.'

Abby's heart sank. 'What sort of incident?'

'He had a part-time job in a garage that repaired motorbikes. One day, left alone, he couldn't resist taking one of them for a spin.'

'Oh . . .'

'He brought it back but not before the owner had arrived to pick it up and called the police to report it stolen. There was no damage and in the end all Cal got was a verbal caution, but he lost his job.'

'That would explain his disappearing act when the police arrived, but I'm more worried about Izzy. I'd try calling her, but I'm probably the last person she wants to hear from.'

CHAPTER EIGHTEEN

'Ms Hamilton's phone is going straight to voicemail,' Dee said, 'and there's no one at her apartment. It's possible that she was picked up by the car Lucy saw.'

'But her own car was at the house,' Abby said.

'She was angry with Mr Finch. Maybe they fought and she called a friend.'

'Tom heard them arguing, but you can't seriously think that she might have killed Howard?'

'I'm in no position to think anything, but if she was upset, she might not have wanted to return to the house while you were there.'

'I wasn't hanging around to gloat,' Abby said, 'but she couldn't have walked far without her shoes.'

Dee frowned. 'She wasn't wearing shoes?'

'The heels were sinking into the lawn. They were Louboutins,' she added. 'I saw the soles as she flung them into a bush.'

'Wow. She was that angry about the house?'

'It wasn't just the house. Howard had lied to her about the Linton engagement ring. He told her that I'd sold it, but I gave it back to him a couple of weeks ago. At least, I'd given him the pawn ticket so that he could redeem it. I don't understand why he hadn't done that.'

'Is it valuable?'

'It's a ten-carat Burmese pigeon's-blood ruby with diamonds and worth a very great deal of money.'

'And he expected you to give it back?'

'It was a family piece, on loan to the wife of the oldest son. A hideous thing, I doubt I wore it more than a couple of dozen times during our marriage. It spent most of its life in the bank.'

'Maybe he didn't have the kind of money needed to redeem it.'

'Oh, good grief, no . . . It wasn't that. He'd refused to pay for Tom's school trip unless I did some work on the garden for him, so I pawned it for the exact amount of the trip. Not one percent of its value.'

'But you *were* working in the garden.'

Abby lifted her shoulders in an awkward shrug. 'Yes, well, I thought I'd fixed him, but his response was to refuse to sign the permission slip for Tom to leave the country.'

'And you didn't want Tom to know.'

'It was between me and Howard. And it came on top of his discovery that I hadn't done as I was told and put his name on the deeds to the house when I inherited it from my mother.'

'So he was mad at you before you found the bones.'

'You could say that.'

'And his response was to coerce you into clearing the garden for him? I don't imagine he was paying you.'

Aware that none of this was looking good for her, Abby took a deep breath. 'It was all part of the pressure he was applying to force me to agree to the less-than-generous divorce settlement he was offering.'

'I see.'

'He thought the fact that I owned this house outright let him off the hook. He chose to forget that he'd lived in it rent-free for seventeen years.'

Dee took a moment to absorb that, then said, 'So why would he tell Miss Hamilton that you'd sold the ring? Did he need the money to finance your divorce settlement?'

'You'll have to talk to his solicitors, or his financial advisor, about that. Is there anything else, Dee? There are things that won't wait . . .'

'Just a few more questions. How did Miss Hamilton react to the news that he'd lied to her about the ring?'

'She made a good effort at brushing it off. She said the colour wouldn't suit her, but she was clearly shaken. And then Jake appeared and told her that he'd rented the house.'

'That was when she said she'd kill Howard?'

'It was a figure of speech, Dee. She didn't mean it. Will you let me know when you find her? I could have been kinder . . .'

'Abby, don't do that to yourself. It won't help.'

She sighed. 'No. If that's it, there are a lot of people I need to call. People who'll be waiting for me to turn up and sort out their gardens next week but, more urgently, people who need to know that Howard is dead.'

'Who?'

'Directors of his company, he's a county councillor and he's running for parliament. The local party, his political agent and his solicitor will have to be told. It won't take long for news of his death to reach the media and they all need to be prepared.'

'Leave the solicitors to us. We'll need to talk to them, and your husband's office gave us their details when I spoke to them after you found the bones.'

'Frankly, that would be a relief. Thank you.'

'You might want to call your own solicitors,' she suggested.

'Yes.' This was going to be an almighty mess. She was going to need Freddie. 'I'll do that.'

'I could make some other calls for you?'

'They're personal. Something I have to do myself, although I'm not looking forward to telling Natalie Grant. Howard's PA,' she admitted.

'The woman I spoke to on Thursday? She sounded a bit . . . tense.'

'She's going to be devastated.'

'They're close? You told the DI that she enjoyed the power being Howard's PA gave her.'

'She did. There have been affairs in the past and she covered for him, clearly blaming me for the fact that he needed the distraction. She thought she could do a better job as his wife and his relationship with Izzy seems to have seriously unbalanced her.'

'She saw herself as the next Mrs Finch?'

'It was pure fantasy, but she shouldn't hear about his death on the radio.'

* * *

The politicians and Howard's colleagues offered their condolences, but even the ones Abby knew well didn't hang around to chat. They had their own calls to make.

The clients who'd been expecting her to turn up on Monday were sweet, telling her not to worry. Once the news was out that it was murder, they might not be quite so kind.

Which just left Izzy and Cal.

Izzy would go to her father for protection. Cal didn't have that option, and she sent Lucy a text asking if he'd turned up at Molly's.

'*Not here*,' replied Lucy. She attached a picture of Sophie holding her kitten to the text.

'Dee,' she said, when she returned to the living room, 'I'm a bit concerned about Molly. She's old and a bit confused these days, and I don't want her to be on her own once the press gets involved. If I ask her to come here, do you think someone could pick her up?'

'I could do that.'

'She has a cat. And kittens,' Abby warned. 'They'll have to come too.'

'I can cope with them, but what about Cal?'

'Not there, but I'll text him to let him know where she is. And tell him to come here too.'

'If he's hiding,' Dee told her, 'he'll have turned off his phone and removed the SIM card.'

'I'm hoping he's not that street smart.'

'They're all that street smart,' she said. 'I'll leave a note on the door for him.'

'Thank you. I'll text Lucy and let her know.'

'It might be a good idea, if I wasn't obviously in uniform. Have you got a jacket and scarf I could borrow?'

While Dee covered her uniform, Abby made the call, but Molly was adamant that she would stay put in case Cal came home. 'And there's Mabel.'

'You can bring her and the kittens.'

'She'll just try and bring them back here,' she said. 'What am I going to do, Abby? My sister trusted me. If anything happens to that boy . . .'

'Nothing is going to happen to him,' Abby said, anxious to reassure her. 'You've been great. Found him a job.'

'A job that got him involved in a murder! Penny will blame me.'

She was clearly in a panic at the prospect of telling her sister that her grandson was missing.

'There's no point in worrying her until we know more.'

There was time enough to call her if Cal hadn't turned up by lunchtime tomorrow but, hopefully, hunger would have driven him home long before then.

'Well, if you think that's best.' Abby could hear the relief in her voice.

'I'm sure of it.'

After offering more reassurance, she turned to Dee.

'Molly is insisting on staying put.'

'If I go and pick up the children,' she said, 'I can try and persuade her to come with me.'

'You're welcome to try, but you're going to have to convince Mabel first.'

'Mabel?'

'The cat.'

Meg arrived minutes after Dee had left.

'My mother would have made a casserole, but you wouldn't thank me for anything I'd made so I called in at Cook — hopefully this will keep you going for a day or two.'

She put a large carrier bag on the kitchen table and then swept Abby into a hug before standing back and looking at her.

'What happened?' she asked. 'Jake only knew that Howard had been attacked, the police were all over it and he appeared to be their prime suspect.'

'They haven't arrested him?'

'No, but they took him to the station and he had to hand over his clothes. Fortunately, he was returning to London and had his bag with him.'

'They didn't ask for my clothes, but I fell on Howard and then I tried to give him CPR. They would have been useless as evidence.'

But would have been a very useful way of contaminating what there was if she had been the killer, she realised. As would the police . . .

'You fell on him? Abby, for heaven's sake . . .'

'I found him in the garden, Meg. Someone had hit him with my spade.'

'What!'

'In the throat.'

'Oh my God, that's horrible. Who would do such a thing?'

She shook her head. 'I have no idea, but the spouse is always top of the list of suspects.'

'But you didn't kill him.'

It was a statement, not a question.

'Thank you for that but I was there, Meg. It was my spade, I found him and heaven alone knows I have enough motive to convince a jury.'

'If every woman who was abandoned for a younger woman killed their husband—'

‘Forget the cheating. Think of the money. At the moment the children and I get everything but once married to Izzy all that would change.’

‘Surely he’s sorted that?’

‘I’m sure the new will has been drawn up, but there was no point in signing it until after the wedding, or he’d have had to do it all over again.’

‘In that case, we need to find out who would want him dead,’ Meg said. ‘Why do people kill?’

‘Don’t . . .’

‘Come on, Abs, this is important.’

‘This isn’t Cluedo.’

‘No, it isn’t. It’s your life. Okay, I’ll start. You said it. Money. That’s top of the list.’

‘And it’s not an old novel with defrauded trust funds and fake wills. Howard might be fighting it, and I might have been mad at him, but he knew he was going to have to pay up,’ she said. ‘And I wouldn’t have deprived my children of their father.’

‘You know that,’ Meg said. ‘I know that. But do the police?’

Abby thought about it. ‘In Agatha’s books people sometimes kill to cover up another crime.’

‘Had Howard been up to anything dodgy? On the Planning Committee? Taken a back-hander from some developer?’

Abby shook her head. ‘He was too politically ambitious to get his hands dirty in that way, but he knew Bryan Crawford was up to something grubby and threatened to expose him unless he resigned from the committee.’

‘I remember. It was just before Christmas. According to the paper there were tears when he made his speech about cutting back on workload for family reasons.’

‘There were tears,’ Abby said, ‘but they were about the money he wouldn’t be making. And while Howard was around, he was blocked from any position on the council that he could use to his advantage.’

'That's a reason. Have you told the police?'

'I haven't told them anything, and while Bryan Crawford had a grudge, this wasn't planned. Someone grabbed my spade and lashed out. I don't imagine they meant to kill him.'

'It could have been made to look that way.'

Abby raised her eyebrows. 'That's seriously cynical and anyway, no one, let alone Bryan Crawford, would have known he'd be there.'

'It's a fair guess that he'd go there sometime after the story about the bones, and Crawford could guarantee that you'd be the prime suspect.' Meg paused. 'If he was corrupt, losing the place on the Planning Committee would be a serious blow to his pocket as well as his pride.'

'And he'd let me take the fall?'

'Why not, if he could get away with it?'

'That's . . . horrible.'

'He's not the only one who might bear a grudge. Perhaps one of his little distractions didn't take kindly to being dropped when he remembered he was married. The fact that he'd made the break when he met Izzy Hamilton might have been enough to tip them over the edge.'

'Far enough to commit murder?'

'Not murder, at least not planned, but one of them might have walked up through the wood, wanting to relive past moments of passion in the summerhouse. Maybe hoping to find him there. He was already in a seriously bad mood, and if he'd turned on them, they could have lashed out in a fit of anger.'

'The days of the summerhouse as a place of dalliance are long gone. The floorboards couldn't take the strain, but there was enough ill temper flying around the Lodge this morning to fuel a small war without looking for anyone else.'

'Jake did mention that Izzy went after Howard in a thorough strop.'

'I'd told her that Howard had lied to her about the Linford engagement ring, and then Jake topped that by telling her he was moving into the house.'

'That would do it.'

'That's not all. She said she'd come to do some measuring up, but I think she might have been checking up to make sure Howard and I weren't getting too cosy over the herbaceous border.'

'Paranoid?'

'Pregnant,' Abby said. 'But can you honestly see her picking up a spade, let alone swinging it? She might break one of those perfectly gelled nails.'

'True. But she'd have had it repaired before submitting to a police interview.'

'Meg!'

'Believe me. She'll arrive for her interview dressed in black, in tears and bump prominently on display—'

'Stop!' Abby shook her head, although she knew her friend was right. 'They'll have to find her first.'

'She's missing?'

'Her car is still there, but she was shoeless. She couldn't have walked home.' Before Meg could ask, she said, 'The heels of her Louboutins were sinking into the lawn. She took them off and flung them away.'

'Damn, she *was* mad.'

'It looks as if she called someone to pick her up from the lane.'

'A taxi to the nearest nail bar?'

'Meg!'

'You've got to admit that it's suspicious.'

'It was hot, she was upset. Maybe the thought of walking back up to the house without her shoes was too much.'

'Maybe she had blood on her clothes,' Meg persisted.

'Lucy saw a car leaving by the kitchen garden lane,' Abby admitted. 'She thought it might have hit something as it pulled out, but it didn't stop.'

'Then it won't have been a taxi. All those big houses on Huntsman Hill have security cameras, so hopefully they'll have picked it up. And if the car did hit something there could be paint samples. I could take a look.'

'I'm sure the police are doing that, but I don't want it to be her, Meg. Think of the baby.'

'Think of the expensive lawyers her father will be wheeling out to protect her. You need to focus on your own family, Abs. What have the police said?'

'Nothing. So far they've just asked what happened, but we all have to go to the station tomorrow for fingerprints, DNA and interviews.'

'This is so unfair . . .' She looked around. 'Where are the children?'

'At Molly's. Lucy thought Sophie could do with some kitten distraction and Tom went along to make sure they weren't bothered. My family-friendly copper has gone to pick them up.'

'Then we haven't got long. So, suspects? Who, apart from you, was in the garden?'

'Who wasn't? It was like Piccadilly Circus up there this morning. I took Tom and Cal—'

'Cal?'

'He's Aunt Molly's great-nephew. Following your advice, I've taken him on as temporary help. Jake you know about. Pam Lewis was there briefly too, until Howard arrived. He was absolutely vile to her and she fled.'

'Really? Why would he waste time on Pam when he had you to yell at?'

'She was twitchy whenever he visited Ruth, which irritated him, but this was on a whole new level. He actually accused her of using her visits to the hospital to steal the silver cross his aunt always wore.'

'That sounds out of character. Heaven knows I'm not one of Howard's fans, but he was a politician to his fingertips. The smile may not have been sincere, but it rarely slipped in public.'

'He could certainly pile on the charm for a vote,' Abby agreed, 'but it's been in very short supply recently. He's getting everything he ever wanted, but something was bugging him, and it started before I pawned the Linton ruby.'

‘Perhaps Izzy *did* have something to worry about?’ Meg suggested. ‘Is it possible that after the first thrilling flush of his new life with the beautiful, politically connected and undoubtedly demanding Ms Hamilton, he was missing the easy comfort of a wife who demanded little and provided the full range of housekeeping services?’

‘She sent his shirts to the laundry, and she’d done the Cordon Bleu course in Paris. Howard was living his dream life.’ And despite everything, she was sorry that it had been cut short so brutally. ‘Pam’s been doing some cleaning for you since Ruth died, hasn’t she?’

Meg nodded. ‘Yes. Thanks for putting me in touch with her. She’s a real find.’

‘I have a few things that Ruth left her. I was going to drop them off on my way home but now I’ve no idea when I’ll be able to get out. By tomorrow it won’t just be the *Observer* camped out on my doorstep.’

‘Do you want me to take them?’ Meg offered. ‘It’s on my way.’

‘That would be something off my mind.’

‘You do know that you can call me anytime, Abby? If there’s anything you need?’

‘I know, but I don’t want you dragged into this.’

‘I was there this morning. The police have already asked me to make a statement, so I’m in it, like it or not.’ She sighed. ‘Jake told me about the row he had with Howard.’

‘He was completely shocked when he heard that Howard was dead,’ Abby said. Maybe a touch too quickly, because Meg raised an eyebrow.

‘If you don’t mind me saying so, that sounds a touch defensive. Just how well do you know him?’

CHAPTER NINETEEN

Abby got to her feet. 'No . . .' She walked through to the kitchen, filled the kettle and switched it on, then turned to face Meg, who'd followed her. 'It's not like that.'

'Okay, so what is it like?'

'Nothing. It's nothing,' she repeated when Meg looked unconvinced. 'I didn't expect him to be there this morning. I hung up on him after he'd passed on some gossip about Finch Developments.'

Meg frowned. 'What kind of gossip?'

'Something about the St Catherine's site. The sort that once it gets around can cause all kinds of trouble. He was there this morning to make his peace with me.'

'And then Howard turned up.'

'He was already fit to blow a fuse when Jake began winding him up about renting the house. He poked him hard in the chest and then he turned on me. That's when Jake hit him.'

'Very protective.'

'Don't!' Abby begged. 'Honestly, his first concern when I told him that Howard was dead was that he'd done him some real damage.'

'Hmm . . . So where was everyone else while this was happening? What was your new lad doing?'

'Cal? Tom saw him in the machinery workshop when he should have been cutting back bushes. Howard didn't know him and might have thought he was an opportunist thief . . .'

'With Howard in that mood, I wouldn't have hung around,' Meg said. 'What does he say happened?'

'He's missing too.'

'Oh.' She thought for a moment. 'Where did you find Howard's body?'

'Where I found the baby's bones. Near the summerhouse.'

'If this lad had lashed out, Howard would have been found by the machinery workshop.' She frowned. 'Do you think that his death could have had anything to do with the bones you found?'

'I don't see how . . .'

'But?'

Abby shook her head. 'I can't shake the feeling that if I hadn't unearthed them none of this would have happened.'

'All that stuff in the papers could have stirred up memories,' Meg agreed. 'Someone, the baby's mother or father, could have been drawn to the place.'

'The police suggested that. But why would they attack Howard?'

'You mentioned that he's been in a vile mood lately. Maybe he said something that caught whoever it was on the raw?'

'It's possible. And then there's the gossip about problems at the St Catherine's site. I dismissed it, but could there be any truth in that?' Abby asked.

'I haven't heard anything. The survey was surprisingly good considering the age of the building. Some asbestos, but removal costs were covered in the deal.'

'Surprisingly good?'

'You're thinking that there could have been an element of fraud? A crooked surveyor? Do you know who told Jake that there was a problem?'

'Bryan Crawford.'

'Then it's undoubtedly malice,' Meg agreed, 'but I'll dig around and see if I can find out what he was doing this morning. And I'll give Steve a call. He's on his way to Cornwall for the week with his family but he'll want to know what's happened.' The kettle switched itself off. 'Do you want a cup of tea?'

Abby shook her head. 'No. I keep switching it on. Doing something to occupy my hands.'

'You need something a lot stronger than tea, but let's stick to the records for now. With all the coming and going, did you get a chance to look at them?'

'No, but I do have Ruth's gardening journals. I hoped they might give me a date when the rose was planted.'

'That would be a start.'

'Actually, when I was looking at them, I did find something . . .'

Abby went into the mudroom and searched through the bags until she found the one she'd been looking at.

'There's a photograph tucked in the back of this one,' she said, taking it from its hiding place.

Meg glanced at it. 'A maid? She's so young! What was the school leaving age back then?'

'Fifteen, I think.'

'It's a bit . . .'

'What?'

'There's something about the way she's looking at whoever's holding the camera.'

'Shy?'

'Shy but eager. Almost as if she's expecting a treat . . .' She gave a little shiver as she handed it back. 'Did George like young girls?'

'You're not seriously suggesting . . . ?'

'That baby had a father, and young girls, living in, have always been vulnerable.'

'Well, yes, but look at her. She's as plain as a pikestaff and that uniform is ugly enough to deaden the ardour of anyone.'

'You're missing the point. It's not glamour that's the attraction. It's that she's young. Untouched.'

'No . . .' Abby, horrified put her hand to her mouth.

'I'll bet there were more photographs with fewer clothes. I wonder if they're hidden somewhere in the house. Have you still got the keys?'

'I never saw George with a camera,' she protested.

'What about Ruth?'

'No!'

'I know you want it to have been the gardener's baby, Abs, but according to the newspaper it had been buried in some style.'

'And where did they get that information?' she demanded, dropping the journal on the kitchen table, wishing she'd never opened it. 'Howard was right. I should have just covered them up.'

'You know you couldn't do that, and whatever happened, it isn't your fault.'

The photograph had slipped onto the floor and Meg stooped to pick it up. 'Abby?'

'What?'

'I know she's very young and skinny under that ghastly dress but take a closer look. Doesn't Pam have a port wine stain like that on her neck?'

Abby rubbed her thumb over the photograph, hoping that it was just a dirt. But it wasn't on the surface . . .

'It can't be her!'

'When I took her on as a cleaner,' Meg said, 'I had to fill in all the usual forms. She goes into rentals to clean so we run routine criminal background checks. Nothing came up, but she told me that she'd only started working at the Lodge after they closed St Catherine's.'

'That's what Ruth said too, but once you see the likeness . . . It is her, isn't it?'

'I'm almost certain.'

'It explains a lot. Howard was trying to move his aunt into a care home but, out of the blue, she installed Pam in the house as her carer.'

'Did she say how she knew her?'

'They met at church, according to Ruth. Howard was furious, but the vicar confirmed it and his aunt wouldn't be budged.'

'But why would she lie? Is there anything in the journal?'

'I haven't had a chance to read it yet. But there's something else. Ruth left Pam a Tiffany lamp. This morning she told me that she remembered her bringing it home. I thought she was mixing things up. She does get muddled . . .'

'So?'

'The lamp was in the house before I married Howard.'

'Well that pretty much confirms it.'

'Maybe. This morning, after Howard accused her of stealing, she dropped the box and the lamp broke. She's going to be very upset about that.'

Meg lifted an eyebrow. 'And you'd like me to make her a cup of tea and encourage her to talk about it?'

'It's a lot to ask.'

'I'm as keen to know what happened as you are, Abs. If she is the mother of the baby . . .' She didn't finish the sentence. 'Will you tell the police about this?'

'I don't imagine the bones of a long-dead baby are very high on their list of priorities right now. And at the moment there's nothing to tell.'

* * *

The report of Howard's death "in suspicious circumstances" broke on the local radio station's early evening news broadcast.

There was a short statement from the chair of Howard's political party. The usual regret at the loss of a man destined to rise high in public service, profound condolences to his loved ones — how tactful was that! — and his many friends in Maybridge.

This was followed by DI Glover appealing for anyone who had been in the vicinity of Linton Lodge between 10 a.m. and 12 p.m. and had seen a car leaving the property to come forward.

Having been warned, the curtains had been closed, the office landline switched to silent, leaving the answering machine to pick up any calls, and Lucy's and Tom's mobiles turned off.

Neither of them had been happy about that.

'People will say hurtful things on social media,' Abby told them, 'and if you respond, it will only make things worse.'

She had no doubt that her friends and clients would all be approached by the local press.

She'd sent a warning and apology to the heads of both schools and posted on the parents' WhatsApp groups, but there was little else she could do.

Several people sent messages of condolence, and then her phone rang and Emma's name flashed up.

'Abby . . . I've just seen your message on the school WhatsApp group. I don't know what to say. How are you?'

'Honestly, Em, I don't know. It doesn't seem real.'

'I can imagine. How are the children coping?'

'It hasn't fully sunk in,' she said, but she knew how it would be. They'd wake up and for a moment wouldn't remember, and then it would all rush back . . .

'You do know that if there's anything Nick or I can do, you only have to ask?'

'Yes. And thank you.'

'We're going to the caravan tomorrow for half term, but, if it would help, Sophie could come with us. If she doesn't settle, I could bring her home.'

'You'll be in Wales!'

'A couple of hours in the car, and we've known Sophie since she was a baby. She's Cara's sister from another mister. I'd ask you all to come, but—'

'But it's a caravan,' Abby said. 'I know and it's unbelievably kind of you, but the police will want me here.'

'They can't suspect you . . .'

'They've got to have me on the list. Howard was killed with my spade and I found him.'

'It's ridiculous,' Emma protested. 'You wouldn't hurt a fly. Have you any idea who might be responsible?'

'Honestly? No . . . It feels like something out of *Midsomer Murders*.'

'In that case, don't agree to meet anyone in Linton Woods at midnight, if you hear suspicious noises don't go tripping outside in your slippers to investigate and, if you do find a vital clue, don't mention that you know whodunnit in Mrs Shah's shop, because the killer is bound to overhear you.'

Abby managed a laugh. 'Good advice.'

'And Abby, I mean it about Sophie.'

'Thanks. I do appreciate the offer, but I think she needs to be with Lucy and Tom right now.'

Within an hour of the radio broadcast, the internet was buzzing with rumours, details of their marital rift and speculation on who'd want to kill Howard.

Some of his previous "diversions" came out of the woodwork to throw in their pennyworth.

The consensus appeared to be that he always ran back to his wife, leaving the clear suggestion that Izzy Hamilton was about to be dumped and she'd lashed out in anger.

As for her, group wisdom suggested that the only reason she took him back after his affairs was her determination to get her hands on Linton Lodge and its acres of garden.

There were a number of suggestions that his role as chair of the Planning Committee could have made him enemies. Several unpopular decisions were raised by disgruntled locals who'd had their applications turned down.

And the possibility of problems at the St Catherine's site came up.

Abby had the sense that someone was really pushing that.

But she was the one in the spotlight.

The spurned wife who was about to lose Linton Lodge to a younger, more glamorous woman. And there were plenty of photographs of both her and Izzy.

The ones of her showed her hot and sweaty with dirt under her fingernails. Izzy's, in contrast, were all from the

County Chronicle wearing designer gowns, with immaculate hair and make-up. Very much the proverbial trophy wife in waiting.

Realising she was being drawn in, tempted to strike back at people who knew nothing about her or Howard, she followed her own advice and stopped obsessively checking her phone.

A police constable, who'd arrived earlier, left the comfort of the kitchen to take up his post guarding the front door from the press, to move on the nosy who lingered outside and gather in the flowers and cards and donations of food that began to arrive from neighbours, friends and clients.

Dee called in later to let her know that there was still no news of Cal.

'What about Izzy?'

'She's apparently under sedation. Not well enough to be interviewed.'

'At least she's being looked after.'

'And not just by her doctor. Her lawyer has her back,' she said, 'but she won't be able to avoid our questions forever.'

'You're treating her as a suspect?'

'She was there, she was angry and she fled the scene. That makes her a person of interest.'

'You might want to speak to Councillor Bryan Crawford,' Abby said. 'He has a hefty grudge against Howard and made some pretty nasty threats a few months ago.'

'Threats? What kind of threats?' Dee asked.

'Nothing specific, just generic "watch your back" stuff after Howard had caught him up to no good and forced him to resign from the planning committee. He was genuinely fit to kill. And he's been spreading rumours, trying to stir up trouble for Finch Developments.'

'I'll pass that on. Meanwhile, DI Glover has asked if you could all come to the station in the morning to give your statements.'

'What time?'

'About ten? I'll come and pick you up. Is there anything I can do for you before I go?'

'No . . .' Abby began, then hesitated.

'What?'

'Could you call Jake Sullivan and let him know that we're all okay? He wanted to come to the house, but I don't want gossips making something out of nothing and I'm not sure how secure a mobile phone will be. You hear such things . . .'

'You should be safe enough if you're using your Wi-Fi, but I'll pass on your message.'

'Thank you, Dee. You've been a huge support.'

'If you think of anything that might help us find out who did this, Abby . . .'

'I understand.'

Sophie was weepy at bedtime and didn't want to be alone, so after the comfort of hot chocolate, Abby tucked her up in her own bed and settled down beside her, chatting to her until, eventually, she'd drifted off.

Lucy and Tom talked for a while in Lucy's room before Tom took himself off to bed and the house fell silent.

Abby tried to sleep, but whenever she closed her eyes she could see Howard's body, the dirt, the bloody gouge in his throat where the sharp edge of the spade had struck him.

Something about it niggled at her. It was as if the image was trying to tell her something . . .

And why on earth had Howard been there?

Was it just curiosity? Or, having walked away from Tom, had memories drawn him to the hidden garden, the summerhouse . . .

Had Jake been there, waiting for her? Hoping that she might have changed her mind?

Or had Izzy, still fizzing with anger, discovered him there, lost in the past? What could he have said to her that would cause her to abandon her car and call someone, a friend, her mother, maybe even a cab, to pick her up?

Wretched about the row with Tom, did he tell her that it had been their secret place? That it was where Lucy had been conceived?

Had it been one betrayal too many and she'd lost it?

The police would surely have checked with the local taxi companies. And any CCTV from the houses along Huntsman Hill.

Finally, she eased herself out of bed, planning to go down and fetch the journal with the photograph in the back. Maybe check to see if there were other photographs.

Before she went downstairs, she looked in on Lucy to make sure she wasn't lying awake.

She wasn't lying awake.

She wasn't there.

CHAPTER TWENTY

Abby checked the bathroom, then went downstairs in case Lucy had come down to get a drink, but the house was quiet. There was only the ticking of the grandfather clock in the hall and the settling of old timber after the warm day.

She opened the drawer where she'd told the kids to put their phones. Lucy's was missing.

Muttering an expletive, she ran back upstairs. 'Tom!'

He grunted. 'Whasup?'

'Lucy's gone.' He struggled, blinking, to sit up. 'She's taken her phone. Do you know anything about this?'

'What? No . . . Yes . . . I told the silly cow not to get involved . . .'

'Cal?' She didn't wait for a confirmation. 'Has he been in touch with you?'

'He doesn't fancy me,' he said, smirking.

'This is not a laughing matter,' Abby snapped. 'Where is he?'

'Hiding out in one of the kitchen garden stores.'

'But the police searched there.'

'He stayed out of the way until they'd finished. Lucy made me promise not to say anything, but I didn't think she'd be this stupid.'

'We'll discuss that later. I have to get there before Cal gets that old motorcycle going.'

'What motorcycle?' He saw her look. 'I'll come with you,' he said, rolling out of bed.

'No, I need you to stay here with Sophie. Take your phone, and if Lucy comes back, with or without Cal, call me.'

Abby flung on some clothes, grabbed a torch and let herself quietly out of the back door.

With the policeman guarding the front of the house and the possibility of lurking newsmen, she couldn't take the car, but Lucy would be on foot.

The bolt on the back gate was drawn, confirming her belief that she'd gone down the narrow lane at the back of the garden and then taken to the woods. The same route she would have used that morning on her mission to warn Tom.

There was a nearly full moon, and she ran a good half-mile, panting with the effort, until she reached the edge of the trees. Thick with leaves, they cut off what light there was and she was forced to slow down and turn on her torch. Aware there was bound to be at least one officer to keep the press and the ghoulish away from the scene of Howard's murder, she angled the beam down onto the path and moved more cautiously.

The path through the woods was steep and overgrown, and the woods were full of alien sounds that had her constantly twisting and turning, half expecting something to leap out at her. Trying not to think about Em's warning . . .

Forcing herself to ignore the rustling of small mammals going about their business, the grabbing thorns of wandering brambles that lay in wait to snag on clothes and skin, she pushed on, only letting out the tiniest squeak as one caught at her cheek.

Heart pounding, a stitch in her side, she stopped for a moment to catch her breath and, in the silence, became aware that her own heavy breathing was being repeated half a second later.

She told herself that it was an echo, the sound bouncing off the trees, but when she held her breath, the breathing continued.

She was not alone . . .

If she'd been watching one of her favourite TV cop dramas, this was the moment she'd have been shouting at the stupid woman who'd gone outside — *'It's the murderer! Run! Call the police . . .'*

Running was not an option and, holding the torch defensively, she froze against the gnarled trunk of an old oak tree, telling herself that it was probably a policeman, patrolling the grounds . . .

Cue the sound of hollow laughter.

The breathing got louder, there was a shuffle among last winter's leaf fall and then the largest badger she'd ever seen waddled, huffing and puffing, onto the path in front of her.

It paused for a moment to sniff the air, turning in her direction, green eyes glowing neon bright in the torchlight before she slumped against the tree, sucking in lungfuls of air.

It would, Abby told herself as she moved on, give Emma a laugh. She might even laugh about it herself one day. Maybe when she was telling her grandchildren the story.

The moon was high and full and, after the dark of the woods, it seemed like daylight as she stepped out into the garden.

The big gate squeaked on its hinges as she let herself into the kitchen garden and she paused for a moment to listen. Nothing.

Moving quietly, she made for the machinery room where Tom had seen Cal. The room with the old motorcycle.

The door, like the gate, needed oil, but whoever was inside wasn't quick enough to cut the light from a small torch.

Hers was more powerful, and she swept it up towards the partly boarded rafters.

'Come on down,' she said. 'Both of you.'

There was silence, then creaking as one of them made their way to edge. It was Cal who slid over and dropped down first, holding out his hands to catch Lucy as she followed him.

'Dad saw Cal in here and thought he was a thief,' Lucy began before Abby could start in. 'When he saw the police, he thought he was in trouble.'

'Oh, he's in trouble, and so are you. But not with the police, although I can't say the same for the three of us if the officer guarding the crime scene hears us. Let's get out of here.'

'Hello? Who's there?'

Oh shoot . . . Too late . . .

She stepped outside. 'It's Mrs Finch, Officer.'

He flashed a torch in her face. 'Have you got any identification?'

'She's my mum,' Lucy said, stepping out behind her.

'And my boss,' Cal added.

'And this is my driving licence.' Grateful for the instinct to stick her wallet, along with her phone, in her back pocket, Abby handed it to the officer, who shone his torch on it before returning it with a nod.

'What are you doing here?'

'Cal was hiding because he was scared,' Lucy said before she could answer. 'I thought if I came and talked to him, he might listen to sense.'

'You're Cal Henderson? My sergeant's been looking for you.'

'I'll bring him to the station tomorrow, officer,' Abby said. 'But it's been a tough day, and right now I think we all need to go home and get some sleep.'

'Just wait there,' he said. 'I have to call this in.' He stepped away and spoke briefly into the communication device clipped to his uniform.

'I'm really sorry, Mum, but Cal—'

'I know all about Cal.' She wanted to be angry with Lucy. She could have come to all kinds of harm running around in the middle of the night. But at her age Abby was pretty sure that she'd have done the same for Jake, and right now her only feeling was one of relief. 'They just want to know if you saw anything.'

'I didn't. When Lucy's dad started shouting at me, I ran.'

'He didn't catch you?'

'He stopped when he heard someone calling him.'

'Did you see who?'

He shook his head. 'It was a woman's voice and she sounded angry, but by then I was heading for the wall.'

Izzy . . .

'I'm really sorry to hear what happened to him, Mrs Finch. And for causing so much trouble.'

'Just tell the police what you heard—'

'Mrs Finch?' The PC was back. 'If you'll all come with me to the house, they're sending a car for you.'

'There was no need for that. We could have walked—'

'I don't think they're offering us a taxi service,' Cal muttered, grimly.

'What? No! I have to get home. Tom is waiting for us. And if Sophie wakes up and I'm not there . . .'

Tears welled up in Lucy's eyes. 'I'm so sorry!'

'It'll be okay,' Abby said, hugging her. 'Come on. The sooner we get this over with . . .'

By the time they reached the front of the house a police car was waiting for them.

'I was told to make sure you all got safely home, Mrs Finch,' the driver said, ushering them in, 'and to ask you all to stay there until someone collects you in the morning. The DI will talk to you then.'

She heaved a sigh of relief. 'We'll do that. Thank you.'

Fifteen minutes later they were delivered into the care of a very embarrassed young policeman.

'You've made me look a right idiot,' he said.

'I'm really sorry,' Abby said. 'Would a cup of tea and a sandwich help?'

Nothing.

'Cheese on toast?'

He sighed. 'Oh, go on, then.'

She left Lucy slicing enough cheese to feed the five thousand while she went to check on Sophie, who hadn't stirred.

By the time Cal had been fed and a bed made up for him in Tom's room — he wanted to go back to Molly's, but she wasn't risking him doing another bunk — the sky was glimmering with the silvery pink edge that heralded dawn.

Abby, too wound up to sleep, sent Lucy to join Sophie so that she wouldn't wake up alone, then set about clearing up the kitchen.

That done, she took the bag containing the earliest journals into the sitting room and, since she had no idea when the rose was planted, she curled up on the sofa with the first one.

From the beginning, it was more than a simple gardening journal. There were details about the household, the staff, the family.

Clearly, as a very young bride, Ruth had been frustrated at having to live with her brother-in-law, who was a good deal older than her husband and controlled every part of their lives.

George had no money of his own. His older brother, as first-born son, had inherited everything — the house, the business — and George's future was entirely in his older brother's hands. Moving away, making a life for himself, must have seemed impossible.

Ruth let a little of her feelings spill onto the page, and then a small red cross began to appear regularly, a heart-breaking sign that another month had passed without the promise of a baby.

Was that why Ruth had been so unwelcoming to her? Because of her apparently effortless fertility?

Abby had planned to skim quickly through the journals but found herself helplessly drawn into life at the Lodge. It was clear that, as she failed to give George an heir, Ruth had turned to the garden as an escape from the suffocating atmosphere of the house and the man who ruled it.

And there were little rebellions.

When he'd dismissed a gardener without notice for some minor misdemeanour, Ruth, clearly outraged, had given him a week's wages from her own allowance and had written him a glowing reference.

And then there were the young live-in maids who'd come to them from the children's home under the patronage of the Finch family.

They hadn't stayed long, swiftly leaving the drudgery of service for higher wages and more freedom in the tobacco factories of Bristol.

Ruth, maybe envying their chance to get away, had given each of them a post office book with money — enough to get them home if they needed it — and a silver cross to keep them safe in the wicked city.

Mention of the cross made Abby sit up.

Had one of them come back pregnant and asked Ruth for help? Would Ruth have found her somewhere safe to stay? Maybe even creating a fake pregnancy to pass the baby off as her own?

A woman desperate for a child would do almost anything. And if it had been stillborn? Would she have buried it to save the girl from disgrace?

Abby began skimming through the journals, skipping over the description of plants and purchases made when she'd gone to the Chelsea Flower Show, looking for a gap when she'd been away for longer.

There had been a few carefree days, near the end of 1961, when she and George had visited Ruth's mother in London, seen a new musical that had just opened called *The Sound of Music* and done some Christmas shopping.

Then this . . .

We returned home to the shocking news that Pamela Lewis, having stolen money from my brother-in-law's bedside drawer and the kitchen petty cash, has run away.

Pamela Lewis . . .

Abby stared at the name, her heart thumping.

It was true. Pam *had* worked for Ruth as a girl. Why had they both lied about that?

> *I find this so hard to believe. Pamela is the sweetest girl, hard-working, eager to please, and although her belongings have gone, I couldn't leave it at that. At the children's home they gave me her uncle's address, but there was no sign of her there and a neighbour told me that Mr Lewis had come into money and "done a flit" several days ago.*

When she'd talked to Lucy about the reason for her being in St Catherine's, all Pam could tell her was that she'd done something "bad".

Whatever it was, she hadn't run off to spend the money she'd supposedly stolen.

Had her uncle forced her to steal from her employer, then had her locked away in an institution to cover his crime?

Pam was not the sharpest knife in the box and, confused, not knowing what was happening, she'd have said anything he told her.

Or was there something more sinister happening at the Lodge? Because suddenly the departure of so many girls — Patricia, Susan, Jean, Angela — and the fact that Ruth had given them money and a religious symbol that meant so much to her, had an ominous feel.

She'd been away when Pam disappeared.

Meg had asked if George liked young girls, but he'd been in London with Ruth.

When Ruth had given Pam the cross she'd worn all her life and five thousand pounds, had she been thinking of the money she'd given to the girls who'd gone to work in the city?

Did she have a sense of obligation?

Or worse, guilt?

CHAPTER TWENTY-ONE

'Abby?'

A tap on the living-room door jerked her out of a doze.

'Dee . . .' she said, making an effort to pull herself together. 'What time is it?'

'Just gone nine. I knocked but there was no answer. It's not a good idea to leave the back door unlocked.'

'It was unlocked? Cal . . .' She pushed the journal out of sight under a cushion and scrambled to her feet.

'I found this on the door,' Dee said, handing her sticky note.

I've gone to take a shower and get some clean clothes before we have to go to the cop shop. Back soon. C.

She let out a sigh of relief and, caught by a yawn, said, 'Sorry, I haven't had much sleep.'

Dee grinned. 'I heard you'd had an adventurous night.'

'You could say that, but we did find Cal. Or at least Lucy did. You're not in uniform today,' she said, heading for the kitchen.

'As I've already been involved with the discovery of the bones at the Lodge, and with you, I've been co-opted as acting DC onto the team investigating your husband's death.'

'Is that a good thing?'

'I've taken the exams and I'm hoping, if I make a good impression, to make it permanent.'

'Well, good luck with that,' Abby said, struggling to hold in another yawn. 'Tea? Or coffee?' she asked, waving at the expensive machine Howard had bought but hadn't bothered to take with him. Presumably Izzy already had one.

'Tea is fine, but why don't I make it while you get ready?'

'Thanks. I'll rouse everyone, grab a quick wake-up shower, then I'll do something about breakfast.'

Abby knew how this morning would be for the children. And every morning for a while. Waking up and thinking the day was normal and then remembering. It would be like losing him again and again . . .

There was nothing she could do to make that moment go away, but she held them, hugged them, mopped up tears.

Normally, the bickering over breakfast drove her mad. Today she would have welcomed that normality.

* * *

They dropped Sophie off at Molly's for a kitten date, but she clung to her. 'Will you come back?'

'Yes, sweetheart.' She gave her a hug. 'I promise. And when I do, I'll put your hair in French plaits.'

It didn't seem like much of a big deal, but it was enough to reassure her.

Detective Inspector Glover was waiting for them when they arrived at the police station, but he was not alone.

Freddie Jennings was with him.

'Freddie . . . It's good of you to turn out on a Sunday.'

'Under the circumstances I thought you should have a watching brief.'

She nodded. She knew she was innocent, but while the speculation on social media had been expected, it had shaken her. And she had to think about the children.

'I'm very grateful.' She turned to the children. 'Lucy, Tom, this is Mr Jennings, our family solicitor.'

'Call me Freddie,' he said. 'And who's this?'

'Cal, Cal Henderson. He works for me and was in the garden yesterday. I'd like you to take care of him too.'

'Of course.'

He shook hands with each of them before turning to the DI. 'I'll need a few words with my clients before we begin.'

Behind him, Dee said, 'If we could just take fingerprints first?'

'Abby? Are you happy with that arrangement?'

'My fingerprints will be on the spade, Freddie. As will Tom's and possibly Lucy's. And Cal was working with me on Friday. Our prints will be needed for elimination purposes, so the sooner the better.'

Prints taken, they were left alone with Freddie.

'I'll need each of you to go through what happened in the garden. If I can talk to you first, Abby?'

'Yes, of course.'

They left the children with Dee while Freddie took her through what had happened the previous morning. She held nothing back, and told Tom, Lucy and Cal that they were to do the same.

That done, they were taken, one by one, through to the interview room.

Abby, as responsible adult, stayed while the children were interviewed and Freddie took notes.

Inspector Glover had been joined by another officer, a sergeant, who conducted the interviews, while the inspector observed in silence.

'There's nothing to worry about, Tom, I just need to know what happened yesterday morning. Where everyone was, what they were doing. Okay?'

Tom nodded. 'Okay.'

'So, where were you when your dad found you, Tom?'

'I'd gone to fetch the lawn edger from the store in the kitchen garden and I was on my way back.'

'I have a plan of the house and garden. Can you show me where precisely?'

He looked at the plan. 'About there.'

The sergeant nodded. 'You were angry with him? About a school trip?'

'I was angry with him for cheating on my mother.'

'You were seen on CCTV, Tom.'

'What CCTV?' Abby demanded.

'According to the security company who were monitoring the house,' the DI intervened, 'it was installed by your husband when his aunt was in hospital. He was concerned about the house being empty. The camera was well concealed. Apparently, she was very much against them?'

Abby nodded. 'That's true.'

'He didn't bother to mention it to you?'

'He'd moved out by then,' she told him.

The sergeant, having waited patiently during this exchange, resumed questioning Tom.

'You were angry with your father, I understand that, but you said that you didn't need boots because you weren't going to Iceland. What was that about?'

'Dad had been difficult about it.'

'He didn't want you to go?'

Tom shrugged. 'I don't know what his problem was,' he said, colouring up. 'But when he found me he gave me the permission slip.'

'What happened then?'

Tom swallowed. 'He walked away.'

'And yet you were so upset that your sister took you home.'

Tom didn't answer.

'Was he going to look for Miss Hamilton?'

'He doesn't know where his father was going,' Freddie interjected.

'He didn't tell you where he was going?' the inspector asked.

'No,' Tom said.

'What direction did he take?'

'Across the garden. Towards the lake.'

'Did you hear anything else?'

'I heard Izzy shouting at him.'

'Could you hear what she said?'

'She said that Dad was still tied to Mum's apron strings and couldn't let go.'

'And what did he say?'

'I couldn't hear.'

'And what happened to the permission slip?'

Tom shrugged.

'If I tell you that we found pieces of it in the garden . . . ?'

He mumbled something.

'I'm sorry, Tom, I didn't quite get that,' the DI said.

'I tore it up, okay!'

'Did you see him again after that?' the sergeant continued.

He shook his head.

'For the recording, please.'

'No.'

'Thank you, Tom, that's all for now.'

The sergeant then quizzed Lucy about the message she'd taken to Tom. 'About cricket nets, I think you said.'

Lucy glanced at Abby, then said, 'That wasn't true. I didn't want to say anything in front of my sister, but when Dad came looking for Mum yesterday morning, I told him we knew how mean he was being about Tom's trip. He was really angry when he left and I thought I'd better warn Tom what I'd done, but he wasn't answering his phone so I ran up there.'

Inspector Glover had remained silent, simply listening, but now he said, 'While you were at Linton Lodge, Lucy, did you see anyone apart from your brother? Cal Henderson, for instance?'

'The only person I saw was Tom.'

'But you do know Cal?'

'We met at Aunt Molly's house when I picked up a cake she'd made for us. She's not a real aunt,' she added, 'she was my great-grandmother's friend.'

He nodded. 'I know how difficult this must have been, Lucy. Thank you for your honesty.'

Cal was not quite eighteen, so Abby stayed with him too.

'Tell me about yesterday morning, Cal,' the sergeant asked.

He went through everything from the moment he was picked up, from Abby showing him the storerooms where the tools were kept to starting work.

'Why were you in the kitchen garden?'

'My wheelbarrow was full of the stuff I'd cut back, and Abby, Mrs Finch, told me to take it to the kitchen garden so that we could make a bonfire later.'

'And while you were there, you went into one of the storerooms. Were you looking for something to steal?'

'No!'

'Cal is keen on motorbikes,' Abby said. 'I mentioned that there was one in the machinery store.'

'So you thought you'd take a look?'

'I . . . yes. I wanted to see if I'd be able to fix it up. Mrs Finch said I could use it for work.'

'I see.'

'I had the door open and was wiping off the cobwebs when suddenly this huge bloke started yelling at me, calling me a thief . . .'

'Howard didn't know that I'd just taken Cal on as an apprentice,' Abby explained.

'When did that happen?'

'He'd started working for me the day before, but as Lucy told you, his great-aunt is like family.'

The DI straightened a little in his chair. 'What did you do then, Cal?'

'He was between me and the gate, so I ran for the wall.'

'It didn't occur to you to stop and explain yourself?'

'He was angry, man . . . I thought if he caught me, he'd give me a walloping, but then some woman started shouting and he turned around.'

'What was she shouting?'

'"Howard." She said that first and then, really loud, "Howard Finch!"'

'How did she sound?'

'Like a head teacher looking for you when she thinks you've done something really bad.'

There was a moment of silence as every adult in the room remembered that exact moment, that exact tone of voice . . .

The DI was the first to pull himself together. 'Did you see her?'

'No. She was outside somewhere. She couldn't see him. She was just shouting his name.'

'Trying to find him?'

'Yes.'

'I've got the tone,' the sergeant said, 'but did she have an accent of any kind?'

'She was posh,' he said.

'Like Mrs Finch?'

'No. Mrs Finch is sort of posh, but her voice is soft. This was sharper. Higher. The kind of voice that goes through you like a knife.'

'Thank you, Cal. That's very descriptive. What happened then? Did he answer her?'

'No . . . He just said . . .' He looked at Abby. 'He didn't sound happy.'

'Forget I'm here, Cal,' Abby said. 'Just tell the DI what you heard.'

He swallowed. 'He said, "Oh fuck, what's she doing here?"'

'Was the emphasis on the word "she" or "here"?'

Cal thought for a moment. 'He said, "What's *she* doing here?"'

'And then what did he do?'

'He looked at me and shouted that he was going to call the police, and that was when I went over the wall.'

'It's eight foot high.'

'There was a tree thing growing against the wall. I put my foot on that.'

Abby sighed, wondering just how much damage he'd done to one of the espaliered peaches on the south wall.

The DI glanced at her but she shook her head.

'And you heard nothing else?'

'I was out of there.'

'Out of the kitchen garden, maybe, but you didn't leave.'

'No, well, I knew I'd let Mrs Finch down, so I hung about in the woods for a bit so that I could explain.'

'But you didn't see her.'

'No.'

'Did you see anyone?'

'No.' Neither officer spoke. 'Look, I stayed out of sight, right?'

'But you must have heard the search party calling your name.'

'I saw a couple of . . .' He thought better of the word that he'd been about to use. 'I saw a couple of uniforms but I dodged them and then, once they'd searched the kitchen garden, I went back in there. There were boards on the rafters, so I climbed up and hid there.'

'And, later, you sent Lucy a text, telling her where you were.'

'I thought the big guy had called them about the bike. I wanted her to tell her mum that I wasn't going to pinch it. She thought if she told me on the phone what had happened, I'd run.'

'Was she right?'

He shrugged. 'I don't know. I mean *murder* . . . But I didn't expect her to come and get me.'

'Were you going to go home with her?'

'She wasn't taking no for answer, and I couldn't let her go home by herself, but then Mrs Finch turned up.'

He was finally dismissed, and Abby gave his arm a reassuring pat before it was her turn.

'In your original statement, you rather downplayed the incident with Pamela Lewis,' the sergeant said. 'Your husband called her a thief. Suggested that she had manipulated Mrs Ruth Finch in some way.'

'I don't know why he disliked her so much, but he really resented the fact that his aunt had left her some money along with a few personal bits and pieces. It wasn't a huge amount. Just a thank you for taking care of her.'

'You picked up the box she dropped and put it in your car. Where is it now?'

'Megan West delivered it to Pam for me. Pam does some cleaning for the agency.'

'There were some bags too,' the DI said. 'What was in them?'

'Ruth's gardening diaries. I thought, if I read them, I might be able to discover when the rose was planted over the baby's bones.'

'And have you?'

CHAPTER TWENTY-TWO

Abby felt momentarily skewered to her seat while Detective Inspector Glover waited for her reply.

'I haven't had time to read them.'

For a moment she thought he'd demand she hand them over, but he clearly had bigger things to worry about and, having made a note, he said, 'If you do find anything, you will inform us.'

It wasn't a question.

'Of course,' she said.

He sat back. 'From what we heard on the CCTV footage, it's obvious that you and Mr Sullivan had been more than just school friends. That you'd had a relationship.'

'You could hear what we said?' Abby asked, surprised.

'The system has integrated audio.'

'Oh, I didn't realise . . . We had a one-night stand on the evening of the school prom when I was eighteen. Jake left town the next day. I wouldn't call that a relationship,' she told them, wondering what else she'd said that was about to come back to bite her.

'Your husband seemed to take it rather personally.'

'I'd gone there as his date,' she said. 'I'd been told that he had plans of his own that night involving a video camera.

It was a lie, but I didn't discover that until later. He had no trouble finding a substitute date for the evening, but I'd humiliated him.'

'After their fight, Mr Sullivan said that he'd hit him with something harder next time. Is that what happened? Did he find your husband in the garden and hit him with your spade?' the sergeant asked.

'You're asking my client to speculate,' Freddie reminded him. 'She can have no idea what Mr Sullivan did or didn't do.'

'Can you confirm,' the DI said, after the sergeant had taken her through everything she'd said the day before, 'that you'd left the spade by the hole you'd dug on Thursday morning?'

'I'd stuck it in the heap of soil.'

Left on the ground, it would have been a less convenient weapon.

'And which side of the hole was that?'

'On the right.'

'You're certain of that?'

'Yes. I'm left-handed and, for me, it's the natural side to dump soil from a hole, but I imagine you have photographs that will confirm it.'

He smiled and she thought they were done when he said, 'One final question, Mrs Finch. Did you kill your husband?'

Freddie put a hand on her arm. 'You don't have to answer that, Abby.'

She looked at him. 'It's a reasonable question under the circumstances, Freddie, and "no comment" sounds so guilty.'

'No comment means exactly that. No more, no less. And DI Glover knows very well that if he wants to ask you that, he must caution you first.' He turned to the DI. 'Unless you're going to do that, Inspector, we're done.'

'This appears to have been a heat-of-the-moment attack,' the DI continued, ignoring the fact that Freddie had closed his notebook and was already on his feet. 'Possibly, in view of your husband's state of mind, one of self-defence.'

'Abby . . .' Freddie warned when she opened her mouth to protest.

'I doubt whoever picked up the spade and swung it at your husband intended to kill him,' DI Glover continued. 'I'd say that we're looking at manslaughter rather than murder. Possibly with mitigating circumstances.'

Freddie's hand tightened on her arm.

'He had already threatened you, Mrs Finch.'

'Excuse me, Detective Inspector Glover, but can I be clear? Are you inviting me to confess to the lesser charge of manslaughter?'

'Abby . . .'

'I did not attack my husband, Inspector. He was dead when I found him.'

He nodded and rose to his feet. 'Thank you for your patience, Mrs Finch,' he said, picking up the file in front of him. 'You can join your children while I have your statements typed up. As soon as you've signed them, you'll be free to go.' He exited the room, followed by the sergeant.

As she stood up, Abby discovered that her legs were like jelly and she sat down again, rather abruptly.

'That was . . . humiliating.'

Freddie handed her a paper cup filled with water. 'You did really well.'

'Until I lost it at the last minute.'

'You didn't lose it. You told the DI the truth. But Cal's report about the woman he heard shouting was interesting. It had to have been Izzy.'

'I suppose . . .' She took a moment to think. 'I know he was in a temper, but Howard was infatuated with her. I just can't imagine him saying that.'

'Who else could it have been?'

'Not Pam. She would have run a mile if she'd seen him.' She shook her head. 'There's something else,' she said. 'Something niggling at the back of my mind.'

'Something you saw? Heard?'

'I don't know. Let's go and make sure the children are okay.' Except they weren't children. They'd been interviewed by the police about the death of their father and nothing in their lives would ever be the same again.

* * *

Tom leapt to his feet as soon as she entered the room where they were waiting with Dee.

'What did they say?'

'Nothing, Tom. They just took me through what happened. As soon as we've signed our statements, we can go home.'

The relief in his face, the sag of his shoulders spoke volumes. He'd clearly been afraid that she was about to be arrested for Howard's death.

Aware that hugging him would cause him off-the-scale embarrassment, she did her best to engage him in conversation while they waited but got only monosyllabic answers.

DI Glover eventually returned with their statements, and Freddie read through all four while the inspector waited.

Abby signed hers and she was about to slide it back across the desk when the niggle that had been bothering her finally resolved itself.

'Oh . . .' she said. 'That's it!'

'Abby . . .' Freddie warned.

'No, this is important, Freddie,' she said. 'I've just realised that whoever attacked Howard must have been right-handed.'

DI Glover paused. 'Right-handed? What makes you say that, Mrs Finch?'

She swallowed, seeing it as clearly as if she'd been there. The hands grabbing for the spade, pulling it out of the heap of soil and swinging it. Howard falling to his knees, choking, trying to get his breath. The attacker, realising what they'd done, flinging the spade away and running . . .

Was that who she'd heard?

It was so real that for a moment the room swam, and she dropped the pen she'd been holding, her hand flying to her mouth to stop herself from crying out.

'Enough, Inspector,' Freddie said, ushering them from the room and out into the fresh air.

'Lucy, Tom, can you wait in the car with Cal while I have a word with your mother?' Freddie asked.

'Thank you,' she said, when they'd gone.

'Can you tell me why you have the impression that Howard's killer is right-handed?' he asked.

'It's not just a vague impression. I could see it . . .' She closed her eyes. 'It's all there in high definition and I'm never going to be able to get that picture out of my head. The blood on the left-hand side of the spade. The angle of the wound . . .'

'Don't—'

'But it's important.' She turned to look at him. 'Left-handed, it would have been backhand, awkward. He'd have had time to move, avoid the blow . . .'

'If that's the case, the pathologist must have already suggested that the attacker was right-handed. It's why the DI pushed you on which side of the hole you'd left the spade. And, having observed you sign your statement, he will know that you were telling the truth about being left-handed.'

'And so is Tom.'

'He was strung up tight as a drum in there,' Freddie said.

'He was afraid I was going to be charged with killing Howard.'

'And Cal Henderson was on edge too. I suspect he did see someone, and so do the police.'

'I could see that, but why would he lie? He only came to Maybridge a few days ago. He doesn't know anyone here.'

'Probably just nerves.'

'He has had dealings with the police before.'

'I thought he might. Tell me about the ring.'

'Hideous thing. It's too big to wear except on special occasions but worth a ridiculous amount of money. Maybe Howard was planning to sell it.'

'Was he short of cash?'

'Not as far as I know. He'd just inherited Ruth's estate, and now she's dead, the house was his and he can do what he wants with it. Has he been pleading poverty over the divorce settlement?'

'Well, yes, but that's standard. I didn't believe him.'

'I did hear a rumour about contamination at the St Catherine's site,' she said.

'Really? That's a concern. I'll look into it.'

'I'm more concerned about Izzy. The police couldn't find her yesterday.'

'I've heard nothing officially but, according to my wife, the WhatsApp gossip is that she's under sedation in a private clinic.'

'Is the baby okay?'

'If I hear anything I'll let you know. In the meantime,' he asked, 'is there anything I can do for you?'

'Set the clock back to Thursday morning?' She shook her head. 'Sorry.'

'It's okay. You're doing amazingly well under the circumstances.'

'I imagine the police will want to see Howard's will?'

'That's for tomorrow. Do you know if you're the main beneficiary?'

'I don't know the details, but unless he made a new one in the last few months, which seems unlikely, then yes, with the children. Which gives me a strong motive,' she said. 'You can see why DI Glover has me at the top of his list. I have the full set. Motive, means and opportunity.'

'It would certainly make his life easy,' he admitted, 'but he's going to have to look harder for his killer.'

'I appreciate your confidence.'

'I'll be in touch with Howard's solicitor in the morning. If there's nothing else?' She shook her head. 'Then I'm going to have a word with DI Glover about the conduct of your interview.'

'He's just trying to get at the truth, Freddie, and I want that as much as he does.'

'I know, but there are to be no interviews without me present,' he warned.

* * *

Dee stopped to pick up Sophie and drop Cal back at Molly's.

'I don't want you to worry about anything, Cal. Mr Jennings is going to take care of you.'

'Thanks, Mrs Finch. I'm sorry I caused so much bother.'

'You're safe, that's all that matters. Just keep an eye on Molly for me. She's worried about what your grandmother will say if she finds out about you getting involved in all this.'

The thought clearly horrified him. 'She won't hear it from me.'

'Good lad. And if either of you need anything, give me a call.'

* * *

'Do you need anything?' Dee asked, as she dropped them off at home to a volley of camera clicks from the gathered press.

'You could remind that lot that the children are all minors so there must be no pictures of them in papers.'

'It will be a pleasure.'

'And you'll let me know what's happening?'

'Of course. And you can give me a call at any time.'

As soon as she got inside, Abby called Izzy's parents but got an answering machine.

'It's Abby Finch . . .' The phone was picked up before she could continue.

'Mrs Finch, I don't think this is at all appropriate.' The woman's voice was stiff with disapproval.

'Lady Hamilton? I know I'm the last person you want to talk to, but I've just heard that Izzy is in a clinic.'

'She collapsed when she heard the news. Clearly you are less affected by your husband's death.'

She'd anticipated hostility. She and Izzy were both suspects, and obviously her ladyship wanted *her* to be the one carted away in handcuffs.

'No less affected, I assure you, but with three children who've just lost their father I don't have the luxury of taking to my bed. I was concerned that the shock might have caused a miscarriage.'

There was silence and for a moment she thought Lady Hamilton had cut the call, but then she said, 'I'm sorry to disappoint you, but the baby is fine. My condolences to your children.'

Then she hung up.

'Are you okay, Mum?'

Realising that Lucy was staring at her, she took a breath and found a smile from somewhere. 'Yes. Yes, I'm fine. I just wanted to be sure that Izzy's baby was okay.'

'Why would you care?'

'Because it's Daddy's baby too, so it will be your brother or sister.'

And because she'd wound up Izzy and sent her after Howard, which meant she had to be one of the last people to have seen him alive.

'I hadn't thought of that. I don't suppose it will be allowed to have anything to do with us.'

'That'll depend on Izzy.' Although, after her mother's response to her call, she thought it extremely unlikely.

'Grown-ups can really mess things up, can't they?' Lucy said.

'I'm afraid so.'

'I didn't mean you!'

'We all play our part, Lucy. We could all be kinder.'

'You're being kind about Izzy and her baby. I'll bet she's not being kind about you.'

'Oh, Lucy, give me a hug.'

They clung to one another for a moment until the sound of tyres on the gravel drive made them both turn.

CHAPTER TWENTY-THREE

Abby froze. Despite what she'd told Tom, every time a car drew up she expected it to be the police with more questions. About Jake, that wretched ring . . .

They all stood there for a moment, but then the constable on guard opened the door and Sophie, nearest, shouted, 'It's Charlotte!'

'What? No, it can't be. They've gone to France for half term . . .' But Lucy was already being swept up in her godmother's arms.

'We were at the beach and haven't been listening to the news, but Mum called me this morning,' she said, encompassing Abby and Sophie in the hug.

'She sent flowers . . .'

'And phoned me. Why didn't you call me?'

'You're supposed to be in France.'

'Simon has to fly to the US for work on Tuesday, so France has been cancelled until July. Not that it would have made any difference. You could all have come.'

'I'm not sure I'd be allowed to leave the country.'

'What?' Charlotte looked shocked. 'They can't suspect you? That's ridiculous. Anyway, we're at the cottage for the week, so pack your bags, you're coming back with me.'

Abby thought with longing of the quiet Somerset cove and the sprawling cottage owned by Charlotte's family where she'd spent so many happy childhood holidays. The chance to get away from the policemen at the door, the ever-waiting cameras across the lane . . .

Except there was no getting away from this. At least not for her.

Charlotte, reading her mind, said, 'The children. Let me take the children.'

'No . . .' Lucy looked stricken. 'We can't leave you on your own.' She turned to Tom. 'And you've got your match.'

'No.' He shrugged. 'I had a text from coach saying that in the circumstances he understands that I won't want to play.' He looked bleak. 'What he means is that they'd rather I didn't turn up.'

'He's just trying to do what's best for everyone,' Abby said. 'He knows that it's going to be horrible for all of you for the next few days. You won't be able to go out without people staring at you, whispering. You won't be able to see your friends. If you're at the cottage, I won't have to worry about you.'

'We'll worry about *you*,' he said.

'There's absolutely no need. Whoever killed your father was right-handed.' She held up her left hand. 'Can you manage to pack?'

He stood there for a long moment.

'Come on, Tom, Soph,' Lucy said, 'I'll help.'

'Don't forget your toothbrushes!'

'I've got this, Mum, and Charlotte is desperate to ask you what happened.'

Neither of them spoke until the children were upstairs.

'What did happen, Abs?'

'Someone hit Howard with my spade. I found him . . .'

Charlotte took her hand. 'I'm so sorry. Is there anything I can do to help?'

'You are helping, in the best way possible, but if there's a problem . . . Sophie . . .'

'We'll take care of her. You can Facetime with them all and if I think she needs her mum, I'll call you. Have the police any idea who was responsible? What was that with the hand?'

'The garden was full of people and most of them were angry, including me, but from what I saw when I found Howard, I'm convinced that whoever struck him was right-handed. Tom was there, so I wanted him to know that.'

'The crime scene people will have worked that out too, right?'

'Let's hope so.'

'I hate the thought of leaving you here on your own. I know Howard had left you and the kids for that ghastly woman, but you were married for a long time. Are you sure you're going to be okay?'

She nodded. 'There are things I have to do, people I need to see. All of that will be a great deal easier if I'm not worrying about the children.'

'I understand, but if you can get away, come and join us.'

* * *

After they'd gone Abby heated one of the ready meals Meg had bought, but she did little more than pick at it.

Had it only been four days ago that she'd met Jake again? Sat with him in the supermarket café drinking tea and eating lemon drizzle cake? Her heart beating just a touch faster than normal . . .

Abandoning the half-eaten food and hoping that fresh air would help, she went out into the garden on legs that felt as if they weren't quite making contact with the ground.

It was exhaustion. She recognised it from the early days with the babies, especially Sophie, when she and Howard had taken it in turns to watch over her.

There had been no late nights at the office, no business weekends away when his baby girl had needed him and, as she sank onto a bench, the tears finally came, pouring down her cheeks.

Weeping for the savage waste of a life.

Weeping for her children, and Izzy's baby, who would grow up without a father.

And for an infant who'd died and been buried without a name.

Could it have been Pam's baby?

The entry in Ruth's journal didn't match the story she'd told Lucy for her social science project. Could Meg be right about what happened? Had she given birth in the house while Ruth was away?

That might account for her being shut away in St Catherine's for "moral delinquency", but if that was the case, there could be only one reason why Howard's grandfather had told his brother that she'd stolen money and run away.

That disturbing thought sent her back to the journals but, after the entry about Pam's disappearance, and Ruth's abortive attempt to find her, there were no more entries in that year.

Concerned, Abby picked up the next year. The first entry was 23 March and it was just one word.

Italy.

The entries were slow to start with. Trains, places, hotels . . .

George had, it seemed, left his brother to take care of business while he'd taken Ruth to Italy on an extended vacation.

The Ruth of the earlier journals would have filled the pages with her impressions, sketches, photographs, but her handwriting didn't flow, and Abby sensed that she was forcing herself to write the bare minimum.

There was no excitement, no joy in new sights, the warmth of an Italian spring.

Remembering her own inability to do more than go through the motions after her mother died, Abby felt the grief coming off the pages.

There was no mention of a death in the family and, fearing that Ruth had suffered a miscarriage, her heart went out to her.

Gradually, though, the sun seemed to bring her back to life and slowly the pages began to be filled with descriptions of places they'd been, the people they'd met. There were sketches and watercolours of landscapes filled with olive groves and slender cypresses. Then, as spring stretched into early summer, there were the hot colours of pelargoniums in pots and bougainvillea tumbling over faded stucco walls in Capri.

All seemed well, until on 21 May the entries stopped and there were no more for the rest of the year.

But in the pocket at the back Abby found a note on Linton Lodge notepaper from Howard Senior's wife, Margaret.

Dear Ruth,

How are you? In his last letter to Howard, George said that Italy has worked its magic and you have recovered not only your strength but your spirits, which is such good news.

Sadly, things haven't been easy here. Howard, as you know, isn't the easiest of men, and yesterday he turned his temper on Peter, blaming the poor boy for a broken vase in the dining room and giving him a beating, when the whole house knew that he'd thrown it against the wall himself in a rage over something.

I suggested I take Peter to stay with my godmother for a week, but of course he wouldn't hear of it. There's no escape for either of us.

Dr Williams has given me something for my nerves, which, frankly, are in shreds, but the truth is that I'm not sure how much longer I can cope. Please, Ruth, you know I wouldn't ask if I were not desperate, and only if you are well enough, but I feel safer with George here. Could you come home soon? Please.

All love,
Margaret

Safer?

Abby was still trying to get her ahead around what Margaret had written when her phone rang.

'Jake . . .'

'How are you?'

'Good question.' Better for hearing his voice. 'I think the term "as well as can be expected" fits the bill.'

'And the children?'

'I don't think it's properly sunk in, but at least they're out of the public gaze. A distant cousin, my oldest and dearest friend, arrived this morning and has taken them to stay with her own children for the half-term break.'

'I'm sure that's good for them. Not so much for you.'

'No,' she admitted, 'but if they were at home they'd just be keeping their heads down, avoiding whatever nastiness is thrown in their direction. Grieving for their father . . .'

'And you? What will you be doing? I don't imagine working is an option.'

'No. It would help keep my mind off things, but I can hardly turn up at my clients' homes with a load of sharp objects while I'm a murder suspect. As it is I'm likely to lose the more nervous among them.'

'Could Cal cover for you? Cut the grass, if nothing else?'

'Actually, that's not a bad idea. Thanks.'

'You're welcome.'

'Am I? I feel terrible for dragging you into this.'

'I wasn't dragged, I pushed my way in. I've got meetings, but I'll be back as soon as I can get away. I don't suppose you'd want to be seen eating out, so I'll sneak in the back way with a takeaway. Call me if you need anything.'

'Jake—'

'I'll be in touch.'

'Wait—' But he'd ended the call, no doubt deliberately, before she could tell him that he should stay away.

For a moment, the thought warmed her and then, telling herself to get a grip, she turned to the dozens of texts on her phone, deleting or skipping past most of them until she saw the one from Meg.

'I tried calling but the line was busy. I gave Pam her box and she cried when she saw the lamp. I made her a cup of tea and asked her to tell me about it, but she said Mr Howard had sworn her to secrecy. She got so agitated that I didn't dare push her. But Howard? Really? That doesn't make any kind of sense.'

As Abby read the message, a chill ran down her spine.

Mr Howard . . .

That wasn't her Howard. That had to be his grandfather, Howard Senior. The man with the portrait in the hall of Linton Lodge painted in his robes as mayor of Maybridge.

The man who'd ruled Linton Lodge, and the lives of everyone who lived and worked there. The kind of man who blamed his son for his own accidents and left his wife begging for her sister-in-law to come home because she was afraid.

The kind of man who would have thought it beneath him to notice a maid. Who, under normal circumstances, would never see her because she'd have to be up early to get her work done in the house before the family was about.

* * *

'Abby? Is anything wrong?' Meg asked, the moment she answered her call.

'No . . . Well, nothing new, at any rate, but I've just read your text. It's not my Howard Pam's talking about. It's his grandfather.'

'What? I don't understand . . .'

'The Howard who built the Finch Memorial Hall in honour of his own father. And I've found an entry in one of the journals. Pam definitely worked at the Lodge as a girl.'

'Oh, sugar lumps. That can't be good.'

'It isn't. George and Ruth went to London to stay with her mother over Easter. When they returned, Howard Senior told them that Pam had stolen money and run away.'

'But . . .'

'Exactly. But. In capital letters. She didn't run anywhere. She was shut away in St Catherine's.'

'Did it happen then? That could have been later.'

'That's a thought,' she said, clutching at straws. 'I can check the date in Lucy's project file.'

'But that won't answer the big question. Is she the baby's mother?'

'She couldn't have hidden it from Ruth, surely?'

'Some women barely show and that shapeless dress barely touched her. She might not have known she was pregnant. You read about women who think they're just constipated when giving birth.'

'True. Pam was very young. She's a dear, but not the sharpest knife in the box.'

For a moment, neither of them spoke, then Meg said what Abby was thinking.

'It doesn't add up, does it? If Howard Senior had discovered that she was pregnant, he would have left Ruth to deal with it or sent her back to her family like something out of a Victorian melodrama.'

'She didn't have a family. Her parents were dead and her uncle stuck her in a children's home. Reading between the lines, though, it's obvious that Ruth had her doubts.'

'Maybe she gave birth in secret, panicked, grabbed whatever money she could find and ran.'

'Leaving the baby behind?'

'If it was stillborn . . .'

'She'd have been terrified,' Abby said. 'Hysterical . . . That could explain why she ended up in St Catherine's.'

'Yes . . . Abby, I'm sorry, I have an appointment in ten minutes, but I haven't forgotten about Bryan Crawford. I'll call you.'

CHAPTER TWENTY-FOUR

Abby sat for a moment, clinging to the hope that it had happened just as Meg suggested.

Pam, terrified, could well have taken the money and run. She wanted that to be the case, but it just didn't fit.

There was nothing in the journal about a baby and, while Howard Senior might well have had reason to bury it, if he had there would have been no shawl, no box, no cross. All he'd have done was dig a hole deep enough to make sure that the animals wouldn't dig it up.

The burial had a woman's hand all over it. Ruth's hand . . . It had to be.

Lucy had printed out several copies of her project and used the office binder to turn them into presentation copies. She'd even made a copy to give to Pam, but she'd been afraid it might upset her and it was still on the bookshelf.

Abby knew that Lucy had been deeply shocked by the comments on the photocopy of Pam's committal to St Catherine's and, when she found it, she could understand why.

> *Samuel Lewis, Pamela's uncle, has confirmed that her mother died in childbirth and her father had "buggered off" when she was five years old. Unable to cope, he'd taken her to St*

Michael's children's home, where he'd done his best to keep in touch with her.

According to him she'd struggled at school and, on leaving, was found a job in service, but would steal anything that wasn't nailed down and was a "dirty girl" who would go with any man for a few coppers. He described her as a danger to decent men.

There was no mention of a pregnancy.

Her uncle's horrendous description of Pam was so at odds with Ruth's that Abby was convinced that he'd forced her to steal for him and then had her locked up in a place where no one would believe her.

It would tie in with what Howard Senior had told Ruth — that she'd stolen money and run away. There was just one thing wrong with that.

According to Lucy's project, the Mental Health Act, which passed in 1959 and came into force in November 1960, had abolished the practice of locking up girls for promiscuity — although many women hadn't been released for many years and, if there was no family to take them in, had become institutionalised.

That had been Pam's fate.

But Pam hadn't been shut away in that ghastly place until 31 March 1961.

Whatever she'd done, she should never have been there.

Her life had been stolen from her.

The question was, by whom?

Her uncle's damning statement had been used to keep her there, but who would have had the power to persuade the gatekeepers to ignore the change in the law?

This had happened around Easter and, checking the date on her search engine, she discovered that 31 March was in fact Good Friday, a bank holiday, when there wouldn't have been a sitting magistrate.

The whole thing smelled of a cover-up and it all pointed to the fact that Pam had been the mother of that poor baby.

Young, not knowing what was happening to her, she must have been terrified.

She was going to have to talk to her, but it wasn't something that could be done on the phone. She'd have to go and see her.

She could just slip out of the back way to avoid the newsmen, but after Saturday night's escapade, she didn't want to get the PC guarding the door into more trouble.

'Harry . . .'

He turned to look at her.

'I'm going—' Her phone began to ring. 'Sorry, I have to take this . . . Dee? Is there any news?'

'Yes.'

One word, but it had a doom-laden quality and Abby's stomach lurched as she shut the door.

'It's not good news, is it?'

'I told you we were going to do some DNA tests. It seems that Howard and the baby you found are a direct match.'

'No!'

'I'm sorry, but there's no mistake.'

'No, that's not right. It can't have been Howard's baby.'

'What makes you so sure? You met at school, but were you dating all that time?'

'No,' she admitted. 'I was at university. We didn't see one another again until after I'd graduated.'

'What about Howard?'

'He went into the family business straight from school.'

'Which means there were three years when he was dating here in Maybridge and you were away?'

Abby, forced to admit that was the case, sank onto the nearest chair.

'I know you said the rose was flowering before you were married, but can you be certain how long before that it had been planted?'

About to explain that she had been looking for the date in the journals, she thought better of it. They hadn't been interested when she told them what she'd taken from the house, but now dating the rose was important, and they might be concerned that she'd destroy any evidence implicating Howard in the burial.

'Abby?'

'The garden was completely overgrown by then.'

'The perfect hiding place.'

There seemed little point in continuing to stress that the rose had been well established. 'I took the remains of the rose through to the kitchen garden to burn, Dee. For obvious reasons that never happened, but I believe if an expert were to look at the trunk, they would be able to tell approximately how old it is.'

'Is that possible?'

'They date trees by counting the growth rings. It's called dendrochronology.'

'Okay. I'll pass that information along.'

'DI Glover won't release this to the press? Please,' she begged. 'I don't want the children hearing this. It's just speculation.'

'It's a little more than that, but it won't be released unless it becomes relevant to the enquiry.'

'That's not much of a guarantee.'

'It's the best I can do.' She paused. 'How are you doing?'

'I'm not used to staring at nothing but four walls, but I can't inflict myself on my clients until things are clearer — assuming they'll want a murder suspect designing their borders.' She paused, hoping for a denial. It didn't come. 'Has Izzy been interviewed?'

'Not yet. Her lawyer brought in a written statement this morning. She claims that she didn't see Howard on Saturday morning and, too upset to return to the house, she called a friend to pick her up.'

'But that's not true. Tom told you that he heard them arguing.'

'He overheard an argument.'

'It was about me, Dee. About him being tied to my apron strings. Who else would it be?'

'I'm sure the DI will follow that up. We do know that she was picked up in a black four-by-four. Not the car that Lucy thinks she saw, although it's possible that was just someone using the lane to turn around and misjudging the gap.'

'You haven't got that one on camera?'

'The houses in this area tend to have long drives and their cameras are focussed on the area close to the house. We're checking all the cars that passed the traffic camera into town, and on the Longbourne Road, but if they went uphill, it's all country lanes and we've got nothing unless they drove into Linton Lovell.'

'If the noise Lucy heard was the car hitting something, there will be traces of paint,' she said.

'Forensics have been there. Maybe we'll get a result. Or at least someone we can cross off our list.'

They had a list. Was she at the top of it?

'How did Natalie Grant take the news?' she asked, not wanting to think about that.

'We haven't been able to speak to her. She wasn't in when an officer called to break the news and ask her a few questions.'

'No one warned her?'

'I'm sorry. I know you were concerned about her.'

'Yes . . .' Natalie would undoubtedly blame her for the fact that she'd heard about Howard's death on the news, and she'd be right. She should have called her. 'She was in a state the last time I spoke to her.'

'A state?'

'She said she knew that it was all over.'

'What did she mean by that?'

'I suspect she meant her life. Not literally. Her dreams of being promoted from Howard's "office wife" to the real thing.'

'With any justification?'

'Natalie is a couple of years older than me. Howard's indiscretions tended to be younger.'

'She didn't take that as a sign that she should move on?'

'Her view was that they were down to my inadequacy as his wife. She clearly thought that once she'd replaced me, he wouldn't need his "silly girls". I warned him that it would end in tears, but it amused him. He enjoyed the "lovering".'

'Lovering?'

'Mother/lover?' Abby said.

'You're absolutely sure that there was nothing more in the relationship?' Dee pressed.

'Absolutely. If there had been an affair, Natalie would have been history the minute it was over. She was far too good a PA for him to risk that.'

'I see. What sort of car did she drive? Do you know?'

'She has one of those little Fiats. Pale blue. If she's not at home, she has a sister living in Longbourne. It's possible that she might have gone to weep on her shoulder.'

'Do you have a name?'

'Nicole, I think. I don't know her surname. Maybe someone at the office will be able to help.'

'Hopefully we'll find her there,' she said. 'I'm sorry I haven't got more news for you.'

'Whatever it is, it won't be good. Have you finished at the house? I'd like to pick up the rose I left there. It's in a pot and, in this weather, it will be struggling without water.'

'I can pick it up and drop it off here—'

'And there's that old motorbike that Cal was going to fix up,' she added, quickly. 'I thought, since we can't do anything, that he might as well make a start.'

'Won't everything have to be valued? For probate?'

'It's not worth much, but I'll inform Howard's solicitors that I've taken it.'

'Okay. I'll check with SOCO and let you know when they're finished.'

Once Dee had ended the call, Abby googled DNA and discovered that a male match was through the Y-chromosome, and it could go back generations.

Despite Dee's natural scepticism, she knew that Howard wasn't the father. He would never have given her one of the roses when he proposed if he'd known what was lying beneath it. Although it might explain Ruth's sharpness when she saw it.

But the hard fact remained that one of the Finch men had fathered the baby.

She was staring at a family tree that one of the children had put together for a primary school project, when Meg called her.

'I'm sorry I had to rush off, but I've spoken to someone I know in the council offices. Bryan Crawford was supposed to be at a lunch given by the Chamber of Commerce for potential investors in the town. He didn't show up.'

Abby's mouth dried. 'That's . . .'

'The man would be first in line for a free bag of crisps and a shandy in the Dog and Duck,' Meg said. 'It would take something very big to keep him from smoked salmon and champagne.'

'Maybe he was sick.'

'Maybe someone should ask him,' Meg suggested. 'But on a lighter note, now that the Lodge is off the market until after probate, I've found something riverside to tide Jake over until I can find what he's looking for.'

'He'll be grateful.'

'And he'll be in Maybridge.'

'Meg . . .'

'I know. If Howard was just a philandering ex it would be simple. Death complicates things. Have the police told you anything?'

'Only that Howard's DNA is a match for the baby.'

'What!'

'They're convinced he's the father, but it could be any male in his family. I've been checking dates on the family tree against Pam's disappearance.'

'George?' Meg suggested.

'He wasn't there when Pam disappeared.'

'That doesn't mean he's not the father.'

'I suppose not.'

'Were there any other boys in that generation?'

Abby pondered this. 'Three that lived. Howard James, Howard's grandfather. Henry, who died as an infant, and I think there was a girl who was stillborn and possibly some miscarriages as there was a gap. Then Stephen who was killed at Dunkirk, and finally George, who was the youngest.'

'It could have been Stephen. Could the rose have been that old?'

'Pushing it a bit, I'd have said.'

'Back to George, then. Was he in the army?' Meg asked. 'Wouldn't his generation have done National Service?'

'No one has ever mentioned it. Maybe he had flat feet, or after losing one son in action, maybe his father could have pulled some strings . . .' She stopped.

'Abby?'

'Pam was locked away on the thirty-first of March, the weekend she's supposed to have run away. It was Easter, Meg. Good Friday. Who would have the power to have a girl locked up in St Catherine's on a holiday weekend?'

She thought for a moment. '*Omigod*. A doctor.'

'Maybe. But who would have summoned him? Had the influence to get round the law?'

'Wasn't Howard Senior mayor of Maybridge?' Meg asked.

'Mayor, magistrate . . . on the board of all kinds of charities.'

'Possibly a governor of St Catherine's?'

'We could check, but even if he wasn't,' Abby said, 'he'd have known someone who was.'

'You're thinking there was dodgy business there?'

'You have to admit that it's suspicious.'

'It does, but we seem to have got fixated on Pam. The baby could have arrived much later. What about your Howard's father?'

'Peter?'

'The piece in the *Observer* said that he died of a gunshot wound after his wife left him for her lover. They didn't say as much, but the implication was suicide.'

'You're suggesting she left because she discovered that he'd got the scullery maid up the duff and he killed himself? It was the nineteen-eighties, Meg. The school leaving age had been raised and no one was taking in orphans to scrub the floors.'

'You're saying that they didn't have staff at Linton Lodge?'

'They had a live-in housekeeper,' she admitted, 'but by then, the rest of the staff would have come in daily.'

'Entitled men have never stopped taking advantage of powerless women, Abs.'

'I know, but if Peter had been doing the whole *droit de seigneur* thing, Sarah wouldn't have abandoned her baby and run away, she'd have divorced the hell out of him.'

'You're discounting the lover?'

'I'm not discounting anything. That's what's so frustrating. The subject of Howard's mother was strictly off limits. All I know about her is her name.'

'Maybe we could find something on one of those ancestor-tracing sites,' Meg said. 'She must have had family, but we're getting off the point. You need a date for that rose before the papers get wind of it.'

'Yes . . .' She let the subject of Sarah's disappearance go. 'I can't have the children believing, even for a moment, that their father could have done this.'

'What are you going to do?'

Abby drew in a deep breath. 'I'm going to have to talk to Pam.'

CHAPTER TWENTY-FIVE

Abby was considering what to wear — widow black or a pair of jeans — when Charlotte called to let her know they'd arrived safely.

'How are they?'

'It could have gone either way with Sophie, but Grace was so excited to see her and show her everything that the moment passed. Lucy's on her phone, and Tom and Archie are talking cricket with Simon. So far, so normal. Are you okay?'

'Happier now the children are out of this.'

'We'll take good care of them, and if you need to talk, I'm here.'

'Thanks. I may take you up on that.'

But first, Pam.

She settled on the jeans, compromising with a black T-shirt and, as an afterthought, grabbed a shopping bag. Not the "Crazy Gardening Lady" one.

'Harry, I'm going to get a few things from the shop. Milk, cheese . . . a bottle of gin,' she added, hoping to raise a smile.

'Are you sure, Mrs Finch?' He nodded in the direction of the newsmen hanging around on the other side of the road. 'They aren't the only ones with cameras.'

'What are they waiting for?'

'A shot of you being carted away in handcuffs,' he replied.

'Oh, cheers,' she said. 'Tell the silly beggars I'll make them a cup of tea when I get back. If they're lucky I'll go easy on the weedkiller.'

'Now, now,' he said, but she'd finally got him grinning.

She switched on the car radio without thinking and found herself listening to the local news bulletin.

... continue to investigate the death of prominent Maybridge businessman Howard Finch.

They were called to Linton Lodge on Saturday morning after Mr Finch's body was found by his estranged wife, garden designer Abigail Finch.

The police are appealing for anyone who was in the area of Huntsman Hill between eleven a.m. and one p.m. on Saturday to contact them.

Last week, the remains of a baby were found ...

Abby hit the off button. She didn't want to hear rehashed speculation and innuendo, she wanted answers.

She had planned to stop at the corner shop on the way home, but it occurred to her that some good biscuits might help the tea go down. And flowers.

There were bunches of rose buds in a bucket outside the shop in all colours. She chose a deep pink and, once inside, she picked up bread, cheese, tomatoes and chocolate biscuits.

Mrs Khan was at the till and greeted her with a hug and condolences. 'Oh, my dear, you should have phoned. Ajeet would have brought you what you needed.'

'That's really kind of you, but the walls were closing in on me.'

'Of course. How are you? How are your poor children?'

'Bearing up,' she said. 'They're away from all this, staying with their cousins.'

'Family is so important at times like these.'

* * *

Pam looked shocked to see her.

'Shall we put these in water?' Abby suggested when she didn't take the flowers.

'Yes, sorry, thank you.' She reached for a jug. 'I heard about what happened to Mr Howard. The police came. I told them I didn't do it!'

'It's okay, Pam. No one is accusing you of anything.'

'I told them I didn't do anything,' she said, clutching at the cross she was wearing. 'Mrs Ruth gave me this. The nurse was there—'

'I know. And in any case, it was in her will.' She put a hand on her arm to calm her. 'I'm really sorry about the way Howard spoke to you.'

'You don't have to be sorry. You have always been kind, but men like him do bad things and they're never sorry.'

Not true. Howard was always sorry. He'd been full of apologies after every one of his extramarital escapades.

He'd actually grovelled after Izzy had gone on the offensive, promising that he'd make the divorce as painless as possible, that he'd always be there for the kids.

It was only since Ruth died that he'd become so bad-tempered. She'd put that down to grief, stress . . .

'Did you see Howard later?' she asked, using the small pair of secateurs she always carried in her bag to trim the ends of the roses. 'When he came down the garden?'

'I was sitting on the bench, crying for my lamp.'

'The bench by the summerhouse?'

'No.' She shook her head. 'That was Mrs Ruth's garden. It was her private place.'

'I wonder why she abandoned it?' Abby said casually, not looking at Pam, as she arranged the roses in the jug. 'Left it to go wild.'

'She said it made her sad. She didn't want to go there anymore. She wouldn't have liked what you've been doing there.'

'Howard wanted to restore it, make it the way it used to be, as a memorial for his aunt.'

'She wouldn't have liked it,' Pam repeated.

Abby turned to look at her. She said she hadn't been there and yet she knew it was being restored . . .

'Is that because of the baby?'

'I was by the lake,' she said, not answering the question. 'I kept very still so he didn't see me.'

'Very sensible.' Abby picked up the jug and carried it through to the living room and put it on a table under the window. 'Did you see anyone else while you were sitting there?'

'I didn't see anyone,' she said, but she wouldn't make eye contact.

'This is a lovely flat,' Abby said, changing the subject. 'You can see the river from here.'

'I walk there every day. I walked along the river on Saturday, and then through the woods. It's allowed,' she added, defensively.

'It's a public footpath. Anyone can use it.' The bluebells brought hundreds of people to the woods in the spring.

'Mr Howard didn't like it. He tried to get it closed.'

Abby frowned. That wasn't true. Howard may not have liked people tramping through his woods, but it had been a right of way long before the Lodge was built.

Except, of course, it wasn't her Howard who had wanted to block it off. It would have been his grandfather.

'Did you hear anyone?' she asked. 'While you were sitting by the lake?'

'That woman from the police asked me that, but I ran home.'

'Did something frighten you, Pam?'

'I heard a woman shouting. She was very angry.'

'Not Howard?'

She shook her head. 'Miss West brought my things, but the lamp was smashed to bits. She made me a cup of tea.'

'And so will I,' Abby said. 'And I've brought some of those chocolate biscuits that you like.' She produced the packet from her bag and went to put on the kettle.

By the time they were on their second cup of tea, and Pam had cleared the plate of biscuits, she was much more relaxed and Abby felt she could risk showing her the photograph.

'I was looking at Mrs Ruth's garden books and I found this in one of them.' She'd scanned the photograph she'd found in Ruth's journal and printed out a copy and now she held it out so that Pam could see. 'I think it's you.'

'No . . .' She shrank back into her chair, putting as much distance as she could between herself and the photograph.

Abby put it down on the small table between them. 'Who took it, Pam?'

She shook her head.

'Was it Ruth?' she prompted.

'No!'

'Mr Howard?' Pam's only response was a squeak of distress. 'What did he promise you, Pam?'

'Can't . . .' More head shaking. 'Mustn't . . . I promised.'

Hating to push her, but certain that this was a story that she had to know, that Pam needed to tell, Abby moved from her chair and knelt in front of her and took her hands. 'He can't hurt you, Pam. He died a long time ago.'

'Mrs Ruth told me that she'd look after me, find me somewhere nice to live, if I promised never to tell.' She clutched at the cross, but she wore a scarf to hide the port wine stain at her neck. 'She made me swear.'

'Mrs Ruth kept her word, Pam. She has looked after you. She found you this lovely flat. And she gave you the lamp.'

'It's broken.'

'Is that what Mr Howard promised you? The pretty lamp?'

She kept her eyes down and her mouth shut.

'It's really important, Pam. The police think I might have killed Howard. My Howard. Mrs Ruth loved him, and whatever she made you promise, she would want you to help me find out who hurt him.'

'Mrs Ruth would do anything for him. He was her boy.'

'He was,' Abby agreed. 'Like her son. She'd want whoever killed him to be punished.'

'And telling you about the photo will help?'

'It might.'

'Just you. Not the police.'

'If that's what you want.'

'It's hard,' she said. 'Thinking about it.'

'I know. Take as long as you need.'

Pam's fingers bit into Abby's hands as she went back in her head more than half a century to the time, before St Catherine's, when the photograph was taken.

'I was in the drawing room cleaning.' She looked at Abby. 'We had to do it before the gentry were about. We weren't supposed to be seen but Mr Howard came in while I was dusting. I just froze, but when he saw me, he smiled and said to carry on as if he wasn't there.'

'That must have been difficult.'

'I tried, but he was watching me, and I was so nervous that I nearly knocked over the lamp.'

Abby felt as if she'd been holding her breath for a week. 'What happened, Pam?'

'He caught it, held my hand, took the duster from me and did it himself, then he kissed my cheek and said, "Our secret." I nearly wet myself . . .'

'I can imagine,' Abby said.

'After that he was there every morning.'

'Dusting the lamp for you and kissing your cheek?'

Pam blushed.

Not just her cheek . . .

'He was very handsome, and when I told him that I thought the lamp was the prettiest thing I'd ever seen, he asked if I'd like one in my room,' she said, 'and I told him I'd do anything for something so pretty.'

Oh, Pam . . .

Abby tried to imagine a naive young girl being offered something so special. An innocent for whom "anything" must have meant no more than the worst cleaning job she could think of.

'I thought he'd want the boathouse scrubbed out, but he just wanted to take a photograph of me.'

Abby looked at the black-and-white picture of the young girl that lay between them.

'This photograph?'

Pam didn't look at it.

'What did you say?'

'I said if Mrs Ruth found out I'd lose my place. She'd told me that I was never to talk to Mr Howard, but I didn't tell him that.'

'What did he say?'

'He said he understood and I thought he'd forgotten, but then Mrs Ruth and Mr George went to stay with her mother for Easter. He was supposed to be going away with his wife and little boy.'

'But he didn't go.'

'No. He stayed behind and he said if I went down to the boathouse after I finished work, he'd take the photograph and I could have my lamp. It was beautiful then. The boathouse.'

By the time Abby had married Howard, it was already in a bad state, but it had been easy to see how it had once been.

'There were rooms upstairs,' Pam said. 'A sitting room with big armchairs, a cupboard with glasses and drinks. And a bedroom. Mr Howard used to sleep there sometimes. When his friends came for parties.'

'There were no friends when you were there?'

'No. Just me and Mr Howard.'

'What happened, Pam?'

'He gave me a drink,' she said. 'It was green and tasted like mint and was warm as it went down. I liked it and he gave me some more and then he started taking photographs, clicking away, click, click, click . . .'

'He took a lot of photographs?'

She nodded. 'Then he said that my dress was ugly and he had a prettier one for me to wear in the bedroom.'

'Oh, Pam . . .'

'He was smiling and the lamp was so pretty, but I felt a bit dizzy and couldn't manage the buttons so he came and undid them for me. The dress fell on the floor and it was so funny and I was giggling and he kissed me on the lips and that was nice, but then he was touching me, pulling up my petticoat, holding me and putting his hand between my legs. I knew that was wrong, but when I tried to tell him, to push him away . . .' Tears were pouring down her face now.

'It's okay, Pam, I understand.'

'He was so strong, Abby. He pushed me back against the bed, pulled down my knickers and stuck his thing in me . . .'

Abby wanted to tell her to stop, but she was away in the past reliving the nightmare . . .

'It hurt and I screamed, begging him to stop, but he didn't, and I kept screaming until he hit me. I couldn't struggle after that because I wasn't there anymore.'

Abby, sick to her stomach, could not begin to imagine the fear, the pain this supposed pillar of the community had inflicted as he'd beaten and raped a defenceless, fifteen-year-old girl . . .

'What happened afterwards, Pam?'

'The doctor came. My head hurt and I didn't know where I was. I thought he was going to help me, but I didn't struggle when he did it to me, in case he hit me too.'

Oh, dear God . . .

'When I woke up, I didn't know where I was. I heard my uncle's voice and I thought he was going to take me home, but he left me there. No one ever came for me. Not my uncle, not Mrs Ruth . . . They told me I'd been very bad and that I had to stay there until I learned to be good.'

'Ruth tried to find you, Pam, but she didn't know where you were.'

'She said. When I saw her in church, she asked what had happened to me and I told her what Mr Howard had done.'

'Is that when she took you to stay with her at the Lodge?'

'I didn't want to go there, but she said there was no one else there. Only her. She told me that she would look after me, but I had to promise not to tell anyone what had happened because it would hurt young Mr Howard.'

Abby swallowed. Ruth would have done anything to protect Howard.

'I told her that it didn't matter what I said. I'd told them at St Catherine's but no one had believed me. But she made me hold her cross and swear . . .'

Abby had been surprised about the cross, but Ruth, on her death bed, had given it to Pam to wear as a constant reminder of her promise not to tell.

'I've broken my swear, Abby. Will I go to hell?'

'No! No, you won't. Ruth should never have made you swear.'

'She took me away from that horrible hostel they put me in when St Catherine's closed. I would have done anything for her.'

And Ruth would have done anything to protect Howard's political career.

Had those other girls been less gullible than Pam and left before they suffered the same fate? Or had they been more calculating, trading their only value for what they could get out of the old goat and his vile friends in those boathouse parties before they made their escape?

His wife must have known what he was like. Heaven alone knew what he'd done to her before she'd had a total breakdown, spending the rest of her life in a nursing home, leaving Ruth to raise Peter.

And Ruth . . . Had she turned a blind eye while the girls from the children's home were left to their fate?

Giving them money and a silver cross to ease her conscience when they'd had enough, or he'd tired of them.

Thinking them no better than they ought to be . . .

It was, after all, what she'd thought of her.

Howard Senior had seen only easy prey, but Pam had fought, and no doubt afraid of what she'd do or say, he'd had her locked away.

Ruth hadn't taken Pam in out of kindness.

She looked after her to ensure her silence, and the awful thing was that, like Ruth, she wanted to protect her family, her children, from this ghastly revelation. Beg Pam to keep her secret.

But while no amount of money could ever compensate for what had been done to her, she was certainly entitled to more than the five thousand pounds that Ruth had left her.

She had just one more question.

'Pam, afterwards, when you were in St Catherine's, did you have a baby?'

'No babies for me,' she said, sadly. 'If I'd had a baby, they would have had to take me to the hospital, and I could have run away.'

'I'm so sorry for what happened to you.'

'Mrs Ruth told me that God had punished him for what he did to me.'

'Did she?'

Abby thought it was more likely to have been the whisky than the hand of God that had sent him plummeting down those stairs.

'My Howard, young Mr Howard, looked very much like his grandfather, Pam. Was that why you were so afraid of him?'

'He called me a thief, but Mrs Ruth gave me her cross so that I would never forget my swear. And she said I should live in this flat and have the lamp . . .' She looked at it, eyes streaming with tears. 'Will I have to leave now?'

Abby looked around and realised what Meg had meant. This block, near the park, was prime real estate. It was a mystery how Ruth had managed to get Pam housed there. Or whether she would be able to stay now that Ruth was dead.

'What did she tell you about the flat, Pam?'

'That it was mine for all my life.'

'If that's what she told you, I'm sure that's right,' she said, but she would have to look into it to make sure. 'And maybe we can get the lamp repaired too,' she said, although why she would want it beggared belief.

Pam looked at it for a moment and maybe the same thought occurred to her, because without warning she seized it and hurled it across the room.

CHAPTER TWENTY-SIX

'Meg . . . are you busy?'

Abby was sitting at one of the café tables in the cobblestone courtyard of the Red Lion.

The old coaching inn had been turned into a centre for designers and craftsmen and, in the corner of the courtyard, the Buttery bakery and café offered the best cakes and pastries in town.

The sun was shining, there were buckets of flowers outside the flower shop next door, hanging baskets everywhere overflowing with bright blooms, but she was shivering.

'Abby? What's happened?'

'I've been talking to Pam and I'm a bit shaky.' More than a bit. She wasn't sure how she'd made it this far, only that she didn't feel fit to drive and didn't want to go home until she'd cleared her head of what she'd heard. 'I'm at the Buttery. Can you come?'

'Five minutes.'

Meg's office was in the town centre. She was there in three, went in and ordered tea and walnut cake, carried them out into the sunshine and sat down.

'Not cake . . .'

'You look as if you've seen a ghost. You need the carbs,' she said. 'Now, tell me, what's happened?'

She told her.

'And Ruth swore her to secrecy?'

'It wasn't to protect that dreadful man's reputation and George was dead by then. She did it for Howard. She knew that if the story ever came out, it would be the end of his political ambitions.'

'I suppose.' Meg sipped the tea. 'Did you ask her about the baby?'

'She said there was no baby.'

'And you believed her?'

'She was sad. And angry. She threw the lamp against the wall.'

'It's a lot for anyone to keep bottled up, Abs, and with that beard Izzy made him grow, Howard looked very much like his grandfather.'

'I know, but—'

'She was already frightened, and fear is a motive for murder. If Howard found her in the garden and, already angry, said something, or did something that brought it all back, she might, for a moment, have thought it was the old man come back to hurt her . . .'

'You're saying that she could have lashed out.'

'Face it, Abs, it's a possibility, but I can see that you don't want to believe it.'

'After all she's suffered? What do you think? And she said she never went near that part of the garden because it made Ruth sad.'

'Well, we both know why. Pam might be a bit slow, Abby, but she's not stupid. And despite her age, she's had a lifetime of scrubbing floors. She's very strong.'

And despite saying that she wouldn't go there, she had known about the restoration.

'If it wasn't Pam's baby, there could be another woman out there who suffered the same fate. If she'd seen the story in the *Observer* and gone there to see where her baby had been buried, seen Howard . . .'

'You've found nothing in the journals to date the rose?'

'Not so far. Ruth was meticulous about detailing the date of planting anything special, with the name of the grower, usually with a catalogue photograph or a watercolour sketch, but so far nothing.'

'That's suspicious in itself. What about the household accounts?'

'I'd have to go through the Lodge archives. If I could just find a receipt, or an entry in the accounts to prove when the rose was bought . . .'

'Have you still got the keys I gave you?'

'Yes. I asked Dee Newcombe about picking some things up, but she said she'd let me know when they'd finished in the garden.'

'Now the police have finished using the kitchen I'm going to have to go and check for damage.' She grinned. 'If they've been using Ruth's delicate china cups, any breakages will make a hole in the chief constable's budget. Where does your bodyguard think you are?'

'I told him I was popping to the corner shop for milk and gin.'

Meg laughed. 'Let's hope he doesn't get it into his head that you're sitting on a park bench getting sozzled or he'll send out a search party. Come on, let's go.'

Fifteen minutes later Meg drove her four-by-four through the gates of Linton Lodge but instead of pulling up in front of the house, she carried on round to the kitchen courtyard.

Abby climbed down and looked around, half expecting a challenge from a constable on watch, but all she could hear was the drumming of her pulse in her ears.

'Okay?' Meg asked.

'Barely . . .'

Abby shook off a sense of the creeps, of being watched, unlocked the kitchen door and Meg switched off the alarm.

'I'd better change that for security,' she said. 'Heaven knows who's been in and out of here and I'll bet Izzy Hamilton has a key.'

She punched in some numbers.

'All done. It's your birthday. Day, month, year.'

'I should be able to remember that. Did you know that Howard had installed concealed CCTV cameras?'

'Why concealed? Surely the point is to warn off potential burglars.'

'Apparently Ruth was paranoid about being spied on, but the point is that the police know every word that was spoken on the doorstep that morning. They asked if Jake and I are in a relationship.'

'Awkward. Has he been in touch?'

'He called to let me know that he's coming to Maybridge later in the week.'

'Great. The rental I've found him is a bit quirky, but I think he's going to love it. Now, where are these archives?'

'Upstairs in one of the attic rooms, according to Lucy. Apparently, there's a record of every penny spent from the moment they opened up the ground to lay the foundations.'

'It'll be up the backstairs, then. Servants were only allowed on the main staircase when no one was about, and then only to remove dust and apply polish.'

Two flights led to a corridor with attic rooms that had once been servants' quarters and storage rooms.

'I've never been up here,' Abby said, looking in the first room, which was furnished with a modicum of comfort and had a fireplace for which some poor skivvy would have had to carry up the coal. 'Housekeeper?'

'I imagine so,' Meg said. The next few rooms were smaller, each furnished with a narrow bedstead, an upright wooden chair and a small wardrobe. No rug, no fireplace. Not one jot of comfort.

'Pam would have slept in one of these,' Abby said.

Beyond them were box rooms, used for storage.

'What is all this stuff?' Meg asked, looking into a room filled with boxes and trunks.

'I don't know. Not the accounts,' she said, but Meg had already opened the lid of the nearest trunk. 'Oh, this is criminal.'

'What?' Abby glanced back at the jumble of clothes, which looked as if they had been taken from their hangers and tossed into the trunk, then turned back to a pile of photo albums she'd found, opening the one at the top. Each page had a tissue layer to protect it, and as she lifted the first one, her heart stopped in her throat as she saw a studio portrait of a toddler.

'This is Armani, Abby. And there's a Betty Jackson jacket. And, oh my God, a classic Jean Muir dress just screwed up and thrown in as if it was a rag . . .' She shook it out and held it up. 'Who did they belong to?'

'Margaret, maybe?' Abby suggested, more interested in the photographs. 'She had a breakdown and was eventually moved into residential care.'

'Something rather better than St Catherine's, I imagine.'

'It couldn't be worse.' She stopped. 'Meg, could you check on something for me?'

'If I can.'

'Pam's flat. Is it possible to find out who owns it? I assumed the council had housed her after Ruth went into hospital.'

'Spencer Court? I don't think so. I did wonder how she could afford it. Leave it with me, I'll see what I can find out.' She picked up a jacket. 'Margaret was married to Howard's grandfather? Have I got that right?'

'Yes.'

'Then these clothes can't have been hers. These are later. They're going to need some attention, but they'll be worth good money . . .' She stopped. 'I don't appear to have your attention. What have you found?'

'Photographs . . .'

Meg looked over her shoulder. 'Good grief, that's the infant Howard. Cute with blond curls. And then he grew up.'

'There's a copy of it in a frame on Ruth's desk. His hair got darker as he got older, but Tom looked just like this when he was little.'

She turned over the page. He was wearing the same clothes in the next photograph, but in this one he was sitting on the lap of a woman she had never seen before.

'This must be his mother. Sarah . . . I've never seen a photograph of her before.'

'The one who, according to the *Observer*, abandoned him and ran off with her lover?' She took a closer look.

'She's beautiful.'

'And she's wearing the Jean Muir dress I just found screwed up in the trunk. She must have been desperate not to take that with her . . .' Abby looked at the photograph and then at the dress Meg was holding. 'I am right,' Meg insisted. 'It is this dress?'

'Yes, but if it was a spur-of-the-moment thing, she would only have time to pack the essentials.'

'True, but then, after she'd gone, would someone dump her clothes in a trunk and bring them up here?'

'Under the circumstances they would hardly pack them neatly to await collection.'

'No, but this looks as if it was done in a panic.'

'Or fury. Most men would have thrown them on a bonfire.'

'But Peter was dead,' Abby said.

They both stared at the clothes for a moment then Meg closed the lid of the trunk. 'We're here to find a date for the rose. Abby . . .'

'Yes . . .'

She tore herself away from the photographs, the clothes, and followed Meg.

At the end of the corridor, they found a room lined with shelves on which stood accounts ledgers, files containing receipts and staff record logs going back to 1868, when the house was built.

Against one wall was a table and chair, above which was a land registry map of the land bought by Howard's great-great grandfather, a plan of the house and the architect's drawing of the proposed frontage.

'What will you do with the house?' Meg asked. 'If it comes to you when everything's sorted out?'

'Are you asking as an estate agent or my friend?'

'Both. You could knock it down and have Finch Developments build affordable housing.'

'That wouldn't go down well with the neighbours. Not that it would get past the Planning Committee.'

'True.'

'I wonder if Bryan Crawford will worm his way back onto the committee now that Howard won't be there to block him?'

'Where would Howard keep a record of what he found out?'

'On his laptop.' Which would be at Izzy's.

'We'll worry about that later,' Meg said, looking around. 'Where do we start?'

'Nineteen sixty-one.' Abby took down a ledger and laid it on the table. 'The year that Pam supposedly ran away.'

'You do realise that Ruth, if she was in a hurry, might just have gone to the garden centre, picked up the first rose she saw and paid cash.'

'You clearly didn't know Ruth. And anyway, you couldn't just go to a garden centre and pick up a pot-grown rose at any time of the year back then. It would have been supplied bare root by the grower sometime between November and March.'

'Okay. I'll take 'sixty-two. What am I looking for?'

'The rose is a climber called Blush Noisette, but it might just be listed by the company who supplied it.' She named a few of the best-known rose breeders. 'Take that chair. I'll grab one from the maid's room.'

Abby collected the chair but, on the way back, she stopped for the photograph album.

Meg looked up when she put it on the table, then put her hand on the book.

'Don't go there, Abby. You have enough on your plate.'

'I can't leave it. You saw that photograph. She loved Howard but she never came back for him when Peter died.'

'There could be a dozen reasons for that.'

'A dozen? There's only one that would have kept me away.'

Before Meg could answer, Abby's phone rang. She checked the screen and saw that it was Jake. She took a breath and then let it go to voicemail.

Meg's eyebrows raised a touch. 'You're not going to answer that?'

'Not now.'

'He's concerned.'

'Only because he's involved. He left, Meg. We had that night and then he disappeared without so much as a goodbye.'

'The way you told it, he didn't have much choice.'

'I'm not talking about leaving Maybridge. I understand that, but there was nothing to stop him from picking up a phone, or at least sending a postcard.'

'Maybe you should ask him why he didn't do that.'

'Maybe someone should have asked why Sarah never sent Howard so much as a birthday card,' she said.

'She might have sent them, but if Peter committed suicide and the family blamed her, they would have kept them from him.'

'Tossed them along with her clothes in a trunk?' She turned as if to go and look.

'Abby, don't . . .'

'Suppose she never went anywhere, Meg? That her wardrobes were emptied to support a story. Maybe the baby isn't the only body that's buried out there.'

'You're suggesting that Peter killed her, then shot himself, and the family covered it up?'

'Isn't that what you're thinking?'

'You've been through a lot in the last few days. Maybe your imagination is running wild. Talk to Howard's solicitors,' she urged. 'The family might have cut her off, but I'd bet good money that they know what happened to her.'

Abby swallowed. 'Maybe.'

'Meanwhile, can we get on with finding this rose?'

'Yes. Sorry . . .'

Abby eventually found an entry for a purchase from one of the country's foremost rose breeders in November 1963. 'I think this might be it.'

'It's a bit later than we thought, and there are no details.'

'There'll be a receipt in the files.' Abby stood up, stretching her back, before using her phone to take a photograph of the open ledger showing the entry.

She hunted in her bag and found an old birthday card she'd used to make a shopping list and used it to mark the place before taking down the file marked "Receipts 1963".

It didn't take long to find a receipt for three bare-root roses: *Rosa* "Félicité-Perpétue", *Rosa banksiae* "Lutea" and *Rosa* "Blush Noisette".

'Pam was telling the truth. It can't have been her baby, it's too late.'

But there had been an entry in the journal showing the Lutea rose. It had been well-established by the time Ruth had produced the watercolour, but maybe there would be something there.

'Can we check the staff records?' Meg suggested, bringing her back to the attic room with its ledger-laden shelves.

Abby checked her watch. 'It's gone six.'

'I don't have to be anywhere, and now we've got a date to work back from it shouldn't take long.'

It didn't.

Catherine Mary Porter, listed as "maid of all work", left the Lodge in October 1963. Working back, they discovered that she'd been employed two weeks after Pam's disappearance.

'Cut and dried?' Meg suggested, as Abby used her phone to take photographs of the relevant pages and tore the birthday card to make more bookmarks.

'It looks like it, but it doesn't tell us what happened to her.'

'There's nothing in Ruth's journal?'

'I haven't read much beyond Pam's disappearance. There's a long gap when George took Ruth to Italy for a long holiday. I suspect she may have had a miscarriage. I did find a letter that Howard Senior's wife, Margaret, sent to Ruth, begging her to come home.'

'Why would she do that?'

Remembering her letter, Abby felt a shiver run through her. 'Margaret had had her only child late after a lot of miscarriages, Ruth told me once. She was a lot younger than Margaret. Only just a year older than Lucy when she married George.'

'Ruth had no children of her own?'

'No. But she brought up Peter after Margaret became ill, and then Howard . . .'

'So,' Meg said, 'Catherine Mary Porter. I wonder if she ended up in St Catherine's too? Maybe Pam knows her.'

'Unlikely. It's possible that Pam slipped through the net, but by 1963 the new act would have been well in place.'

'So? What do you think happened to her?'

'Right now, I'm thinking all kinds of things, Meg.' Abby picked up the photo album and hugged it to her chest. 'And I don't want any of them to be true.'

CHAPTER TWENTY-SEVEN

'I have found evidence that the rose was purchased in 1963, Dee, which clears Howard of any involvement in the birth and death of the baby.'

Abby thumbed in the text and attached the photographs she'd taken of the ledger and the receipt and sent it to Dee.

She didn't have to wait long for her phone to ring.

'You've been to the Lodge?'

'I had to prove that Howard had nothing to do with the baby before the press got hold of it.'

'I told you that we weren't going to release that information.'

'And I'm sure you meant it, but can you guarantee that something this juicy won't be leaked?'

Dee sighed. 'Did you remove the documents from the house?'

'No. I left them on the table in the archive room on the top floor of Linton Lodge. I can bring them to the station if you like.'

'No. I'll go and pick them up.'

'Meg West, the partner in Marshall & West, has changed the alarm code. Either I can come with you, or you can get in touch with her to let you in.'

There was a pause. 'I suppose I should thank you, but next time you have a bright idea, don't play detective. Tell me.'

Abby cleared her throat. 'There is something else.'

'Okay . . .'

'I found evidence in the staff log that Pam Lewis worked at the Lodge before she was shut up in St Catherine's. And there's something dodgy about that too. The law had changed. She shouldn't have been there.'

'You're suggesting that she's the mother of the baby you found?' Dee asked.

'No, the rose was bought later. Her replacement was a girl called Catherine Mary Porter. She left the Lodge shortly before the rose was bought.'

'Abby! Why didn't you tell me where we could find all this information? We could have had a team on it ages ago! I don't know what the DI is going to say.'

'He's got a murder on his hands. I didn't think that the illegal burial of a baby that happened decades ago would be very high on his list of priorities. If it ever was.'

'Maybe not, but if you have any other bright ideas, tell me.'

'Yes. I'm sorry,' she said. 'Did you find any fingerprints on the spade?'

'There may be something, but apparently that kind of wooden surface needs specialist techniques to bring up the image. This isn't a television drama. In the real world, forensic investigations take time.'

'I do realise that and I'm sorry for being a nuisance. It's late, you must be off duty and I need to call the children.'

'I'm still in the office and I was about to call and let you know that we've finished with the Lodge. You can collect your rose any time, although I imagine you've already done that.'

'No. I didn't go into the garden. I'll pick it up tomorrow.'

'There's no reason why you shouldn't plant it.'

The thought gave her the shivers, but it reminded her of something she wanted to ask.

'What will happen to the bones, Dee?'

'I don't know. If you were thinking of putting them back where you found them before you plant the new rose,' she said, 'I'm not sure that's possible.'

'No.' The infant was a Finch. 'If you'll let me know when forensics are finished with them, I'll arrange to have him buried in St Michael's. With his family.'

'That's . . .' Abby thought she heard Dee swallow. 'We'll have to wait for the coroner. I'll let you know.'

Abby FaceTimed the children, who were glowing from a day in the sun, then had a word with Charlotte, who assured her that they were fine, then had to be reassured that she was coping.

That was harder.

Not for the first time, Abby wished she had reburied the bones, hadn't started to dig for information. But there were things that, once seen, could never be unseen.

Meanwhile, she had a pile of condolence cards to deal with.

She opened them on autopilot, glancing at the names, recognising the handwriting of old friends and neighbours who, in some cases, had been leaving Christmas and birthday cards at the house since she was born. She took note of their kind messages.

There were more formal notes from the vicar, members of the church, Howard's colleagues and his political connections on the council — even one from the two-faced Bryan Crawford. She put that with the envelopes to be recycled. The rest she set aside to be answered later.

That done, she took a deep breath and faced the flashing light on the answering machine.

Assuming that the earlier ones would be a mix of condolences and the press, she started with the most recent.

The first, left just before five, was from Howard's solicitors.

'Mark Livingstone, Hargreaves, Mitchell and Peacock. The partners have asked me to convey their condolences to your family for your loss, Mrs Finch.'

Her family, not her, she noticed, but they were hardly going to fall over themselves to be sympathetic to the woman who, for all they knew, might have murdered their client.

'The police already have a copy of your husband's will and, since we have no way of knowing when his body will be released for burial, we will not wait for a formal reading. Perhaps you could let me know when it will be convenient for you to come to the office.'

She had intended to take Meg's advice and ask them about the disappearance of Sarah Finch. The tone of Mark Livingstone's message suggested they were going to deal with her at arm's length while holding their noses.

They certainly weren't going to share any of the family's dirty little secrets with her. Maybe they'd be more forthcoming with Freddie, but he'd be at home with his wife and family and what she had to tell him would wait until the morning.

There were plenty of messages from the press, which she deleted as soon as they identified themselves, but there were many more from Howard's colleagues, and from her friends and clients, offering their condolences and urging her to contact them if she needed help.

She made a note of those too, so that she could thank them later.

Then there was a message, left on Saturday afternoon, from Natalie Grant.

'You! This is your doing, Abby Finch! My poor Howard is dead and it's all your fault!' The words, screamed into the phone, caught on a sob. *'If you'd let him go, let him come to me, he'd have been safe—'*

There was a crash as she dropped the phone, swearing as she scrabbled about for it. It sounded as if she'd been drinking . . . Abby wanted to hit delete, to stop hearing this, but transfixed by the horror of it, she remained frozen.

'He'd have been safe,' she repeated, on a sob. *'But you clung and clung so he felt trapped, desperate . . . I could have loved him, looked*

after him.' For a moment her voice was low, pleading, barely intelligible, then she was screaming again. '*He's got that little bitch pregnant after all I've done for him . . . All the lies I've told for him* . . .' The sobbing was becoming painful, hysterical, her words harder to make out, but there was a final coherent burst. '*He's a coward . . . lying to you . . . lying to me . . . Lying and lying and lying and now he's dead and my life is over too* . . .' There was more noisy sobbing, but Abby had already grabbed her phone.

'Natalie Grant?' she demanded as soon as Dee picked up. 'Has anyone seen her or spoken to her since Saturday?'

'Is there are problem?'

'I've just picked up a very disturbing message she left on my answering machine on Saturday afternoon. She'd been drinking and sounded completely out of control. I'm afraid she may have done something stupid—'

'I'm on it,' Dee said, not needing her to spell it out. 'Save the message.'

She was still sitting there, shaken by the raw violence of Natalie's outburst, when she heard the back door open, and a familiar voice call her name.

'Jake . . .' She just about got his name out before she burst into tears.

He said nothing, just handed her a tissue from the box on the desk before pulling her up into his arms and holding her until she had herself under control.

'I'm sorry—'

'Don't!' he said. 'Don't apologise.'

'I need some air.'

He held onto her arm as if she might fall, and they went out into the garden and headed for the arbour that her father had built for her mother.

'Can I get you anything?'

Abby shook her head. 'Just tell me that it's going to be all right.'

He sat down and put his arm around her. 'It's going to be all right.' She relaxed into him.

Sitting here, with the sun setting behind them, the cream roses glowing in the shadows and filling the air with vanilla sweetness, she could almost believe him.

After a while she drew a long shuddering breath. 'Thank you.'

'For what?'

'For turning up at exactly the right moment. Knowing exactly what I needed.' She turned to look at him. 'It's your superpower.'

'If I had a superpower, I'd make all this go away for you.'

'No one can do that.'

And comforting as it was to lean against him, she forced herself to pull away, sit up, wipe her hands over her damp cheeks, aware that she must look a fright.

'What are you doing here, Jake? I thought you weren't coming back to Maybridge until later in the week.'

'I did try to call and let you know there was a change of plan.'

'We were in the Lodge looking at the records when you rang.'

'No problem. I grabbed a couple of pizzas and a bottle of red on the off chance. I can leave if you don't want company. Or I could stay and help you eat them?'

She began to laugh. 'As I said, it's your superpower.'

'Stay there. I'll be right back.'

He returned from the kitchen with two pizza boxes, a couple of glasses and a bottle under his arm.

Having put the boxes on the seat and handed Abby the glasses, he produced a corkscrew from his pocket, opened the wine and filled the glasses.

Abby took a sip and groaned. 'What is this?'

'I asked the bloke in the wine shop for something that would warm the soul and lift the spirits.'

'He knows his job.'

They sat for a while, biting into the cheesy-and-tomatoey deliciousness, sipping the wine, and when they were done with the pizza, Jake refilled their glasses. 'Do you want to tell me what happened today?'

'It's been a bad news, very bad news, good news, bad news sort of day. The bad news is that the baby's and Howard's DNA are a match.'

'No. Whatever else I think about him, I don't believe that for a moment.'

'And you're right. The good news is that although the father has to have been a Finch, a search through the archives proved that it could not have been Howard. At least not my Howard.'

'Okay. What's the very bad news?'

'The past is a dangerous place, Jake. It needs a health warning.'

'What have you discovered?'

'What happened to Pam Lewis. Terrible things that I'll never be able to get out of my head.'

'Would it help to share?'

She shook her head.

'Okay. And the other bad news?'

'Nothing solid. Just the feeling that things aren't as they seem. That there are secrets, lies . . . When we were up in the attic at Linton Lodge, looking at the archives, we found Howard's mother's clothes. Expensive, designer stuff just tossed into a trunk.'

'How do you know it was hers?'

'There were photographs of her with Howard when he was just a toddler. Meg was with me, and she spotted that Sarah was wearing one of the dresses.'

'Wasn't she supposed to have run away with a lover?'

'And then disappeared without a trace.' She turned to look at him and he sighed.

'You're not buying it.'

'No.'

'Well, I'm glad you weren't on your own.'

'If I'd been on my own, I wouldn't have looked in the trunk, or noticed the dress. I'd have gone straight for the records.'

'That explains why you were in such a state when I arrived.'

'What? Oh, no. That was Natalie. Howard's PA. She left a message on my machine sometime on Saturday. She'd clearly been drinking.'

'She thought that if she hung on long enough Howard would eventually see the light and take her to his bosom?'

She looked at him. 'Bosom?'

He shrugged. 'Manly chest?'

'What on earth have you been reading?'

'Balance sheets, construction estimates, cash flow projections. Tell me about Natalie.'

'She must have called straight after she heard the news on the radio. That should never have happened. I should have gone to tell her myself.'

'Your children needed you, Abby, and she's an adult. Give yourself a break.'

'I know . . . But she shouldn't have been on her own. I told the police and they assured me they'd go and inform her in person.'

'Maybe she wasn't at home. Or just didn't answer.'

She sighed. 'She was probably already working her way through whatever booze she could lay her hands on.'

'What did she say?'

'She was incoherent, sobbing for most of it, but she was sure as hell blaming me for Howard's death and the fact that her life was over.'

'And you think she may have done something drastic?'

'I've called the police, but if she has taken something it's going to be too late. If I'd listened on Saturday . . .'

'On Saturday someone had killed your husband. It could have been her.'

'What? No . . .'

But then "no" had been her reaction to the idea that anyone present that morning had killed Howard. She knew it was clutching at straws to hope it was the passing madman everyone was so quick to blame in golden-age detective fiction.

If someone had come into the garden and attacked him, it wasn't by chance and Natalie was unhinged enough. But Howard had been with Izzy for months. Why now?

'What time did she leave the message?' Jake asked.

'I'd have to check the machine . . .' She stopped. 'You're wondering if it could have been before his death became public knowledge?'

'Aren't you?'

She thought about the woman Cal had overheard shouting for Howard. And Howard's reaction. He'd have had more patience with Izzy. Whether Izzy had been in a fit state to be reasoned with was another matter.

'Dee asked me to save the message. I'll leave it for her to work out the timeline.'

'Leave it all to her. Is there any progress with the enquiry?' Jake asked.

'Apparently it takes time. I did tell them I thought whoever struck the blow was right-handed. But I'm sure they still have me in the frame.'

'Which is ridiculous. You weren't the one who hit him.'

No. Jake had done it for her. Always the knight errant.

But that was the thing about knights errant. Once they'd done their good deed they were gone. They had other battles to fight. Dragons to slay. Meetings to attend. Accounts to balance.

She needed to remember that.

'Have they been in touch with you since Saturday?' she asked.

'Only to confirm a few details. Such as whether I'm right-handed. Which I am.'

'Jake!'

'Don't worry about it. How are the children bearing up?'

'They're staying with my cousin Charlotte. I think you might have met her. She helped me build the sensory garden in the park.'

'Dark curly hair, laughed a lot?'

'That's her. They appear to have had a good afternoon on the beach with her children.'

'You should join them.'

'I will when things are clearer, but Howard's solicitors want to read the will.'

He frowned. 'Aren't they supposed to wait until after the funeral?'

'Usually, but who knows when that will be. Presumably the police already know the contents, and I just want to get it over and done with so that I know what I'm likely to face.'

'You're anticipating problems?'

'What I'm anticipating is a hard time from Izzy Hamilton. Or rather her lawyers. I suspect they're the ones pushing for the reading so they can start building a case for their client and her offspring to get their just deserts.'

'Or maybe she just wants to know if he's made a new will in her favour.'

'Unlikely. He was young, fit and he'd have had to make a new one once they were married. I can't see Howard doing that twice, although I'm sure his solicitors were urging him to draft one. Whatever happens, she'll have a claim on the estate. Or at least her baby will.'

'And you have three children and a lot of years married to him. Don't let them bully you.'

'Freddie Jennings has my back.'

'Is he up to it?'

'He may not be a fancy London solicitor, but if it wasn't for him, right now half of this house would have been in the divorce settlement grinder.'

'Then you appear to be in safe hands, so let's finish this bottle and I'll leave you in peace.'

'You're not driving . . .' she said, as he emptied the bottle into their glasses.

He looked up, eyes very dark in the dusk. 'Any other time I'd take that as an invitation.'

'Maybe it is.' She kept her eyes on her glass, because looking at him was not such a good idea. 'Maybe I've had too much of this, but right now I really need a hug.'

The hug was duly administered and was everything she'd asked for. The comfort of another body warm against her own, the brush of lips against her hair. That never-let-me-go moment that took her right back to the night of the prom when he'd left her at her back door. And disappeared from her life for over twenty years.

She had to force herself to pull away.

'Better?'

'Yes,' she lied. 'Thank you.'

And because she didn't know what else to do, she picked up the pizza boxes and the empty bottle.

'If you'll take the glasses into the kitchen, I'll put these in the recycling.'

She took a moment to get her breathing under control, and by the time she returned to the kitchen, the glasses had been rinsed and were on the drainer.

'What are you doing tomorrow?' Jake asked.

'I have to talk to Freddie, then I'm taking Cal up to the house to pick up a motorbike and the rose I abandoned. Apart from that, I'm in the hands of the law.'

'So, you could come and look at this property Meg's found for me.'

'Where is it?'

'Longbourne Reach.'

'Oh, nice. River frontage and then some. What time?'

'Give me a call when you're free. A neighbour has the key.'

'It's vacant?'

'Ready to move into. And in answer to your earlier question, no, I'm not driving. I walked here from the Queen's Head, and despite all inclinations to the contrary, I am going to walk back there.'

CHAPTER TWENTY-EIGHT

After a couple of sleepless nights, and no doubt aided by the wine, Abby was asleep the moment her head hit the pillow.

It was still early when she was woken by the sun edging over the windowsill, but by the time she'd showered, washed her hair and had a morning FaceTime with the children, it was late enough to call Freddie's office.

She had intended to leave a message asking him to call her when he had a moment, but the receptionist put her straight through.

'Abby . . . Is there a problem?'

'It's nothing to do with Howard's death . . .' He listened in silence while she told him what had happened to Pamela Lewis.

'But she's not the baby's mother?'

'She says not, and the rose was bought a couple of years after her supposed runaway. There was another girl working there then. Catherine Mary Porter.'

'And you're afraid that something similar may have happened to her?'

'It's possible. We need to find her.'

'She'll most likely have married, changed her name. It won't be easy.'

'But you will try.'

'If that's what you want. Meanwhile, if Pamela Lewis wants to make a complaint she'll have to go to the police and make a statement. Do you think she'll do that?'

'Honestly? I don't know.'

'Do you feel able to ask her?'

She took a deep breath, knowing what it would mean. 'I have to.'

'Then I'll leave that with you.'

'And I'd like you to try and find Howard's mother. If she's alive, she should know what's happened to her son. Be at the funeral.'

'His solicitors must have tried to find her when Peter died. Apart from any other considerations, she was Howard's mother. There would have been an issue over guardianship. And possibly Peter's will. If he was seriously disturbed by her disappearance, he might not have changed it.'

'I'm sure they went through the motions, but I doubt the family pressed very hard and they wouldn't have gone to the police.'

'Not unless there were suspicious circumstances.'

'The story was that she'd run away with her lover. I'd like to know if anyone actually questioned that. There was a monster in that house, Freddie. I have a letter that Margaret Finch wrote to Ruth years before, begging her to come home from Italy. I had the strong impression that she was frightened of being alone with her husband.'

'Howard Senior?'

'Yes.'

'But Sarah wasn't alone.'

'We don't know that. Her own husband, Peter, would have been at work, and so presumably would George. Ruth could have been out at one of her charitable functions. And who, if he ever existed, was this mysterious lover?' Abby shook her head. 'He doesn't appear to have had a name. It's all smoke and mirrors.'

'Maybe, but this all happened before the internet and social media, and you couldn't track people's movement through their credit cards.'

'She would still have needed money.'

He sighed. 'Yes . . .'

'She had a son, Freddie!'

'Not all women are natural mothers, Abby, but I'll talk to the Finch lawyers. And,' he added before she could interrupt, 'I will make some enquiries of my own.'

'Thank you . . . There's something else.'

'Not another missing woman, I hope.'

'No, it's about the baby. The police have informed me that he has the same DNA as Howard.'

Freddie blew out a long breath.

'It's not his,' she said quickly. 'I've found documents proving that the rose planted over the grave was bought much earlier. But the father was definitely a Finch. I've taken photos of the documents and given them to the police.'

'I'd better have a copy too, but let's leave the police to inform the family lawyers if they feel it's necessary. Have they been in touch about reading Howard's will?'

'I had a message this morning from Mark Livingstone asking me to let him know when it will be convenient to go to their office.'

'He expects you to go to London? That's totally unacceptable.' He sounded uncharacteristically outraged. 'You're needed here and, under the circumstances, I'm going to insist on being present. The children have a right to be there too, if you think that's appropriate.'

'They've gone to stay with my cousin on the coast for half term.'

'I'm glad to hear that, but whatever it says will affect them. And any other bequests are likely to be to local charities.'

'Yes, of course. I'll call them now—'

'You can leave that to me, Abby. I'll offer them the use of my conference room and it will be an opportunity to ask about the whereabouts of Howard's mother, since she should also be present.'

* * *

Freddie was dealing with Howard's lawyers, Dee was looking for Natalie, the children were safe with Charlotte and the press appeared to have given up on seeing her arrested and found better things to do than loiter across the road.

Restless, unable to settle to anything, she went to pick up Cal, who was in Molly's garden making good use of a hoe.

'Putting in some practice?'

He straightened. 'Mrs Finch . . .'

'I thought we'd agreed that you would call me Abby.'

'Oh. Okay. It didn't seem right in the police station.' He gestured at the border he was working on. 'There are some weeds.'

'You're doing a good job.'

'Thanks.'

'I'll just go and say hello to Molly, then we'll go and pick up that bike.' Then a thought struck her. 'I'm assuming you do have a helmet?'

'Yes, and I've passed my basic training, but I haven't taken a test.'

'That's okay. It's got a small enough engine for you to ride it legally as a learner. There might be some old L plates in the store but, if you're ready, I'll pay for you to take a test.'

'Really?' His eyes lit up. 'You're not going to fire me?'

'Saturday was a one-off,' she said, 'but Molly was really worried when you disappeared — mostly, I have to admit, about what your grandmother would say if anything had happened to you.'

'Gran is always on her back. Nagging her about something. Mum told me that they've always been like that.'

'How are you finding her?'

'Aunt Molly?' He shrugged. 'I don't know. Gran said that she's too old to be living on her own and to keep an eye on her. I think she suspects she might have Alzheimer's.'

'What do you think?'

'She talks to herself. Is that normal?'

'I think it goes with living on your own, although I talk to plants, encouraging them to get on with it.'

'Oh, well, yes, I talk to bikes when I'm working on them but not people who aren't there.' He shrugged. 'The other day I heard her saying, "Just washing the dishes, Gordon, and then I'll pop down to see you . . ." Uncle Gordon's been dead for years.'

'I imagine she was going to stop by his grave on her way to church.'

'Maybe, but then later, after church, she was going on about making scones and telling him that she had the strawberry jam he liked.'

Abby was fighting hard to keep a straight face.

'Anything else?'

'Well, she keeps calling me Joe.'

'Who's Joe?'

'My grandad. Apparently, I look a lot like him. And this morning, when she was hanging out the washing, I heard her say, "I'll see you soon, Jane." She stopped when she saw me, laughed at herself and told me to ignore a silly old woman. But it's a bit creepy.'

'I can see that you might find it a bit disconcerting, but honestly, Cal, it sounds as if she's aware of what she's doing, and I have to admit that there are moments when something will come into my head that I want to tell my mother.'

'And you say it out loud?'

'I do. Sometimes the children catch me, and they think I'm crazy too.' Cal was looking at her as if she had two heads, she realised. 'Your aunt misses Gordon. And Jane was my grandmother. They were best friends all their lives until my gran died.'

'She isn't going loopy, then?'

'A bit forgetful, perhaps. But she is looking tired.' And the fact that she thought she'd be seeing Jane soon was worrying, because Jane had been dead for years too. 'We'll both keep an eye on her, and you can always talk to me if you're worried. For now, put your tools away, and as soon as I've had a word with Molly we'll go and get the bike.'

'Could I use the workshop? There's not a lot of room here and no tools.'

'I'm not sure that's going to be possible, but you could work at my house. There's plenty of room.'

'Oh, right.' If he was disappointed not to have the run of the workshop, he didn't show it. On the contrary he appeared to be delighted. 'That would be great.'

And then the penny dropped. He thought Lucy would be there.

'Cal . . .'

He waited, but she shook her head. Lucy was growing up. Boys were going to be part of her daughter's life and she was going to have to get used to it.

'You've got ten minutes.'

'Abby . . .' He hesitated. 'Are you okay?'

'Honestly? I don't know, Cal, but thank you for asking.' And, touched by his concern, she was smiling as she walked into Molly's kitchen.

She was half dozing in an armchair.

'Jane . . .' For a moment she looked overjoyed but then faltered. 'Oh, Abby. You look so much like your grandmother. I'll put the kettle on.' She struggled to get up.

'No, don't disturb yourself, Molly, I'm not stopping. I just wanted to ask about the kittens.'

'Oh, right.' She subsided against the cushions with obvious relief. 'I went to talk to Gordon this morning and the walk up the hill took it out of me.'

'Don't do that. Call me, anytime, and I'll give you a lift.'

'You've got your hands full.'

'Not at the moment. Can I get you anything?'

She shook her head. 'No, dear. I'll be fine when I've had a rest and Mabel is taking good care of the kittens.'

'I'm sure, but one of Sophie's friends is desperate for one. Are they all spoken for?'

'I'm keeping the ginger-and-white tabby, there are your two, but she can have either of the other two.'

'That's wonderful. Thank you. She's away at the moment, but I'll take pictures and she can choose.'

She'd just texted the pictures to Emma when Dee called.

'I wanted you to know that we've found Natalie Grant. She was taken to A&E by her sister on Saturday evening.'

'Is she okay?'

'She appears to have drunk rather a lot, taken some pills and then cut herself on a broken glass. Whether deliberately or not we can't say. Fortunately, she managed to call her sister before she passed out.'

'Thank heavens for that. How is she?'

'She spent the night in hospital, but she's been discharged and, for the moment, staying in Longbourne with her sister, but I'm not sure that this is entirely down to Howard's death,' Dee said. 'When we contacted her office, we were informed that she was given a redundancy notice just before close of business on Friday afternoon.'

'Redundancy?' Abby repeated, shocked.

'With immediate effect. She was asked to clear her desk, hand over her keys and was escorted from the building.'

'It takes a lot for me to feel sorry for her, but that's brutal.' She shook her head in disbelief that Howard could have treated her so shabbily. 'I assume that Izzy had a taste of the Natalie treatment and told Howard to get rid of her.' Something she should have done years ago. 'But is it legal to make someone redundant if the job still exists?'

'It doesn't. It seems that your husband resigned last week from his role as managing director of the company in order to concentrate on his political career. They were going to issue a statement on Monday.'

'I had no idea.'

'I was assured that Ms Grant had been given a very generous package based on her length of service, along with a substantial bonus.'

'Generous! Substantial! Damn it, Dee, I can't believe that he'd get HR to do his dirty work while he was out of the country.'

'It does rather suggest that he anticipated her reaction. We're investigating the possibility that she was the woman who Cal overheard shouting for him on Saturday.'

'Have you any evidence for that?'

'Forensics are working on it, but there's a scrape on the nearside wing of her car and it's the same colour as the traces of paint found on a post where Lucy saw the car leaving the Lodge. I'm on my way to interview her now.'

'Will you tell her . . .'

'Tell her what?'

'Nothing.'

'It might help her to know that you were concerned, Abby.'

'I rather doubt that.'

'Then I'll leave it. One piece of news I do have for you is about Bryan Crawford. He was at a Chamber of Commerce lunch on Saturday, so he's off the suspect list.'

Abby recalled her conversation with Meg. 'Is that what he told you?'

'He wasn't in his office. I spoke to his assistant.' Dee sounded suspicious now.

'Maybe you should check again, because my information is that he didn't turn up.'

'You've been making your own enquiries?' Dee sighed. 'Of course you have.'

'I'm sorry.'

There was a disbelieving *humph* from the other end of the phone. 'Thank you for the information. I'll tell the DI.'

She ended the call and it dawned on her that Molly had been listening. 'That was the police. Howard's personal assistant has taken his death very badly.'

'One of his other women, is she?'

'No. She had bigger ambitions than that.'

'More fool her. And that woman he's hooked up with has had a lucky escape. They're a bad family. I told your mother that. I told her not to let you marry him.'

'He was very good to her, Molly.'

She shrugged. 'Well, he never had a mother of his own and Ruth Finch was a cold fish . . .' She saw Cal standing in the doorway. 'All done with the weeding, Joe?'

Abby caught Cal's eye. Maybe she'd been fooling herself. She'd have to talk to Penny.

CHAPTER TWENTY-NINE

Abby drove Cal to the Lodge via the kitchen garden entrance and stopped to see what Natalie had, allegedly, hit.

All that remained of the gates that had once kept the garden secure was a wooden post. Having taken a substantial hit, the rotten wood had given way and it was now lying on its side, the *PRIVATE, NO THROUGH ROAD* sign leaning at a drunken angle.

Both bore traces of pale blue paint that was the same colour as Natalie's precious Fiat 500.

'Damn . . .'

It was a gap wide enough for a truck and her car was very small. She must have been in a seriously disturbed state to have misjudged it so badly.

She climbed back in the van and sat there for a moment. She hadn't wanted it to be Natalie. Damn it, she didn't want it to be anyone . . .

Well, maybe Bryan Crawford. Where had he been on Saturday?

'Are you okay, Abby?'

'No, Cal. I know someone killed Howard, but the thought that it was someone I know, someone he knew . . .'

She shook her head and drove on, then reversed up to the kitchen garden gates. 'Open them up.'

Cal jumped out and pulled open the two tall gates, and she backed up to the store and climbed out.

'I'll leave you to load up the bike and any tools you think you might need while I go and rescue the rose.'

'I could go and fetch it for you,' he offered.

'Thanks, but I'll be okay.'

Reluctant as she was to return to that part of the garden, it was something she had to face.

New growth was already beginning of soften the edges of the shrubs she'd cut back to clear the path, and she stopped to trim a few of the untidier branches with her trusty secateurs, delaying the moment when she'd have to face the place where Howard had died.

There was always one more branch that needed trimming, but the sound of a crash startled her and, without thinking, she rushed into the garden.

'Who are you?' she demanded, as two men turned at her approach. 'What are you doing here?'

Stupid question. What they were doing was obvious.

Behind them, the summerhouse furniture had been removed and stacked up on one side. The remains of the clematis, which would have been a joyous riot of pink just a couple of weeks earlier, had been hacked down and lay in a dying heap. The summerhouse door had been removed, as had the windows.

'Geoff Mallard,' the older man said. 'Mallard Construction Services. Mr Finch asked us to demolish the summerhouse and clear the site.'

'When was this?'

'A couple of months ago.' He produced a Finch Developments works order from his pocket and handed it to her. 'We explained that we wouldn't be able to it do before the end of May and he said to just get on with it when we could. We rang the doorbell, but there was no answer. Can I ask who you are?'

‘I’m Mrs Finch,’ she said, handing back the paper. ‘Howard’s wife.’ She’d stopped thinking of herself as that and it felt odd saying it, but it gave her some authority. ‘His widow,’ she added, her voice not quite steady as she said the word for the first time.

He frowned. ‘Mr Finch is dead?’

‘It was on the news, Mr Mallard.’ She gestured in the direction of a piece of police tape caught on a branch above their heads. ‘Until yesterday, this was a crime scene.’

‘I’m very sorry for your loss, ma’am. We could come back at a more convenient time . . . ?’

‘What? Oh, no . . .’ If she hadn’t decided to pick up the rose today, she would have arrived to find a large space where the summerhouse had once stood. ‘You can’t leave it like that. One strong gust and it’ll fall down.’

‘The floor’s rotten,’ he agreed. ‘It was put down on wooden sleepers rather than proper stone foundations and the ground has subsided near the back, causing extra stress. Whoever put it up didn’t do a very good job.’

It had been neglected and past its best when she and Howard, both living at home, had cleaned it up and made it their private passion pad.

Impossible now to recognise those two young people, losing themselves in the heat of the moment with no thought for the future.

‘We’ll get on then, if that’s okay . . . Mrs Finch?’ he prompted.

‘Yes. Yes of course.’

She paused for a moment at the place Howard had died, where an infant had been buried, then she picked up the rose.

There was another crash and some swearing as the two men tugged away the deck.

‘Sorry, ma’am.’

‘Don’t move!’

Mr Mallard looked down at his feet as Abby stepped forward and picked up a bunch of white rose buds about to be crushed under his boot.

They had been protected from the sun but they'd been there for several days and the petals were browning at the edges, the leaves limp. Whoever had left them had tied them with a baby-blue ribbon and there was a card. Using just the tip of her finger on one corner, Abby eased it open and her heart lurched as she read it: *With love, Mummy.*

The baby's mother, maybe Catherine Mary Porter, had been here to leave flowers for her dead baby.

It had to have been sometime on Friday, after the headlines in the *Observer*, but they hadn't been there when she'd arrived on Saturday morning.

Who could have moved them? Not thrown them away — as Howard, angry at the publicity, might have done — but hidden them?

* * *

Abby hadn't been home long when Molly tapped on the kitchen door and came in, bearing a cake tin.

'I made you a cherry cake,' she said. 'I know it's your favourite.'

'Oh, Molly, you shouldn't be baking in this heat. Sit down and I'll make you a cup of tea.'

'I had to make one for the WI. I'm on tea duty so I can't stop, but I'll just catch my breath.'

She was breathing heavily and looked a bit waxy. 'Maybe you should give it a miss. I'll run you home.'

'I'll be fine in a minute, and they're relying on me.'

Abby knew better than to suggest that she didn't look up to it and handed her a glass of water. 'Take your time. I'll run you down to the parish hall.'

'Oh, well, thank you. I won't say no.'

'And call me if you need a lift home.'

'Someone will bring me,' she said, then frowned. 'There was something else. Oh, yes, the vicar asked me to tell you not to worry about the plant stall.'

It took Abby a moment. 'Oh, right . . . the church fete.' She glanced across at the noticeboard, but the flyer was now hidden under a takeaway menu. 'It's not for a few weeks?'

'It's the last Saturday in June.'

'Well, let's see how things go.' She was taking nothing for granted. The police might still arrest her. 'If I can't do it, Cal could run the stall.'

He could come along anyway. He'd be a draw in a manly Earthly Designs gardening apron, and she'd make sure he had a stack of her leaflets to hand out. And if he was there, Lucy was sure to volunteer. Result.

* * *

She'd dropped off Molly at the parish hall and was just pulling out of the car park when a car stopped in front of her, blocking the exit. She lowered the window to stick her head out and ask them to move when she realised that it was Bryan Crawford and, too late, she remembered that his mother was chair of the WI.

She waited patiently while he helped her out and saw her safely inside, then he walked across to where she was waiting. It was a hot day and the window was down, so she was unable to stare ahead and ignore him.

'What the hell have you been saying to the police?' he demanded.

Quietly cursing the broken air-conditioning, she turned to face him. He was wearing a pair of large-framed dark glasses, but they didn't quite cover the bruise on his cheek. 'They asked me who might have wanted Howard dead and I remembered the threats you made after he forced you to resign from the Planning Committee.'

'That was just hot air. I was nowhere near Linton Lodge on Saturday. I was—'

'I know that your assistant told the police that you were at a Chamber of Commerce lunch. That makes him an accessory.'

'He just checked the diary. He didn't know I hadn't made it.'

'Well, the police know the truth, so you'll be getting another visit from them. Where were you on Saturday morning, Councillor?'

'That's none of your damn business.'

'Maybe not, but the police will want to know. I hope you have a convincing alibi.' Suddenly he wasn't making eye contact and she knew . . . 'Oh, right. Did your wife find out? Or was it the woman's husband who gave you that black eye?'

He glared at her, then turned and walked stiffly to his car before driving off with a squeal of tyres. He was off the suspect list, but he wasn't going to enjoy his interview with the police. She just hoped he remembered that there was a speed camera on the bend or he'd get a ticket to add to his woes.

* * *

'I see you've lost the police and media presence,' Jake said when he picked her up later.

'What? Oh, yes. I'm hoping that's a sign that I'm off the suspect list.'

'No one who's ever met you could believe you could kill anyone, Abby.'

'I appreciate that, Jake. I'm afraid that Meg thought I was being a bit defensive on your behalf.'

'Did she think I'd killed Howard?'

'You were there, Jake.'

'But you didn't think I was guilty.'

'There was a moment when you appeared with his blood on your shirt,' she admitted, 'but I saw your face when I told you he was dead. Your shock was genuine.'

'That's because, for one ghastly moment, I thought I might have killed him. He walked away after I punched him, but he could have collapsed . . .'

'It wasn't just that, Jake. I knew that if he'd done or said something bad enough for you to strike him with my spade, you'd have been the one calling the paramedics. And you'd have stayed to do what you could to help him.'

'I hope so, but the impulse to run must be very strong.'

'Someone did,' Abby said. 'Anyway, what did the police say?'

'Apparently, there would have been a fine spray over whoever struck him. I still had a smear where I wiped my hand, so it was clear I hadn't changed my shirt and there was no spray.'

'They wouldn't have been able to tell on my overalls,' she said. 'I was covered in his blood.'

'But you're left-handed,' he said, reaching to start the engine.

'Jake, wait . . .'

He looked at her. 'Are you okay, Abby? Stupid question, of course you're not, but you don't have to put on a face for me. I know you're going through a rough time and if you rather not do this—'

'I was at the Lodge this morning with Cal,' she said.

'Really? You need to stay away from there.'

'It was just to pick up the motorbike and my rose. Ten minutes . . . But I found this.'

She took out her phone and showed him the photograph of the faded roses.

'Someone left flowers? Was there a card?' he asked. 'Was it Izzy?'

'They weren't for Howard. They were for the baby.' She thumbed to the photograph she'd taken of the card. Looked again at the round, almost childish handwriting and frowned, certain that she'd seen something very like it recently.

Could it have been on one of the dozens of condolence cards that were still arriving?

Jake took the phone and used his fingers to blow up the picture.

'Written with a ballpoint pen with blue ink.'

'Left-handed or right-handed, Sherlock?' Abby asked.

He shook his head and handed it back. 'Above my pay grade, but it proves that the mother is still alive,' Jake said, 'and living in the area.'

'Or maybe someone who knows her story left them there. I'm assuming they were left where I found the bones, but someone had pushed them under the summerhouse. Out of sight.'

'What were you doing under the summerhouse?'

'Nothing. A couple of men turned up this morning to demolish it. It seems that Howard arranged it a while ago and they hadn't heard the news. They moved the deck while I was there and that's when I saw the roses.'

'They couldn't have got there on their own.'

'No.'

'It had to have been Howard.'

'I can imagine him picking them up and throwing them away,' Abby admitted, unhappily. 'What I can't see is him pushing them out of sight under the summerhouse. Not his style.'

'No,' Jake agreed, somewhat wryly. 'What did you do with them?'

'I put them back where the mother left them.'

'And you haven't told the police?'

'No.'

'Are you going to?'

'I don't know.'

He said nothing.

'You think I should?' she asked.

'There's something you're not telling me.'

She shook her head. 'It's nothing . . . At least, just a feeling that I've seen the handwriting somewhere before.'

'Be careful, Abby.'

'I only touched the corner of the card.'

'You know that's not what I meant. I really think you should give it to the police.'

'And I'm thinking about the mother, but there is something else.'

'Why do I get the feeling that we won't be house-viewing today.'

'No! I mean, yes.' She was torn now. 'I want to look at this house with you, but I need to know when the summerhouse was built.'

'Because of the flowers?'

'No. Well, not directly. The men told me that it had rotted because it was built on wooden sleepers and the ground beneath it had subsided.'

'Then I'm glad I didn't go in there.'

'You didn't? The police said that the door was open.'

'Not when I was there. I didn't have a key and I didn't hang around. I knew I'd behaved like an idiot and wanted to get my head straight before I talked to you again. Is that the right answer?'

She smiled, shook her head. 'The idiot part is right, but that's not the question.'

'Am I likely to know the answer?'

'It's rhetorical.'

'So there is no answer?'

'Only hypotheses.'

'Try me.'

'Okay. This is the question. Why, if you owned a quarry full of the stuff, wouldn't you put down proper stone foundations?'

'Time?' he suggested, without having to think about it. 'If you wanted it done quickly.' Which was exactly what she'd been afraid of. 'Or it could be a question of cost. It was a big summerhouse. You'd need a lot of manpower to excavate the base. Although I suppose Finch, or a friendly subcontractor, would have one of those small diggers.'

'Which leaves only one explanation.'

'Abby?'

'If you'd buried someone and were going to cover up the evidence with a summerhouse, you wouldn't want anyone, no matter how friendly, going in with a digger or levelling the site. You'd want it thrown up as quickly as possible.'

'You think there's a body buried there?' Jake asked, horrified.

'It would explain the subsidence,' she said. 'As the body rotted—'

'I've got it,' he said, quickly.

'Sarah Finch disappeared without a trace, Jake.'

'And you think that she might never have left Linton Lodge? Do you have any evidence to back that up?'

'I know what happened to Pam Lewis. There was a monster who preyed on young women living in that house.'

'Sarah was married, with a child.'

'I've seen a photograph of her, and she had the kind of ethereal beauty that would appeal . . .' The thought was too awful to put into words. 'There wasn't a handy supply of innocent orphans to work as scullery maids by then. It was all middle-aged dailies.'

'That's . . .' He shook his head. 'No, I don't want to think what that might be. Have you mentioned this to the police?'

'Not yet. I'm not sure that I can persuade Pam to talk to them, and you're right, the rest is no more than suspicion. I've asked Freddie to institute his own search for Sarah. And Catherine Mary Porter. But I need to have another look in the archives.'

'Who is Catherine Mary Porter?'

'I found her in the staff records. She worked at the Lodge after Pam. She left a few weeks before the rose was bought.'

'And you think she could be the mother of the baby?'

'The dates fit and if it is her, the flowers prove that she's still in the area.'

'I know this is going to sound patronising, Abs, but are you sure this obsession with finding the baby's mother, finding Sarah Finch, isn't just a distraction from dealing with what happened to Howard?'

'Patronising as hell, Jake, which doesn't mean you're wrong. But I have this weird feeling that it's all somehow connected.'

'I can see why you'd feel that. Everything happened at the same time and in the same place, but it has to be a coincidence. You need to put it out of your head and join your children.'

'It was Lucy who started this. She made me see how important it is to find the baby's mother and she's going to want to know what I've been doing.'

'Getting yourself worked up?' he suggested.

'I've already discovered what happened to Pam.'

'And now you want to find out what happened to Sarah.'

'And Catherine. I'm going to have her baby buried in the Finch vault and she should be there to see it done decently.'

'These are long-buried secrets, Abby. She may not want to be found. Exposed . . .'

'If I find her I won't expose her, or force her to do anything, but she should have that choice.'

'Okay. Here's what I suggest. We look at this fabulous property Meg found for me, have a late lunch, and then go to the Lodge and see if we can find out when the summerhouse was built.'

Abby didn't immediately answer.

'Or we could do it the other way around?' he suggested. 'Search, house, dinner?'

'Isn't Meg going to meet us at the house?'

'No. She's arranged for Laura, who lives next door, to let us in whenever we turn up.'

'Oh. Right.' Desperate as she was to get to the archives, common sense suggested that Jake's itinerary worked better. 'The first two will take a couple of hours tops, but the search could take a while. Let's do it your way.'

* * *

'It's a houseboat, Jake.'

'Well observed.'

'Did you know?'

'Meg described it as a beautifully appointed bijou riverside residence. She omitted to mention that it was afloat. Maybe she thought it would put me off.'

'And are you? Put off?'

'I wanted river frontage and, you have to admit, it delivers. It has everything I need, in a great location. And the neighbours seem friendly.'

The neighbour who had the key was tall, well-endowed and wearing shorts that revealed every inch of the kind of tanned legs that stopped traffic. She lived cheek by jowl at the next mooring, and there had been ample time to admire her features as she had lingered, bending over rather more than was necessary to demonstrate the storage space on board.

'I'm sure you'd never want for a drop of milk for your morning coffee,' Abby agreed.

They were sitting in the garden of the Pike and Heron, a riverside pub famed for its food that was not a hundred metres along the towpath from the houseboat.

'I take it black,' he replied, without looking up from the menu.

Aware that she'd exposed a possessiveness that she had no right to be harbouring — she had nothing to offer Jake — she said, 'I thought you wanted a garden?'

'Laura has a roof garden. I'm sure she'd be keen to offer advice.'

Abby, aware that she was being teased, refused to rise to the bait.

'Or I could invite a garden designer I know to create one for me. Somewhere fragrant to sit on long summer evenings.' Jake glanced up. 'With a bit of luck, she'd stick around for a glass of wine while we watched the sunset from the deck.'

'Jake . . .'

'Bring the family. I'll buy a boat. I'll need one when Meg finds me the perfect riverside house with a garden for you to makeover. I'm having the steak,' he said, before she could object.

The sad fact was that she didn't want to object. She wanted those fragrant evenings and everything that went with it. She just didn't see how it could be possible.

'Have you made up your mind?' he asked.

'No . . . Can I ask you something?'

He looked up from the menu. 'Anything.'

'Have you ever tried to find your mother?'

His face went blank.

Not *that* anything . . .

'I'm sorry, it's none of my business,' she said, rapidly scanning the menu. 'I'll have the crab linguine.'

While Jake went to place their order at the bar, she drew in a long breath.

* * *

'It's not here.' Abby, having been through years of accounts, searching for the purchase record for the summerhouse, sat back, defeated.

'The family owned a construction company. It could have been done on the books,' Jake said.

'You're suggesting the company paid for it?'

'And put it through as some site expense. Or maybe a subcontractor did it as a favour.'

Abby thought of the new wall at the front of her house, the extension that had been built by one of Finch's subcontractors. Howard had said he'd paid for it, but she knew how the construction industry worked.

'I'll have to go back to the journals. I should probably have started there.'

'I don't think you should be on your own while you're doing that. Can I help?'

About to say that she'd wasted enough of his time for one day, Abby thought about the empty house, the hours of reading that should have been a pleasure, but which had turned into a horror story.

'Thanks,' she said. 'That would be very helpful.'

* * *

'I've got it.'

Jake, who had somehow ended up beside her on the sofa, leaned closer to show her the page he'd found.

A wonderful week in Cornwall with little Howard, putting all the horror behind us. How I'd love to have stayed there. I dreaded the thought of coming back to the Lodge, but of course George has his work and his eagerness to return became all the more understandable when I saw what he'd done.

While we've been away, he's had a summerhouse built in the little garden that he always referred to as my retreat. He'd noticed that it had become neglected and decided to have it cleared and put to rights while we were away.

He said that the summerhouse is somewhere for me to write and paint. A place to get away from the house and all the unhappiness.

He's such a dear man and because I've done what I can to protect him, he has no idea why I stopped going down to the part of the garden that used to be my special place. My refuge. I can't disappoint him but it's going to be very hard to spend time there.

'Oh, good grief,' Abby said. 'Poor Ruth. What a nightmare.'

'I'm not sure I sympathise with her. Instead of confronting the situation, she'd been covering up what had been going on for years.'

'Who would have believed her? That vile man would probably have had her locked up . . .' She stopped.

'What?'

'That's what happened to Margaret. Howard's grandmother. They said she'd had a breakdown, but I saw a letter she wrote begging Ruth to come home from Italy. She was frightened, Jake.'

And when Margaret was locked away, childless Ruth had Peter all to herself.

'Abby?'

She shook her head. 'Nothing.'

He didn't look convinced. 'It seems that George didn't know about the baby buried under the rose.'

'No. And if he had the summerhouse built for Ruth there can't be a body beneath it.'

'Are you sure?'

'Yes. He was a dear man. Kind. And he loved Ruth. He wouldn't have done that to her.'

'So he's not your monster?'

She shook her head. 'No. It was his older brother. Howard Senior. You saw his portrait in the hall.'

'Howard with whiskers?'

'Don't!' she said. 'God knows, Howard had his faults, but he wasn't anything like that predatory man.'

'No. I'm sorry.'

For a moment they could have heard a pin drop, then Abby broke the silence. 'What year is that journal?'

Jake checked the spine. 'Nineteen eighty-seven.'

'Of course. "*All the unhappiness . . .*" Sarah disappeared, Howard senior fell down the stairs and broke his neck and Peter shot himself that year.'

'None of that is mentioned.'

'I'm not surprised. She'd raised Peter. It must have been like losing her own child.' But she'd had Howard to take his place. History repeating itself . . . 'I imagine the journal was the last thing on her mind.'

'How closely did all those things happen?'

'I'm not sure.'

'You don't have the dates?'

'No, but there's a family tree. Maybe that will help.' They went across the hall to the office. 'No dates,' she said, 'just the year. I suppose that's normal for a family tree.'

'There must be death certificates.'

'Well, yes, obviously, but does it actually matter?'

'The devil is in the detail, Abs. In what order did it happen? When exactly did Sarah disappear?'

She thought for a moment, then shook her head. 'I don't know.'

'Someone must have that information. The lawyers?'

'They're coming down tomorrow morning for the will reading. Maybe they'll have some answers to Freddie's questions.'

'Let's hope so.' He glanced at his watch. 'It's late and you need to be sharp tomorrow. In the meantime, I'll find out when those two men died.'

'You think that if Howard Senior died before Sarah left, then she's probably still alive?'

'Not necessarily. If she was having an affair, Peter might have killed her and dumped her body in the river. It would explain why he shot himself.'

'No!' That was a scenario that had never occurred to her and, sickened, she took a step back. 'I didn't think there could be anything worse than I've already imagined.'

'But you already thought . . . Oh, shit.' He wrapped his arms around her and pulled her close, holding her tight. 'I'm sorry. You've been so tough, so determined to find the truth.'

With the pad of his thumb, he wiped away a tear that had seeped onto her cheek. She felt the touch of his breath as he kissed her forehead. Holding her, just as he had once before . . .

It would be so easy for the evening to end the same way, but she couldn't let that happen.

'Jake . . .'

He didn't hear the warning note, or chose not to, but he didn't resist when she pulled away.

'It's okay,' she said, rubbing her palms across her damp cheeks. 'I'm fine now.'

'Are you? Really? I don't want to leave you with nightmares.'

'There's not much you can do about that.'

'I could hold you . . . At least let me stay on the sofa.'

'And leave your car outside all night for my neighbours to see? Can you imagine the gossip? Go. I'll be okay.'

He didn't look convinced, but he didn't try and change her mind. 'Will I see you tomorrow when you're done with the lawyers?'

'Shouldn't you be running your company?'

'Even the boss is entitled to a few days off to move house. I'm counting on you to help me move in.'

'Don't . . .' He shouldn't count on her for anything. 'I'm sure your new neighbour will be delighted to help you make up the bed.'

'You could be right, but there's only one woman I want at my housewarming. Give me a call when you're done with the lawyers. We'll take it from there.'

He touched his hand to her cheek, and then she was watching his car slide silently out into the road and away towards the town.

She stood there for a while, wondering if she was an idiot, but then a security light in her neighbour's house came on as something moved in their garden. A cat, a fox . . . Unnerved by the dark shadows, the fact that the world and his wife knew she was alone, she stepped back inside and, having shut the door, bolted it.

She looked at the journal where Jake had left it on the arm of the sofa and, knowing that she wouldn't sleep, she picked it up and went back to find out what had happened before the holiday in Cornwall.

Ruth's mother had been taken ill that year. She'd been away for weeks and then the old lady had died, and George had joined her for the funeral. That had taken place on 22 February 1987.

The flowers and the service were all described in great detail. Then the will had been read, with everything left to Ruth, including the London house. There was clearly a lot that had to be done, but two days later, on 24 February, they had returned to Linton Lodge. But there was nothing about Sarah's disappearance. Nothing about the death of Howard Senior, or Peter. There was nothing until they had returned from Cornwall months later.

CHAPTER THIRTY

The following morning, Abby, wearing the grey dress she'd worn to Ruth's funeral, arrived at Freddie's office five minutes before nine thirty — the time set for the reading of Howard's will.

'I'm afraid we've got the full house,' he warned. 'Mark Livingstone and Suzanna Peacock from Hargreaves, Mitchell and Peacock. There's Daniel Winter, a lawyer from Finch Developments, and Sir James Hamilton is here with his lawyer, although he didn't get an invitation from me.'

'No, well, I was never in doubt which side Howard's lawyers would be on. Have they given you any information about Sarah? I was hoping they might know the exact date she left Linton Lodge.'

'Not yet, I'm afraid. Suzanna Peacock has informed me that they would have to bring up files from their storage facility before they could offer any answers to something that happened so long ago, and that would involve a cost.'

Abby nodded solemnly. Since she'd had doubts about her theory that Sarah was buried in the garden, she couldn't help but think about the other possibilities. She'd had nightmares about Sarah's weighted body lying at the bottom of the river, and even here, in Freddie's sun-filled office, a little shiver goosed her flesh.

'And, as yet,' he continued, 'I've no information as to the whereabouts of Catherine Mary Porter.'

'She's local, I'm sure of it, but as you said, probably married with a new name.'

'It does make tracing women that much more difficult, and we do need to talk about a budget. Searches like this are not cheap.'

'I understand.'

'I'm not sure you do, but this is not the time. Are you ready?'

She nodded and Freddie walked her into the conference room, introduced everyone present and then sat beside her while Suzanna Peacock read Howard's will.

It had been written, as she expected, just after George died. There were a number of bequests to local charities, but Howard had left her his majority shares in Finch Developments, no doubt in the hope that Tom would eventually join the company. She had also been left half of the remainder of his estate. The other half was to be divided and held in trust for his surviving children.

Abby frowned. 'Surviving children?'

'He was still a young man when he wrote this,' Suzanna explained. 'He was allowing for the possibility of further issue.'

'He was very fond of children,' Abby said, then looked at Sir James. 'Smart of him to make things so easy. Hopefully we can arrange a settlement for Izzy without getting the lawyers too heavily involved. How is she?'

'Much better, thank you, Mrs Finch. She has gone to the police station with her mother this morning. She was not in the best state of mind when she made her statement and fears she may have muddled some things.'

'I'm sure they'll understand.'

Susanna Peacock cleared her throat. 'I'm not sure what you were expecting, Mrs Finch, but the assets aren't as large as Howard anticipated when he wrote his will. His aunt had liquidated a large portion of her estate shortly before she died to buy a property in Maybridge, with instructions that a Miss Pamela Lewis was to live there for the remainder of her life.'

Abby sighed with relief. It explained why he was so angry with Pam. She knew he'd been relying on his aunt's legacy to help fund the apartment he'd need in London. With that money gone, the Linton ring was going to have to do that.

'You don't seem surprised, Mrs Finch.' Mark Livingstone, who had said nothing until now, gave her a thoughtful look. 'Howard was thoroughly shocked by the discovery, and his first thought was to try and retrieve the property.'

'Why did he change his mind?'

'His aunt left him a letter with her will. Once he'd read it, he asked if he could use our shredder.'

Abby nodded. That made sense too.

Howard had read Ruth's letter and destroyed it rather than risk anyone else seeing it. Ever. But it would have confirmed everything that Pam had told her and possibly a lot more.

It certainly explained why Howard had been so short-tempered at a time when everything he'd ever wanted appeared to be falling into his lap.

'Should Miss Lewis need care,' Suzanna continued, when she was sure that nothing more was going to be said, 'the property is to be used to provide financial assistance. At the end of her life, either the property or any financial residue will return to Howard's estate to be divided as laid out in his will.'

Abby had been wondering how on earth she could recompense Pam for what had been done to her but, much to her relief, Ruth had seen to it.

'Do you have any questions, Mrs Finch?'

'Are there any legal obstacles to selling Linton Lodge?'

'I imagine that it will have to be sold to apportion the legacies.'

'In that case I wonder if it would be possible, as part of my inheritance, for me to keep part of the garden? I'd like the walled kitchen garden for my business and the small garden that Ruth called her "retreat". It's where Howard died, and the baby's bones were found.'

'The estate will have to be valued for probate, but that portion can be valued separately at the same time if you wish.'

'Thank you.'

The meeting broke up. Daniel Winter offered his condolences and suggested a meeting when she felt able to spare the time, and then Sir James said, 'Could I have a word, Mrs Finch?' She waited. 'First, I want to apologise for the way my wife spoke to you when you called the other day.'

'She was worried about Izzy.'

'She was, but that does not excuse what she said to you.'

Abby remembered how she felt after that phone call and thought that Lady Hamilton should be the one apologising, but if Sir James wanted to proceed in a friendly manner, that suited her.

'Why don't we put it down to the stress of the moment and move on?' she suggested.

'That's gracious of you.'

Gracious. That was a first.

'There was something else?'

'I wanted to assure you that Izzy is not expecting a settlement from the estate for herself. Howard has provided for all his children equally in his will, which is fair, and my daughter not only owns her own home but is well provided for with a trust fund set up by her grandparents.'

'That's Izzy's decision. Maybe she should have a few days to think about it. When she feels up to it, she could give me a call so that we can meet to discuss the funeral arrangements.'

'I'll pass that on.'

'Mrs Finch . . .'

She turned to Suzanna Peacock. 'Ms Peacock. Thank you for coming to Maybridge.'

'Mr Jennings made an eloquent case. I understand that you asked him to make enquiries about the whereabouts of Sarah Finch.'

'I did.'

'I want to assure you that we're not being obstructive, but we can't help you. I have taken time to look at the files. I can confirm that we did our best to find Sarah after her husband died, which was the first we'd heard of her disappearance. She was, after all, Howard's next of kin. I have to say that the family were not helpful, and the private investigator we engaged could find no trace of her, or the supposed lover.'

'You don't know exactly when she disappeared?'

'I'm afraid not.'

'I understand. Thank you for making the effort.'

'We did advise that after the statutory seven years an application should be made to have her declared dead, but George and Ruth Finch would not hear of it.'

'Because it would all be dragged up again and people would ask questions about what had really happened to her.'

'I couldn't say.'

'But what about Peter's will? Did he make a new one before he . . . before he had his accident?'

'No, but he had nothing very much to leave. His father held the purse strings and under the terms of his will the estate went in its entirety to his surviving brother, George Finch.'

'Isn't that unusual?'

'Peter didn't survive him long enough to inherit. What little he did leave is held in our client account for Sarah. I'm sorry I don't have more information for you, Mrs Finch.'

She considered telling the woman what she'd discovered about Howard Senior, but she had made Pam a promise and it would have to be her decision.

'If you could let me have the details of the arrangements made by Ruth for the apartment. I don't think Miss Lewis quite understands the situation. I'd like to reassure her.'

'Of course. I'll send you copies of the paperwork.'

'Thank you. And thank you for being so frank, Ms Peacock.'

'We'll deal with the valuation of Linton Lodge for probate. Once that's granted, I'll be in touch about the area of garden that you'd like to keep so that we can amend the Land Registry documents.'

'Thank you.'

The room began to empty and Freddie re-joined her. 'Well, that went better than I could have hoped. Did you learn anything about Howard's mother?'

'Only that the family were uncooperative when the lawyers tried to find her. I think something terrible happened to her, Freddie. If Peter was involved and the family knew, or guessed, they would have done anything to protect him, and the family's reputation.'

'You can't know that, Abby.'

'I know that someone buried a baby and the mother disappeared.'

'I realise that this feels very personal to you, but perhaps, for your own peace of mind, you should let it go.'

'You're the second person to tell me that, Freddie, but I can't. Until I've done everything possible it will always be there. Unfinished business. Please keep looking for Sarah and for Catherine Mary Porter.'

CHAPTER THIRTY-ONE

There were voicemail messages from both Jake and Meg waiting for her when Abby left Freddie's office, but she needed some space.

She needed to speak to the children, to hear things that didn't involve past secrets and hideous suspicions. She sent them both a brief text, telling them that everything was okay, but that she was going for a walk and would call them later.

She took the riverside path that led out of town until she found a bench and sat there, watching toddlers feeding the ducks while she listened to Sophie chatter about what she'd found in a rock pool and Tom telling her about a boat trip to a small island, with Lucy chiming in to say that they'd seen dolphins.

Normal, happy things.

'How was it this morning?' Charlotte asked when they were done.

'Better than I could have hoped, to be honest. Apart from a few charitable bequests, Howard left half to me and half to be divided between his surviving children.'

'Surviving? Did he actually write that in a will?'

'It's lawyer language to cover all eventualities. It does mean that Izzy's baby is included, so that makes things easier.'

'She'll want some of yours.'

'Not according to her father. It seems that she's minted in her own right, but I want to hear it from her. If we can settle everything without lawyers making a meal of it, we'll all be better off, both emotionally and financially.'

'Well, that all sounds like good news. So, when are you coming to join us?'

'How are the children?' she asked, avoiding the question. 'Really?'

'Doing pretty well, all things considered. We've had a few tears, although Lucy is doing her best to hide them. And Tom has moments when he wants to be left alone. Sophie is full of beans one minute but then remembers and feels guilty for being happy. Grace knows how that feels from when her grandmother died, and she's being very supportive.'

'Like you were with me.'

'And like us, they'll be friends for life.'

'I can't thank you enough for this.'

'It's the least I can do, but what's keeping you there? Have the police made any progress? They can't think you're responsible for what happened to Howard.'

'I don't think so, but stuff has happened and there are people I need to speak to. I'll explain when I see you.'

'Abby, Howard may not have been the world's greatest husband, but you were together a long time. You need time to grieve. I know how you are, and I'm begging you not to take on the troubles of the world.'

'Three out of three . . .'

'What?'

'Nothing,' she said. 'I hear you.' It would be wonderful to walk away from this and forget about Pam and Sarah. Forget about Izzy and Natalie. Forget about Jake and the temptation of the houseboat. 'I'm getting a low-battery warning. I'll be with you as soon as I can,' she promised.

'Tomorrow.'

'Maybe the day after.'

She had intended to walk along the river, but she'd driven into town and, having picked up her car, she drove up to the Lodge. Everyone was urging her to put the past behind her, to move on, and this was where she hoped to start a new future.

She drove in through the kitchen garden lane, mentally making a note to ensure that access was included when the land was transferred to her.

The retreat she would leave to nature, undisturbed, just as Ruth had wanted it. She'd plant the replacement rose and then leave it as a sanctuary dedicated to those lost and found.

The kitchen garden was different. It was going to be a fresh start for her. A chance to pick up the career she abandoned to look after her mother. To raise her children. A chance to resurrect the dream that one day she might win a gold medal for one of the small gardens at Chelsea.

She spent a while taking photographs and making sketches in the notebook she always carried with her. Checking the peach trees for damage where Cal had climbed over the wall. Planning, in her mind's eye, the raised beds she'd need. The restoration of the glass house built against the south wall. Choosing the storeroom that she'd convert into an office and design studio.

Imagining it all freshly painted in the Earthly Designs green with the name in gold.

Spirits revived a little, she headed down to the river, planning to walk along the towpath towards Longbourne, and found herself confronted with the past in the shape of the old boathouse.

It must have been quite a sight in its day. Upstairs there had been a balcony and she could imagine the family sitting there, drinking cocktails as they watched the sun slip down. A place for family and friends to relax after a day on the river.

The door was open, presumably shut carelessly by the police search team.

Sunlight filtered through the rotting gates that opened onto the river, lighting the still, scummy water of the wet dock. In an instant all the pleasure went out of her day as she stared at it, wondering if Sarah's decaying body, wrapped in a blanket, a silver cross in her hand and weighted down in an old tin trunk, was down there. A macabre echo of the baby she'd found.

Lost in dark thoughts she jumped as she heard a sound from the floor above.

A squirrel, or maybe a nesting bird . . .

There were drifts of feathers on the floor and caught in cobwebs. Birds had roosted here, and the place stank of damp and mice. Or maybe it was rats.

The sound came again. Too heavy for something the size of a rat. It sounded more like someone shifting a little for comfort, although with the roof partly collapsed, comfort would be in short supply.

The stairs, open treads that would have once gleamed with care, were now cracked and rotten in places where the rain had come in.

The dust that had gathered over years had been recently disturbed. Someone had evidently risked walking up them.

She looked up. 'Hello? Is there anyone there?'

Silence.

'It's okay, I'm not the police, but it really isn't safe up there.'

Nothing.

She looked again at the stairs. Someone had made it up them. A poor homeless soul sleeping rough? A drunk who'd wandered in and might fall? A kid, hiding out . . .

Concerned, she began to ease herself up the stairs, testing the treads as she went, staying close to the wall where they seemed firmer.

'Stay away, Abby Finch!'

She froze. Not a drunk or a homeless kid . . .

'Don't come up here if you know what's good for you!'

'Natalie?'

'You've got it in one, now bugger off and leave me alone.'

'I can't do that.'

'Then stay and we can both weep for what we've lost.'

'I understand what you're going through, but please, come down,' Abby begged. 'Come home with me, and whatever's happened, we can sort it out.'

'*Sort it out*,' she repeated in a whiney voice that was supposed to be Abby. 'Get lost, you patronising cow.'

Abby let out a long slow breath. Okaaaay . . . Maybe that hadn't been her best idea.

'If you don't want to come home with me, at least let me take you to your sister.'

'The police are there. I saw them coming for me.'

She'd seen them coming and legged it out of the back door and over the fence? That wasn't good.

'They weren't coming for you, Natalie,' she said, fingers mentally crossed. 'They just want to ask if you saw anything on Saturday morning,' she said. 'You were there, weren't you?'

No answer.

The stair creaked ominously as she took another step.

'Come one step nearer and I'll jump, and then you'll have both me and Howard on your conscience.'

'I didn't kill Howard,' Abby said, her voice a lot steadier than her racketing heartrate.

'You hung onto him when I'd have loved him . . . I'm warning you!'

'If you jump,' Abby pointed out, 'you'll just fall in the river.'

'That's okay,' she said, but her voice was shaking now. 'I can't swim.'

'Then I'd have to jump in and rescue you. Think how much you'd hate that.'

'Do that,' she urged. 'I'll take you down with me and die happy. I'm going to jump right now . . .'

'Don't!' It was clear that Natalie was seriously disturbed, and this wasn't a situation she was equipped to deal with. 'You win. I'm going,' she said, as she eased her phone out of her bag.

'Don't you get it, Abby? No one wins. Not me, not Izzy Hamilton and everyone knows that you lost years ago . . .'

'No . . .' The word was out of her mouth before she could stop it.

Natalie laughed and Abby wanted to scream at her that it hadn't been like that. They'd been a family.

'You're pathetic, Abby. Clinging on like ivy . . .'

She took a breath, reminding herself that Natalie needed help, but as she hesitated over who best to call, her phone beeped a warning and the screen went black.

'Don't bother calling anyone,' Natalie called. 'I'll be dead before they come.'

'No rush,' she said. 'My phone is out of battery.'

Aware that Natalie had called her sister after taking pills, Abby doubted that she'd jump unless provoked. And, right now, she was the provocation.

'I'm going to get it charged—'

'You're going to leave me?'

That sounded more like panic . . .

'Half an hour,' she said. 'Are you hungry? Can I bring you a sandwich? Tea?'

'Fuck off.'

'On my way . . .' She backed carefully down the stairs, made sure to bang the door as she left, and then began to run along the towpath hoping to find someone with a phone.

Normally, on a sunny afternoon there would be dozens of people about, but today it was deserted, and in desperation she began to wave and shout at a passing boat.

'Have you got a phone? It's an emergency!'

The man at the helm eased into the bank. 'What's up?'

'It's too complicated . . .'

She didn't have Dee's number so had to dial the emergency services. 'Police . . . I need to speak to speak to Dee Newcombe in Maybridge . . .' The delay seemed endless but eventually she was put through to Maybridge Police Station. 'Is Dee Newcombe there? Or DI Glover? It's an emergency.' She was asked to wait and then Dee was there, asking her what had happened.

'It's Natalie. She's in the boathouse at the Lodge, threatening to jump. She's upstairs and it isn't safe.'

'Where are you?'

'On the towpath. I had to borrow a phone.'

'Okay. I've got this . . . Go home, Abby. I'll call you when I know what's happened. I mean it. I don't want you there.'

'I know . . .' Her presence wasn't going to help.

She handed the phone back. 'Thank you so much.'

'That sounds like quite a drama.'

'Let's hope not.'

'Can I offer you a lift?' he asked.

She looked at him for the first time. Around forty, rather good looking and definitely hitting on her.

Until now she'd ignored the warnings about going into the woods at midnight, into spooky ruined buildings, even going upstairs when she heard a noise, but getting into a boat with a man she didn't know, even when he'd loaned her his phone, felt like a risk too far.

'Thanks, but I have to pick up my car. I would be grateful if you could hang around in front of the ruined boathouse about five hundred yards downstream. Just in case the woman in there decides to jump.'

'I will if you come with me.'

'Not a good idea. If she sees me, she'll try and pull me in with her.'

'Really? What did you do? Run off with her husband?'

'Actually, she did her best to run off with mine.' But someone else had beat her to it and that might have driven her to kill him. Better not mention that . . . 'The emergency services are on their way.'

'It was worth a try,' he said, grinning. Then, with a wave, he headed downriver in the direction of the boathouse.

She watched him go, knowing that Dee was right, that she could do nothing here. Knowing that nothing could make her move until she knew that Natalie was safe.

CHAPTER THIRTY-TWO

Abby paced a hundred metres one way and then back, waiting, listening. She doubted they'd approach with blues and twos blaring, they'd come in quietly, but Natalie would be watching for them.

She stopped.

Natalie wouldn't be watching. She wouldn't have waited for the police to arrive. As soon as she was sure she was alone, she'd have been down the stairs and out of there.

She ran back, but too late.

'She's not here,' Dee said.

'Dammit, I should have stayed, but my phone died. She saw you coming at her sister's and thought you were going to arrest her.'

'Any thoughts on where she might go now?'

'I've no idea. I didn't see her car.'

'We took it in for forensic testing.'

'Oh . . . She really is a suspect?'

'She was there. At the moment that's all we have. She was there and she's running.'

'She's seriously disturbed, Dee. She was threatening to jump and take me with her.'

'Then I'm very glad you didn't stay. Do you want a lift home?'

'No, thanks. My car's at the house.'

'Where? I didn't see it.'

'I came in by the lane. It's by the kitchen garden.'

'That's the way we came in and if you came in that old Volvo estate, it isn't there now. Did you, by any chance, leave the keys in it?'

'No. I was planning a walk and they're in my pocket . . . Oh.'

'Oh?'

'Tom once managed to lock it with the keys inside. There's an emergency spare taped under the wheel arch.'

'Would Natalie have known about that?'

'She was in the office when I went to borrow Howard's key. He suggested I get a spare cut to hide somewhere on the car. She was the one who suggested the wheel arch was the safest place. To be honest, I'd forgotten it was there.'

'Well, we don't know where she's gone, but we do know how. Remind me of the reg and I'll put out a traffic alert for your car. Do you want that lift now?'

'No, thanks. I've given the neighbours enough entertainment without arriving home in a police car and I was planning on a walk.'

'Do try and stay out of trouble.'

'Yes, ma'am.'

'I'm not a DI yet.'

'But you will be.'

Dee shook her head but was grinning as she walked away.

The river had lost its charm and Abby, unwilling to run into her good Samaritan, walked back up through the garden and took the woodland path home.

She paused to take a look at the retreat garden, wondering what she could do to make it more meaningful. A plaque? A sundial, maybe? A statue of some sort?

The huge bare patch where the summerhouse had once stood was shocking. She walked across to see where the ground was cracked and had subsided. She bent and picked up a lump of dry earth, crumbling it between her fingers. Clay . . . Great for roses, bad for foundations . . .

As she stood up and turned, she saw that there were fresh flowers lying in the baby's grave.

Not more white rosebuds.

These were bright red, the petals like splashes of blood. The sight sickened her. She wanted to grab them and fling them away.

Was that how Howard had felt when he saw those rosebuds? When he'd read the card? Knowing what had been done, knowing what it had cost him. Wanting to get them out of sight before anyone else saw them.

The mother must have been there that morning when they were all in the garden. Between the time she'd been there after sorting out Cal, and Howard's arrival.

Was that who she'd heard in the woods?

She took a step back, turned and fetched a spade from the tool store in the kitchen garden and began to shovel the pile of earth back into the hole.

Covering the faded white rosebuds and the sad little card.

Covering the blood-coloured roses left by poor, deluded, Natalie.

When she'd finished, she cleaned the spade and returned it to the clip on the wall, washed her hands and then walked home, thinking about the two lots of roses.

The dozen white buds were exactly like the ones she'd bought for Pam from the corner shop. They were sold everywhere. Supermarkets, garage forecourts . . .

The red roses on the other hand, were Trumpeter. Not the long-stemmed kind you'd buy from a florist, but a repeat-flowering floribunda and with the short, untidy stems that suggested they'd been cut from a garden.

She'd put half a dozen in a small bed in her own front garden a few years earlier as part of the neighbourhood decorations for the Queen's diamond jubilee, underplanting them with blue and white violas that she'd later replaced with the violet-purple flower spikes of nepeta.

She stopped, struck by a sudden horrible thought.

'No . . .'

Natalie . . . She couldn't have. Someone would have seen her.

Or maybe not. Her cottage was in the narrow lane that had once led to the Old Mill. Restored and now working again, with a shop and a café, it had needed better access from the main road. Mill Lane had become a very quiet cul-de-sac.

The only people who drove down it now were residents, visitors or delivery vans. And, of course, Natalie, who had never missed an excuse to show up with papers Howard needed for a meeting the next day, or a signature that couldn't wait if he was going to be out of the office.

Any excuse to demonstrate her own immaculate appearance in contrast to the harried mother dealing with three young children at teatime.

She would have seen the red roses flourishing in her front garden many times. Had she thought that they were a suitable tribute for Howard?

Despite the fact she was expecting it, it was still a shock when Abby saw that the nepeta had been trampled and her perfect little rose bushes, just coming into full bloom, had been mercilessly hacked.

She didn't move for a moment, just looking at the scattered mess of petals and leaves, grateful that the children weren't here. That Lucy hadn't been here on her own.

She took a deep breath.

Unlike poor Howard, the garden would recover. With a little care it would all be back up and blooming again in a few weeks, but seeing the destruction drove any doubt from her mind that it had been Natalie, out of control, who had found him in the garden and lashed out . . .

'Abby!'

She looked around as June, one of her neighbours hailed her from across the lane.

'I'm so sorry about your roses. I was watering my pots when I saw that woman walk in, bold as you like and start hacking at them.'

'Cal wasn't there?'

'Is that the young man working on the motorbike? He got a phone call and went out just before she arrived. Is he staying with you?'

'No. He's Molly's great-nephew. He's staying with her for a while. She thought he'd be bored so I've given him a job.'

'Is Molly all right? I thought, when I saw her on Sunday, that she wasn't quite herself. She didn't seem to remember who I was. Kept calling me Penny.'

'She's upset about Howard.'

June nodded. 'Yes, of course. Such a shock. I know he wasn't . . . Well, you know, but it was a terrible thing to happen and then that woman walking into your garden, bold as brass, and hacking at your roses.'

'She had a knife?'

'Not a gardening knife. It was a big old kitchen knife. Sheer vandalism. I shouted at her and I would have gone over there, but Beattie stopped me.'

'Beattie was right, June. Your safety is much more important. Can you remember what time this happened?'

'I saw you go out when I fetched the milk in. That would be about quarter past nine. Then we had breakfast. After that I thought the pots could do with a water and brought the hose round. Your lad went off about then. Just after eleven?'

Abby nodded. That would have given Natalie time to leave the flowers in the garden and then go down to the boathouse.

'You went off in your car,' June said, 'but you walked back. Have you had a breakdown?'

'Not exactly. Someone borrowed it.'

'Borrowed?'

'I'll get it back.' Whether it would be in one piece was another matter.

June didn't look convinced. 'They shouldn't have taken that policeman away.'

'I'm sure he has a lot more important things to do.'

'You take care,' June called after her as she crossed back to her own side of the lane.

The bike was propped up in front of the garage, her toolbox beside it, a spanner dropped on the path. She would be having words with Cal, she thought, as she headed for her side gate.

As she opened it, she saw a scatter of rose petals on the path and caught her breath. Had Natalie wreaked her revenge in the back garden too? But nothing had been disturbed.

Natalie had been on foot and used the garden as a short cut through to the woods. Even so, her legs were a little shaky as she let herself in through the mudroom.

It was lunchtime but she wasn't hungry and, having changed into the comfort of soft old jeans and a T-shirt, she went through to the office and looked at the photograph of Sarah with the infant Howard.

What had happened to that lovely young woman with all her life ahead of her? How different would Howard have been if he'd been brought up by two loving parents . . .

She didn't believe for a moment that Sarah would have abandoned her baby and she didn't believe in the lover. But what did she believe? What was true?

She reached for a notebook.

24.02.1987 Ruth's mother's funeral

26.02.1987 Ruth and George return to Linton Lodge

She needed the dates when Howard Senior and Peter died. She called Jake.

'Abby. I've been thinking about you. How did it go this morning?'

'The will was pretty much as expected. Half to me, half to be divided between his surviving children.'

'Surviving . . . That simplifies things.'

'Yes. And according to her father, Izzy doesn't want anything for herself.'

'Get it in writing,' he advised.

'I'll leave that to Freddie. Right now I'm trying to figure out a timeline for what happened in 1987. Have you managed to find those dates for me?'

He sighed. 'If I tell you, will you come and rescue me? Laura came over to invite me to a welcome supper. I had to tell her, regretfully, that I had made other plans for the evening. We did have other plans, didn't we?'

'Jake, I'm sorry, but while the will reading went without incident, the rest of the day hasn't been that hot.'

She briefly told him about her run in with Natalie.

'If she's on the loose with a knife, you shouldn't be on your own. I'll pick you up, I'll cook, I'll ply you with wine to make the world feel like a better place and, since neither of us will then be in a fit state to drive, I'll make up the spare bed.' That came out as a question, but the thought of an evening alone in the house with a crazed Natalie at large was not exactly enthralling.

'Make up the spare bed and I'll save you from Laura,' she promised. 'If you're sure that's what you want?'

He hesitated. 'What I want is a conversation for another day, but here's what I found out. Howard James Finch, born the second of January 1919, died the twenty-sixth of February 1983—'

'What? No . . .'

'I have a copy of his death certificate in my hand.'

'But that was the day that Ruth and George came back from London.'

'And the day he died from injuries sustained in a fall.'

'So, were they there when it happened? Or did they come home and find him? And had Sarah already left?'

'I'm afraid the death certificate doesn't give those details.'

'No . . . Someone should have a word with the registrar about that. What about Peter?'

'He died of gunshot wounds on the fourth of March 1983.'

'Just six days after his father. I thought there was a bigger gap between their deaths. I'm surprised the newspaper didn't make more of it.'

'Maybe they didn't check the dates. Or they might just have been cautious. The verdict was accidental death, and I don't imagine Howard would have taken kindly to them implying anything else.'

'No. They concentrated more on Sarah and Peter.'

'The implication was that Sarah left before either of them died, but what if she didn't?' Abby suggested. 'I've been back through the journal. There's nothing in there about her leaving, with or without her lover. There was the entry about them returning home on the twenty-sixth, but it stops there. There's nothing after that until their return from the holiday in Cornwall.'

Jake said nothing.

'Something happened on the day that Ruth and George returned.'

'Abby . . .'

'Did he kill her, Jake? Did he kill her and then Peter found them and threw his father down the stairs and then, because George and Ruth wanted it all hushed up, he shot himself?'

CHAPTER THIRTY-THREE

'That's a bit of a leap, Abby.'

'Is it? Really?'

'Unless a body turns up, we'll never know. And actually, Abs, I wonder if it's better that we don't.'

'Better?' she demanded. 'What about justice for Sarah? For Peter?'

'I understand your passion, but think of your kids. If you drag all this out into the open, the story will haunt them for the rest of their lives.'

'And if I bury this, I'll be like Ruth. She hid the truth, protecting her family at the expense of those girls.'

'You said yourself that no one would have believed her, Abby.'

'Not then,' she admitted, 'but she kept on covering it up to protect Howard and his political ambitions. That's why he didn't give Izzy the Linford ring. When Ruth found out what had happened to Pam she not only took her in, but used her money to buy her the flat she lives in now.'

'Do you know that or is just conjecture?'

'I know it. Pam told me about being made to swear on Ruth's cross and, when she was dying, she gave it to her to wear, Jake. A permanent reminder.'

'That's . . .'

'Yes, it is. The business with the flat came out at the will reading. Ruth's estate came up nearly a million short, but she'd left Howard a letter which he put through the shredder before he left the lawyer's office.'

'A million?'

'The price of a flat in Spencer Court, furnishing it, providing funds for the management costs for who knows how long.'

'That must have come as a shock.'

'Not just financially — he was planning to use the money to buy a place in London — but emotionally. It goes a long way to explain why he'd been in such a foul mood these last few weeks. Why he'd been so damned mean.'

'Ruth Finch sounds like a formidable woman.'

'I can't begin to imagine how frustrating it must have been for certain women of that generation. Marriage put a stop to whatever ambitions they may have had. They were expected to stay home, take care of their husband and have babies.'

And if there were no babies . . .

She shivered.

'I wonder if she took care of any other women,' she said. 'The baby's mother . . . I might be able to find traces of that in her financial records.'

'Leave it, Abby. If you must play detective, concentrate on Howard. Justice for him and for your children.'

'I think that's a wrap. Natalie was in the garden around the time that Howard was killed, she evaded the police at her sister's and this morning she stole my car. The police are hunting for her now.'

'Then leave it to them. I'll pick you up at six thirty and tomorrow you should go and join your children for what's left of half term.'

He was right, she realised. There was nothing more she could do here.

She'd just put the phone down when it rang again and she snatched it up, hoping for news of Natalie.

'Abby . . . ?'

Not Dee. It was Izzy Hamilton, sounding uncharacteristically uncertain.

'Izzy . . . How are you?'

'I don't know. I still can't believe . . .' She took a breath and gathered herself, more the political powerhouse she would have been for Howard. 'How are your children?'

'Sad, angry . . . Everything you'd expect. They're with my cousin and her children on the coast.'

'It must be a relief to get them away from all of this.'

'It's a reprieve. It's school next week, which will be difficult, and I don't imagine the newspapers are done with us. They'll be all over the funeral.'

'That's why I'm calling you. Daddy said you wanted to talk to me about that.'

'And the will, Izzy, but there's no rush. When you feel up to it.'

'Could we talk now? I'm anxious to get it settled and I think we need to present a united front.'

Definitely brought up to be a politician's wife, Abby thought, but she'd gone to university, had a law degree. This was the twenty-first century, for heaven's sake. With her brains and background, she should have been encouraged to have bigger ambitions than hosting tea parties. Instead of marrying the potential candidate, she should be thinking about standing for parliament herself.

'Are you free now?' Izzy asked.

Abby could have done without it after today, but if she was going to join the children, they had better get it over with.

'I am,' Abby said. 'Where shall we do this? Yours or mine? Or would you prefer neutral ground?'

'Nowhere public, and I'm staying with my parents so, if you don't mind, I'd prefer to come to you.'

For that, read: *Mummy wouldn't have you in the house.*

'Not a problem.'

'Thank you. I'll be about twenty minutes.'

Abby looked at the phone. That was a very different Izzy from the one on Saturday morning. Subdued. Polite . . .

She should probably be on her guard.

It was a fraction more than twenty minutes later when Abby heard a car pull onto the drive.

She went to the front door and found Izzy still sitting in the driver's seat, hands tensed on the wheel. The silk scarf and the sunglasses were still the same, but she was paler and the sex appeal was dialled down. But then there were no men around.

She gave herself a mental slap and forced a smile.

'Come on in,' she called. 'I don't bite.'

'No,' Izzy said, releasing her grip and climbing from the car with a lot less bounce than on Saturday morning. 'That would be me.'

'It's the hormones,' she said, then took a closer look. 'How are you?'

'Don't be kind, Abby . . .' She turned away to wipe the dampness from her cheek with her fingers. 'What happened to your roses?'

'Someone making a statement.'

'They stole them?' she asked, shocked. 'Is that what the spanner's for? In case they come back for more?'

'No, that's just a careless boy,' she said as she bent to pick it up. 'Come in, Izzy. Can I get you anything?'

'I don't want to put you to any trouble.'

'Well, I've had a very mixed day so far and need a cup of strong tea, but I'm happy to make you whatever you'd like. Fresh mint? Earl Grey? Coffee?'

'Not coffee. Earl Grey would be lovely.'

'Not a problem. Come on through,' she said, leading the way through to the kitchen.

'Kitchen company?' Izzy asked.

'We could do the best china in the sitting room if you prefer,' she said, putting the spanner on the island, 'but I thought we'd be more relaxed in here.'

'No, please. I'm honoured. Kitchens are for friends. I know that's not possible after the way I spoke to you on

Saturday . . . To be honest, I was quite shocked when Daddy said you wanted to talk to me.'

'I quite shocked myself when I suggested it,' Abby said, putting on the kettle and taking down a couple of mugs. 'But we've both sustained a loss and there's nothing to be gained from being at daggers drawn.'

'No,' she said, about to ease herself onto one of the breakfast bar stools.

'You'll be more comfortable sitting at the table. Or on the sofa, although it's rather low.'

'I seem to have doubled in size overnight so I'll give the sofa a miss,' she said, pulling out a chair.

'Your father mentioned that you were going to the police station to make a new statement?'

'Yes . . . When the lawyers suggested I make a written statement I panicked and told them I hadn't seen Howard.'

'But you had. Tom saw you.'

'They already knew? They must think I killed him, and I was angry enough. About you being there and being right about the garden. About him lying about the house and the ring.'

'I shouldn't have told you that.'

'I would have, in your place.' She shook her head. 'Paris was lovely, he did everything to make it perfect, but I knew something was wrong and when I found him, I told him to sort himself out.'

'"Cut the apron strings" is what I heard.'

'Oh. Well, yes. And then I felt a bit dizzy so I walked away and found a seat. I knew I'd gone over the top and, once I'd got my breath back, I was going to find him and talk to him, but he was with that wretched woman from the office.'

'Natalie?'

'She was so passive aggressive. Completely out of order. I don't know how you stood her all those years. Howard had promised he'd get rid of her.'

'She was made redundant while you were away. I imagine that's why she was there. To have it out with him. Where did you see them?'

'By the walled garden. She was yelling and crying, and Howard had his arms around her, trying to calm her down. I should have realised, but it felt like another betrayal.'

'Did you speak to them?'

'No. They didn't see me and by then I was so upset that I walked down to the gate at the bottom of the garden and called a friend to pick me up. I didn't kill him, Abby.'

'I never thought you had.'

'I'm afraid I wasn't that generous about you.'

'No, well, I was the one with the all the motives, but fortunately the police don't seem to think it was me.'

'Thank goodness for that.' She looked around. 'This open plan is lovely. You cook, eat and you even have a sofa where you can sit and relax and almost feel as if you're in the garden.'

'The extension was built five years ago when it became obvious that we needed more room,' she said, opening the bi-fold doors to let in the scent of the lilac her mother had planted when she was born. 'And Howard had this dining table made from planks of an old oak that had to be felled at the Lodge. We've converted the old dining room into a room for the children. Somewhere for them to be with their friends, play games, watch television . . .'

'Get away from the adults?'

'And for the adults to get away from the children,' she replied, wryly.

She made tea while Izzy settled herself and took out a notebook and pen. She'd come prepared for business.

'Can I say right now that I am genuinely sorry that you won't have the life you planned with Howard,' Abby said, putting the cake that Molly had brought on a plate. 'For both him and you.'

'That's generous of you . . . *OMG*, cake. I'm starving.'

'That's good news. I've got an awful lot of cake to get through.' She crossed to the dresser for her mother's antique cake forks, hoping to find some napkins without "Happy Birthday" or balloons on them.

'I imagine your neighbours baked for you.'

'They did. The freezer is full of cakes and casseroles.'

'And they brought you flowers and cards,' she said. 'That's quite a stack you have on the dresser.'

'That's just today's,' she said. 'I haven't had a chance to open them yet.' Abby frowned. Could that have been where she'd seen the handwriting? Not on these, but on the envelopes that were now in the recycling bag . . .

'Are you okay, Abby?'

She realised that Izzy was watching her. 'Yes, sorry, I'm trying to find some napkins that aren't totally embarrassing, but I'm afraid it's either birthday balloons or Easter bunnies.'

'Go with the bunnies.'

'Good choice.' The handwriting check could wait until she was on her own and was able to compare it against the photograph on her phone. 'I'm sure you were sent flowers,' she said as she joined Izzy.

'Loads,' she admitted. 'I was quite gagging on the scent of lilies. But no one brought cake.'

'I don't suppose anyone imagined you ate it.'

And, she thought, *they had a cook who would undoubtedly have taken exception to donations of anything less than Fortnum hampers.*

'You're right. I must have been in nursery the last time I had a slice of cherry cake.'

Taking the hint, Abby cut a couple of slices and handed Izzy a plate. 'This is from Aunt Molly and it's probably the best cherry cake you'll ever eat. But on the subject of nursery, the children were wondering if they'd ever have a chance to get to know their new baby brother or sister.'

'Sister. It's a girl.'

'I'll bet Howard was thrilled.'

'Yes. I thought he'd want a boy, but when we had the scan he was delighted.'

Abby remembered those moments, the joy . . . 'He was a good father, Izzy.'

'I know. It was so hard for him to leave your children. He kept putting it off, which is why I forced the issue and, to be honest, I was beginning to wonder if he regretted it. He's been so off lately that I was afraid he was going to come back to you.'

'No, Izzy. The marriage had staggered on because neither of us had a good reason to end it. The baby sorted that and, to be honest, once I was over the shock, it was a relief.' She fished out the teabags and handed Izzy a mug and the milk. 'His bad mood had nothing to do with us. It was to do with whatever was in a letter his aunt left him.'

'Daddy mentioned it. Was it something about his mother, do you think?'

'Maybe . . .' What had Ruth known about her disappearance? She shook her head. 'We'll never know.' Changing the subject, she said, 'I do realise that your little girl will have a very different life from my children, and I don't suppose your mother will approve, but she'll be their sister and they do want to know her.'

'My mother is totally in the doghouse for the way she spoke to you. I've never seen my father so angry. He was going to apologise . . . ?'

'He did and so have you. Maybe, if she came and apologised in person, we could all move on.'

'I'll suggest it.'

'I won't hold my breath.'

'Oh, there's bitchy Abby!' she cried. 'It's so good to meet you.'

They both laughed and, just like that, any tension was gone.

'Daddy said he told you that I didn't expect any of Howard's money for myself.'

'He did, but I wanted to hear it from you. To be sure that you've really thought about it.'

'That's why I wanted to see you. I didn't want you worrying, but apparently the house will have to be sold. Do you mind?'

Abby shook her head. 'I dreaded the thought of living there, but I did always hope that one day I would have the kitchen garden for Earthly Designs. And I'd like to have Ruth's retreat garden where the baby was buried and Howard died.'

'Daddy said, but why?'

'Both George and Howard wanted to restore it to the way it was when Ruth first created it. After she buried the baby . . .'

'*She* buried the baby?'

'It has to have been her. It was why she left it to grow wild. To hide its secrets.'

'But what will you do with it?'

'Let it return to nature. Become a hidden sanctuary in their memory.'

Izzy nodded. 'I'd like that. If I can do anything to help . . . Maybe a stone of some sort? Something simple with Howard's name and dates?'

'Yes, of course. I'm going to ask a stonemason I know to do something for the baby. We have no name or date, but I thought a line from a poem . . .'

'Do you know any more about that?'

'No, but there were flowers left with a card that said, "With love from Mummy".'

'Oh, Abby! That's tragic.'

Izzy's hand went automatically to cradle the infant she was carrying and Abby reached for the other. 'Don't dwell on it.'

'No . . .' Then she laughed. 'Damn it, Abby, look at us both being so nice. My friends wouldn't recognise me.' She shook her head. 'You must have thought I was a total bitch.'

'True, but there have been moments when I could have matched you and then some in the last few weeks.'

About to say something, the sound of the side gate opening caught her attention. 'There's someone in your garden.'

'It'll be Cal. The lad who works for me. He's been doing up his motorbike.' She frowned. 'He apparently had a phone call and left everything, including that spanner. I do hope Molly's okay,' she said, sliding from the stool and going to the open doors. 'Cal?'

There was no reply and she went outside. 'Cal? Are you okay?'

She caught a flicker of movement out of the corner of her eye and half turned but, before she could register who it was or what was happening, something slammed into her jaw.

She tried to speak but had no breath and somehow, without quite knowing how she got there, she was on her hands and knees, her face inches from the stone paving.

'Abby?'

She heard Izzy call her name from what felt like the bottom of the ocean, the scrape of the chair as she pushed it back, coming to see what had happened.

'No . . .' The word was in her head, but no sound emerged. She tried again. 'Run . . .' Her mouth formed the word, but the punch was followed up by a kick to her ribs and the only sound was a groan.

'Stay there.' *Natalie.* 'I'll see to you later. First, I'm going to deal with the bitch who stole him from me.'

'Izzy!' She managed to roll away before another kick caught her and she made a grab for her ankle. 'Run!'

Natalie kicked out again, breaking free, and by the time Abby hauled herself to her knees, she'd found the spanner.

CHAPTER THIRTY-FOUR

'No! Please . . .' Abby could hear the terror in Izzy's voice. 'Don't hurt my baby!'

She forced herself to her feet, swaying for a moment as the world spun, and stumbled back into the kitchen to find Izzy trapped against the kitchen island. Abby grabbed the tea tray, sending mugs and cake flying as she swung it at Natalie.

It was plastic and had no weight, but growling with fury at the interruption, Natalie turned on her, spanner raised — giving Izzy a chance to slide away and make a run for it.

'I told you to wait!'

Abby ducked as Natalie swung the spanner at her head. 'Get out of here, Izzy!'

Realising that her quarry was about to escape, Natalie turned between them, the spanner raised, for a moment torn between shutting Abby up and getting at Izzy, who — frozen in fear — hadn't moved.

'Run!' she yelled, swinging the tray again, hoping that Natalie would come for her but, her mind finally made up, she went for Izzy.

'You! This is your fault. You stole him from me and now he's dead!'

She was clearly beyond reason and, dropping the tray, Abby threw herself at Natalie, sending them both crashing to the floor.

She had her arms around her and hung on as Natalie struggled, lashing out with the spanner, out of her mind with rage.

Abby was strong, but she hadn't had time to fill her lungs and, dizzy from the blow to her head, she could feel her strength ebbing away. She wasn't going to be able to hang on for much longer.

'Izzy . . .'

This time it was a plea for help and finally, out of the blue, she saw the flat bottom of a heavy pan swinging through the air and heard the sickening thud as it connected with Natalie's skull.

She made no sound, just collapsed on her, and, pinned to the ground by her weight, Abby lay there for a moment, eyes closed, trying to gather her breath.

'Abby? Are you all right?'

She thought her hearing had been affected by the blow, but when she opened her eyes it wasn't Izzy holding the pan. It was Molly.

'Have I killed her?' she asked.

'I don't know.' She eased herself out from beneath the unconscious woman. 'But someone should call an ambulance.'

'Let that silly cow do it,' Molly said. 'Standing there, doing nothing while you were being killed.'

'Don't, Molly. She was terrified.' She lifted a hand. 'Izzy? Are you okay?'

'N-no . . .' she said. 'My waters just broke . . .'

'What?' She winced as she sat up. 'I thought you had another couple of months to go . . .' Except, of course, if she'd been pregnant for rather longer than Howard had been prepared to admit.

'I'm not due for another couple of weeks but I've been having pains all day. I thought it was just Braxton Hicks.'

'Ambulance, police . . . Oh, good timing,' she said, as Dee appeared from the garden with a uniformed officer.

'We had a call from your neighbour, but I see you've dealt with it.' She turned to the constable. 'Call for an ambulance,' she said, before bending down beside Natalie to check her pulse. 'She's alive, thank goodness. Are you all right, Abby?'

'Nothing to worry about but make that two ambulances. We have a baby on the way.'

'A police car will be quicker.'

'Whatever you say, but will someone call Lady Hamilton?'

'No. Please,' Izzy said. 'She'll make such a drama. Howard was going to be with me.'

'Is there a friend we can call?'

'I don't suppose —' she caught her breath, swore in a decidedly unladylike manner — 'Abby!'

'Okay,' she said, grabbing the hand that Dee offered and making it to her feet. 'I'm not Howard, but I've been there on three occasions when he's done this, so I guess I'm the next best thing.'

'Abby,' Dee warned, 'you need to see a doctor.'

'I'll see one at the hospital. Can I leave you to deal with all this?' she asked Dee. 'Cal should be back soon.'

'I'm here . . .' He pulled a warning face and stepped aside to reveal his grandmother standing behind him. 'I had a call to pick up Gran from the station, but her train was held up and when we got home, we found a message from Aunt Molly saying that she had to see you.'

'Stop waffling, lad,' Penny said, pushing past him but then stopping as she took in the scene: the police constable who'd arrived with Dee, Dee beside the prone Natalie and Molly clutching the pan with one hand and her chest with the other.

'What on earth . . . ?' Then, looking at Molly, Penny took the pan and wrapped her arms around her, her voice infinitely gentle. 'Catherine Mary Porter . . . I can't leave you for a second.'

For a moment no one said a word and then Izzy groaned. 'Please,' she begged, 'can we go?'

* * *

Abby was being checked over in A&E when Lady Hamilton arrived.

'Mrs Finch . . . that's a shocking bruise. I had no idea you'd been hurt . . .'

'I have a headache, but the damage appears to be superficial. How's Izzy?'

'Resting. Her father is with her now, but I had to come and thank you for what you did. I'm not sure what happened, but Izzy said that you saved her life.'

'I think we both need to thank Molly Taylor. She saved us both. And my neighbour for calling the police as soon as she saw Natalie return to the house.'

'Yes, of course. I'll thank them in person. The police said that woman was following Izzy but her car ran out of petrol and she had to walk the last half-mile to your house.'

'The petrol gauge is a bit dodgy.' Her ladyship's eyebrow rose. 'She stole my car earlier today.'

'Oh. I see.' She cleared her throat. 'I have to thank you too, for calling me when you did. So that I could be there when my granddaughter arrived.'

'Whatever she says, a woman needs her mother at those big emotional moments.'

'She said I'd make a drama, didn't she?'

'She was in labour. Nothing you say then counts.'

Her ladyship smiled. It was a politician's smile, all mouth but not quite reaching the eyes. 'Very tactful. You are a kind and decent woman, Mrs Finch.' She took a breath. 'I hope you'll accept my apology for the way I spoke to you when you called the other day. You did nothing to deserve that. I can't imagine what you must have thought of me.'

Abby could have told her, but what would be the point of that? Instead she nodded — a mistake — and winced.

'Both your husband and daughter apologised on your behalf, but I appreciate hearing it from you. Has Izzy decided on a name for the baby?'

'Mary Louise, but she'll be known as May.'

'That's very pretty,' she said, deciding that it might not be the moment to mention that it was her own second name.

'Izzy wants you to be one of her godmothers.'

Despite the apology, it was obvious that her ladyship was not excited by the idea.

'She'll be a bag of emotions at the moment. Give it a few days and she'll probably have forgotten all about it.'

She nodded. 'If you're ready to go home, Baker is outside with the car.'

'Thank you, but I have friends waiting.'

Lady Hamilton turned and saw a grim-faced Jake, an anxious Meg and a patient Dee. 'Oh . . . yes, I see. Then I'll leave you.'

'Will you tell Izzy that I'm delighted about the baby and that I'll be in touch next week if she feels up to it. Or if she is swamped with baby love, she can leave the funeral arrangements to me.'

'I'll tell her,' she said and, with another smile all round as she left them to it, Abby caught a glimpse of Izzy, thirty years on.

Jake hung back as she turned to Dee. 'How's Natalie?'

'In a secure hospital under sedation.'

'She didn't kill Howard. It was Molly.'

'Yes. I had the story from her sister. I'll need a statement from you, but there's no rush. I'll give you a call in a day or two.'

Meg's hug was long and heartfelt. 'Get her out of here, Jake.'

He put his arm around her and, as he headed for the door, it was all she could do not to sag against him.

'You had a personal visit from her ladyship?'

'There was a suggestion of gritted teeth, but she did offer to have her chauffeur take me home.'

'Instead you've got me and you'll only be there long enough to pack a bag. I'm taking you to your children before you can get into any more trouble.'

'That would be wonderful, but I can't go anywhere until I've seen Molly.' She swallowed. 'It was her handwriting on that card I found . . . I've seen it all my life. On birthday cards, on a note just a few days ago.' She looked at him. 'Was I deliberately choosing not to see what was right in front of me?'

'The mind plays tricks, Abby, and you've had a hell of day. Won't this wait?'

She shook her head, made a mental note not to do that again, but as he reached to start the car, she put out a hand and stopped him.

It had been a day of answers, but there was one more question.

'Why did I never hear from you, Jake? After the prom? Sarah Finch isn't the only one who disappeared without a trace.'

'I was an eighteen-year-old with nothing, Abby, and you were heading off to university, your head full of ambition. And maybe I was afraid that you'd regret what happened that night. That you'd be embarrassed and rather I disappeared.'

'No! No, Jake,' she said, taking his hand. 'I was concerned about you. I wrote to you at Bristol, but the letter was returned. I thought you were the one that regretted it.'

'Then I'm an idiot, but I'd thrown away my university place and taken a huge gamble on the future. I had no idea how it would turn out.'

'Do you think I would have cared?'

'All my thinking was concentrated on staying afloat. I did come back once, when my company was beginning to take off.'

'When?'

'Much too late. I didn't expect to find you at home, but I was going to ask your mother where you were. It was a bright June morning when I walked down your lane and there you were, right in front of me, a baby in your arms and waving Howard off somewhere. I suppose that was Tom . . .'

'Oh,' she said. 'That must have been a shock.'

'You could say that. And that's when I made the second biggest mistake of my life. I went back to London and asked Rachael to marry me.'

'Is she okay?'

'Absolutely fine. She's the hot legal brain I offered you.'

'Oh. Right. Did she strip you of all your assets?'

'I knew what I owed her. We're still friends.'

'You're a good man.'

'I hope so, but I should have had more confidence in myself, more confidence in you,' he said. 'But I'd taken a beating that had knocked the superpower out of sync.'

'It's back now.'

'And here to stay.'

She nodded and he started the car, and neither of them spoke until they arrived at Molly's.

'This may take a while, Jake.'

He leaned across and kissed her cheek. 'Take all the time you need. I'm not going anywhere.'

Penny answered her knock. 'I'm sorry it's so late, but I had a text from Cal that Molly collapsed after we left.'

She nodded. 'It's her heart, Abby. The doctor called me a couple of weeks ago to say that he was concerned about her. He didn't think she should be living on her own and I wanted to get Cal away from trouble . . .'

'Two birds, but I wish you'd called me. I didn't realise how confused she'd become.'

'You've had enough to deal with, but she's been asking for you.'

She went upstairs, tapped on the door and went into Molly's bedroom, sat by her bed and took her hand.

'Thank you, Molly. You saved both Izzy and me today. And Izzy's baby. She's had a little girl. Mary Louise.'

'That's pretty. I'm a Mary too. Catherine Marys always used to be called Molly.'

'Did they? But Porter? I thought your name was Blake before you married Gordon?'

'It was. I changed it so that man could never find me. A girl, you say? I'm glad they're both safe.'

'Thanks to you, but I'm afraid you hurt yourself when you swung that pan.'

'No, dear. The hurt isn't new, and it's been getting worse lately. That's why I was coming to tell you . . . Before I ran out of time.'

'About the baby. It was your baby I found?'

'He was such a big strong man, Abby. He forced himself on me. Came up to my room night after night. Never looked at me. Never spoke to me, just did it and left.'

'I know all about Howard James Finch, Molly. You were not the only one.'

'I didn't know I was having a baby. The pain was so bad that I thought I was going to die. I was trying not to scream, but Mrs Ruth heard me and helped me. But when he came, the baby was dead.'

'I'm so sorry.'

'Mrs Ruth cried . . . Then she got some water and made the sign of the cross over him so that he'd go to heaven and said she'd take care of everything.'

'She wrapped him in a blanket and buried him in a beautiful box, Molly, but I wish, when I found him, that you'd told me.'

'I didn't realise until I saw the paper. Then I knew. But I couldn't tell you because it was a secret. I'd sworn to Mrs Ruth that I'd never tell.'

'But Penny knew?'

'Penny came to fetch me. After. She always took care of me.'

And worried about her.

'Did you give your baby a name, Molly?'

'Richard. When Mrs Ruth made the sign of the cross, I called him Richard. After she'd taken him away she sent for my mother, but it was Penny who came.'

'To take you home.'

'Not home. I couldn't go home. My father . . . She took me to a hotel run by people she knew. They gave me a job and it's where I met my dear, dear friend Jane. I'll give her your love when I see her—'

'Molly, no . . .'

'When I see her, I'll tell her that you found my baby for me.'

'You took him flowers.'

'Mrs Ruth was dead and the house was empty. I didn't think anyone would see. I put the flowers in the hole where he'd been and told him I loved him, but then I looked up and that man was standing right there beside me. I thought he'd come back to do it again . . .'

'So you picked up the spade and hit him.'

'He looked so shocked . . .'

'And then you hid the flowers so no one would know you'd been there.'

'I hid the flowers and then I ran. I saw Cal and I think he saw me, but he never said . . .'

'No, Molly, he kept your secret.'

'He's a good boy.'

'Yes, he is.'

'I knew I had to tell Gordon that I'd killed the man who hurt me so that we could never have babies. He was so happy. Except it wasn't him, was it? It was your Howard. I'm so sorry, Abby.'

'Bad things happened to you, Molly, and you were frightened, but I found your flowers and I put them back.'

'Did you? Oh, I am glad.' Her voice was weaker now. 'What will happen to my baby?'

'I'll take care of him.' But after all she'd learned, she wasn't going to put him anywhere near Howard James Finch. 'Would you like me to put him with Gordon?'

'Oh, yes. Then we'll all be together.'

Abby had to swallow hard to shift the lump in her throat.

'Will they lock me up?'

'No. You saved our lives today and I won't let anything bad happen to you. But you should rest now.'

'Yes, I'll have a little sleep.'

Molly smiled and closed her eyes, and Abby bent and kissed Molly's forehead before joining Penny on the landing.

'She phoned me this morning and told me what she'd done. She was coming to tell you and then she was going to the police.'

'She saved us, Penny. Natalie was out of her mind and would have killed us both.'

'That should count for something,' she said. 'How is the mother?'

'Safely delivered of a little girl.'

'Well, that's a blessing.'

'Molly told me that you knew. About the baby.'

'Ruth Finch sent a telegram to our mother, but Molly would never tell us who had done that to her. Our father was a hard old bigot and he blamed Molly. He wouldn't let Mum come for her. Wouldn't have her in the house. I was married by then, so I came and took her to someone I knew who ran a small hotel in Weston. Your great-grandmother, Abby. She took care of her and, when she'd recovered, Molly stayed to work for her.'

'And she met my grandmother.'

'Yes, Jane. And Gordon. He worked there too. Ruth had given me money for Molly and when they married, they used it to buy this house.'

'They always seemed happy.'

'She had a good marriage, but she was damaged and could never have another baby because of what that evil man did to her. Breaking his neck was too easy a death.'

Abby was inclined to agree, but he was beyond justice. 'The police . . .'

'You need to be with your children. I've told that woman detective what happened. I'm going to make a full statement tomorrow.'

'Do you need anything?'

'No. I'll stay and sort everything out. Cal will help me.'

'Then I'll just say goodnight to Molly.'

Abby slipped back into the room and approached the bed. 'Molly . . .'

She took her hand, but when she gave it a gentle squeeze there was no response. She was no longer there.

CHAPTER THIRTY-FIVE

It was a bright summer day when Howard was laid to rest with his family in the Finch family vault in St Michael's church.

Molly and her baby, Richard, had already joined Gordon and this was the final act in the drama.

Abby and her children shared the front pew with Izzy and her baby daughter.

Behind them were Jake, Meg, Penny and Cal, and behind them Sir James and Lady Hamilton.

The church was packed with the great and good of Maybridge. Politicians, members of the business community, all there to pay their respects to a fallen leader.

Dee was there with DI Glover and a large contingent from the press, but there was no black, and definitely no chrysanthemums.

The flowers were from the gardens of friends, neighbours and Linton Lodge. Foxgloves and lupins, tall spikes of rose bay and soft swathes of cow parsley.

The hymns, chosen by the children, were the joyful ones, and as the coffin was lowered into the crypt, Abby held onto her girls' hands, determined that they should all remember the good times with their father. The laughs, the fun . . .

Afterwards, she hugged a tearful Izzy and, despite misgivings, promised that she would be godmother to Mary Louise.

And then, as she turned to gather her children, she saw a slender figure she recognised at the rear of the church. She took a step towards her, reached out a hand, but people crowded between them, wanting to hug her and Izzy. And the next time she looked, the woman had disappeared.

'Abby? Are you okay?'

'She was here, Jake.'

'Who?'

'Sarah . . . Howard's mother.' She saw the way he was looking at her. 'She was at the back of the church. Tall, with silver hair, wearing something floaty in grey.'

'I thought you'd decided that she was dead.'

'Maybe she was a ghost,' Abby said. Except that when she had raised her hand, reaching out across the length of the church, her ghost had smiled and returned the gesture.

THE END

THE JOFFE BOOKS STORY

We began in 2014 when Jasper agreed to publish his mum's much-rejected romance novel and it became a bestseller.

Since then we've grown into the largest independent publisher in the UK. We're extremely proud to publish some of the very best writers in the world, including Joy Ellis, Faith Martin, Caro Ramsay, Helen Forrester, Simon Brett and Robert Goddard. Everyone at Joffe Books loves reading and we never forget that it all begins with the magic of an author telling a story.

We are proud to publish talented first-time authors, as well as established writers whose books we love introducing to a new generation of readers.

We have been shortlisted for Independent Publisher of the Year at the British Book Awards three times, in 2020, 2021 and 2022, and for the Diversity and Inclusivity Award at the Independent Publishing Awards in 2022.

We built this company with your help, and we love to hear from you, so please email us about absolutely anything bookish at feedback@joffebooks.com

If you want to receive free books every Friday and hear about all our new releases, join our mailing list: www.joffebooks.com/contact

And when you tell your friends about us, just remember: it's pronounced Joffe as in coffee or toffee!

www.ingramcontent.com/pod-product-compliance
Lightning Source LLC
La Vergne TN
LVHW091110080826
845145LV00008B/1858

* 9 7 8 1 8 0 4 0 5 8 3 2 9 *